"Get out of my bed," Allisun snapped.

Hunter shook his head, his midnight brown eyes glowing with sympathy. "There's only the one, and my ankle—"

"I'll sleep on the floor." She made to bolt from the bed, but he was quicker, one hand snagging her wrist. She tried to wrench free. "You're hurting me."

"Nay, you are hurting yourself by struggling."

Allisun stilled, but her pulse beat wildly as she stared at her enemy. His eyes bored into hers with an intensity that stripped away everything but this moment. She was vividly conscious of his superior strength, held in check by the force of his will. Inside her, a primitive fear stirred. He could do with her whatever he wanted. None of the tactics her father and brothers had taught her could help her now. She was utterly powerless. But she would not beg. Lifting her chin, she snapped, "Attack me and have done with it."

Dear Reader,

If you've never read a Harlequin Historical novel, you're in for a treat. We offer compelling, richly developed stories that let you escape to the past—written by some of the best writers in the field!

We are very excited about *Pride of Lions,* a new Scottish medieval novel and the latest in THE SUTHERLAND SERIES by Suzanne Barclay. Critics have described her work as "Pure gold!", "Magical!" and "Totally satisfying." In her latest, a knight and a warrioress from enemy clans join forces and fall in love when they are lost within the territory of an evil laird. Don't miss it!

Be sure to look for *The Heart of a Hero,* a darling Western by Judith Stacy. Here, a bad boy turned rancher has thirty days to prove he'll be a good father to his niece and nephew, and enlists the help of the new schoolmarm. *The Knight's Bride* by rising talent Lyn Stone is a heartwarming and humorous tale of a very *true* knight who puts his honorable reputation on the line when he promises to marry the beautiful widow of his best friend.

Rounding out the month is *Burke's Rules,* book two of THE GUARDSMEN series by Pat Tracy. Set in Denver, this story features a perfectly mannered schoolmistress who falls for the "protective" bachelor banker who helps her fund her school. Don't miss this wonderful, sensuous story!

Whatever your tastes in reading, you'll be sure to find a romantic journey back to the past between the covers of a Harlequin Historical® novel.

Sincerely,
Tracy Farrell, Senior Editor

Please address questions and book requests to:
Harlequin Reader Service
U.S.: 3010 Walden Ave., P.O. Box 1325, Buffalo, NY 14269
Canadian: P.O. Box 609, Fort Erie, Ont. L2A 5X3

Suzanne Barclay

Pride of Lions

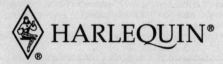

HARLEQUIN®

TORONTO • NEW YORK • LONDON
AMSTERDAM • PARIS • SYDNEY • HAMBURG
STOCKHOLM • ATHENS • TOKYO • MILAN • MADRID
PRAGUE • WARSAW • BUDAPEST • AUCKLAND

ISBN 0-373-29043-8

PRIDE OF LIONS

This edition published by arrangement with Harlequin Books S.A.

® and TM are trademarks of the publisher. Trademarks indicated with
® are registered in the United States Patent and Trademark Office, the
Canadian Trade Marks Office and in other countries.

Printed in U.S.A.

SUZANNE BARCLAY

Suzanne Barclay considers herself sublimely lucky to be writing historical romances. What other career would allow her to watch old Errol Flynn movies and call it research? Or daydream and call it work?

On those rare moments when she can tear herself away from the stories she is creating, she enjoys walking in the woods with her two dogs, Max and Duffy, whipping up exotic meals for her husband of twenty-three years and pawing through the local antique marts for special pieces to decorate her office/study.

Be sure to watch for the next installment in the Sutherland series, _Taming the Lion,_ coming out in June, 1999.

Suzanne freely admits that she has trouble keeping track of all the Sutherlands and Carmichaels who people her stories, and has prepared an updated family tree detailing the various characters, their marriages and their children. To receive a copy, send a large SASE to: Suzanne Barclay, P.O. Box 92054, Rochester, NY 14692.

To my family,
a constant source of pride and joy.

Prologue

Luncarty Tower, the Scottish Borders
July, 1381

The setting sun bathed the crests of the Cheviot Hills in red fire and deepened the shadows in the woods along the creek that flowed past the tower. Soon it would be full dark, and everyone knew the land about was wild and dangerous.

So why in the world was his aunt leaving the safety of Luncarty's stout walls?

His belly tight with apprehension, Hunter Carmichael crept after her, careful to stay well back as she negotiated the steep trail down to the edge of the burn. Her movements were quick and jerky, which was not at all like his graceful aunt, his favorite among his father's five brothers and sisters. But then, she had not been acting like herself all day.

Hunter frowned. Could it be Uncle Jock's fault?

Last night Hunter had heard Brenna and her husband arguing. The sounds of raised voices and weeping had roused him from sleep. He'd lain there in the dark, in the little wall chamber down the hall from theirs and wondered what to do. His parents sometimes disagreed, but they never shouted, and his father would not have made his mother cry.

A shaft of longing knifed through him. He'd enjoyed his summer here with his beloved aunt, but he wished he was home at Carmichael Castle with his parents. He missed his mother's gentle smiles, his father's sage advice and even Father Matthew's lessons in reading and writing and scripture. Uncle Jock didn't hold much with book learning, and had allowed Hunter to roam about, fishing and riding and doing as he pleased. He'd liked that very much indeed, but just now, thinking of home made his throat tighten and his eyes prickle.

Bah, he was ten and three, nearly a man. And it was a man's duty to protect his family, particularly the woman-folk, his father, Ross, had taught him. The memory of those lessons drove Hunter from his warm bed and down the chilly, dark corridor to knock on the door of the master chamber.

"Who the hell's there?" Uncle Jock demanded.

"H-Hunter."

There was some grumbling and cursing, but the door opened. Jock McKie's burly body filled the doorway, clad in loose breeks and a rumpled tunic. "What do ye want?" he demanded.

"I...I heard voices." Hunter peered around his uncle to where his aunt stood by the hearth, her eyes red, her hair tumbling like a black curtain to the waist of her tightly belted bed robe. She looked no older than he, though she was near thirty. The sight of her, so small and unhappy, roused his protective instincts. Pushing past Jock, he went to take her icy hands.

"Are you all right?" Hunter whispered.

"Of course she is," Jock snapped, coming up behind

him. "We were just discussing something, were we not, Brenna?"

"Aye, that's true," she said at once.

Hunter was relieved not to see any bruises on her face. They'd had a soldier at Carmichael who had beaten one of the maids. Bram was his name, and he'd claimed women needed to be hit to keep them in line. Hunter's father had disagreed vehemently. Ross had whipped the man and dismissed him, but the lesson had stayed with Hunter. Though Jock was a head taller than him and weighed twice as much, Hunter decided that if he'd been beating Brenna, he'd thrash Jock. Or try to.

"We were having words, as married people sometimes do, and lost our tempers," his aunt added. "I'm sorry we woke you."

Hunter had pondered that for a moment. "Papa says the rest of us are cursed with Grandfather Lionel's hot temper."

"Meaning Ross does not have one?" she had teased.

"He does, but Mama says it takes longer to come to the boil." Hunter had grinned. "He's trying to teach me to master mine, but…"

"Bah, a bit of fire in a man's gut is what makes him a man," said the Borderer whose clansmen jumped when he spoke. Aye, Jock McKie ruled Luncarty with an iron fist, but in the two months he'd been here, Hunter had never seen him raise his voice or his hand to his wife.

It must be as she'd said, an argument.

Hunter had returned to his room, but he had kept his door open and his ears, too. There'd been no repeat of the loud voices, but after a short time, he had heard hoarse, rhythmic groans. Before this summer, he'd not have known what they were, but two weeks ago, he'd chanced upon a stable lad and a maid trysting behind the barn.

Feeling hot, flustered and a little ashamed to think they were doing *that* at their advanced ages, Hunter had closed his door. His aunt and uncle had obviously made up their quarrel.

But come morning, his aunt had behaved strangely. She'd been too busy for their usual walk, too busy even to sit and talk with him. At first, Hunter had felt as dejected as an abandoned pup. Then he feared that Aunt Brenna knew he'd overheard them coupling last night. But she didn't act embarrassed, more like nervous and preoccupied. She snapped at her maids and harried the servants into what seemed to him, and apparently to them, an unwarranted cleaning spurt.

The mattresses were dragged out to air, the old rushes scraped off the floor of the great hall and a party sent out to cut new ones from along the creek bank. There would be no hot meal that day, declared Brenna the tyrant, for the cook and his helpers were scrubbing down the kitchen.

Jock, chased from the hall by the army of cleaners, had gathered his troopers and ridden off in search of a tavern where they could drink and dice in peace. And doubtless do a bit of wenching, too, judging from the remarks some of the men made.

"Take Hunter with you," Brenna had commanded.

Jock had readily agreed. "'Bout time the lad completed his education," he'd said, winking lewdly.

The notion had been tempting, indeed, for lately Hunter had found himself fascinated by the maids at Luncarty. Young or old, pretty or ugly, the sway of their hips and breasts caused a wild, uncontrollable stirring in his lower body. A longing he was more than curious to satisfy, but his sense of duty was stronger. Hunter had pleaded a bad belly and stayed behind to watch his aunt. For what? He did not know.

She had spent a long time sequestered in Uncle Jock's counting room. When she'd emerged, she was carrying a covered basket. Upon spotting him lurking about, Brenna had sent Hunter on an errand to the blacksmith. He had pretended to go, ducking around a corner to watch for her. When she'd donned her cloak, taken a small basket and headed out of Luncarty, he'd followed covertly.

"I am going down to gather water betony plants," he'd heard her tell the guard on duty at the gate. The man had waved her past with a reminder not to linger too long. After all, Lady Brenna was answerable only to Jock.

Hunter had felt no such strictures. He was her closest kin, and with Jock away, it was up to him to guard his aunt. Especially since she seemed to have gone a bit mad, he thought.

Pulling himself from his musings, Hunter concentrated on his quarry. From Wee Wat Carmichael, the wizened tracker who must be a hundred years old, he had learned the art of following someone without being caught.

Hunter made a game of it, crawling from rock to rock, and bush to bush. But when his aunt entered the woods, her black cloak blended with the shadows, and he nearly lost her. The cracking of a twig to his right gave her away, and he was soon behind her again. Careful to stay back, he watched as she worked her way along the creek bank. She did not pause to look for herbs, but moved quickly through the trees.

The terrain grew rougher and steeper, huge rocks blocking the path as though tossed there by a careless giant. Hunter crawled over and around them, worried because he could not hear Brenna up ahead over the gush of rushing water. The moon had risen, its light peering through the thick canopy of leaves to light the way. Likely Jock was back by now. He'd be worried. Hunter quickened his pace, determined to catch her and coax her into abandoning this search or offering to help her.

He rounded a towering boulder and stopped in his tracks, transfixed by the sight of his aunt...caught fast in a man's arms.

The man was tall and broad shouldered, his red hair gleaming like fire in the moonlight. Some of the McKies were redheaded, but this man was a stranger to Hunter.

Who was he? What was he doing here with Aunt Brenna?

She suddenly moved, pushing free of the man's embrace to stare up at him. Even at this distance, the distress on her face was plain. "Nay. I cannot go with you."

"You must." The man grabbed hold of her shoulders.

"Nay." Brenna twisted in his grip.

Hunter didn't wait to see more. Pulling the sword from his scabbard, he clambered up the rocks. He wished he had more than a light practice blade, but his father had declared he was not yet strong enough to yield a two-handed claymore. Just now, he felt capable of hefting two in her defense. "Let her go!" he cried.

The man whirled, shoving Brenna behind him and drawing his own weapon. The huge claymore gleamed ominously in the half light. "Who the hell are you?" he demanded.

"'Tis my nephew!" Brenna tried to step around the man, but he caught her wrist with his left hand.

"Release her," Hunter shouted, surprised his voice didn't come out a squeak. His opponent was not only larger and better armed, he held the high ground. To reach him, Hunter would have to fight uphill over the rocks. But he'd do it.

"Bloody hell!" the man exclaimed.

"Please." Brenna extended a beseeching hand. "Please go, Hunter, I do not want anything to happen to you."

"I cannot leave you here." Hunter took a step forward, but was stopped by the press of cold steel against his throat.

"Well, well, what have we here?" a deep voice growled in his ear.

Brenna cried out.

"Do not harm him, Owen," ordered the other man.

"Why the hell not?" this Owen grumbled.

"'Tis her nephew. Drop the weapon, lad."

Hunter hesitated, weighing his chances.

"Alex told ye to drop it," Owen repeated, his blade pressing the point.

Whispering a curse, Hunter let his sword clatter to the stones. His eyes locked on his aunt's wide blue ones across the short distance separating them. *I'm sorry,* he mouthed. Then he transferred his gaze to the man who held her.

Alex's eyes were a paler shade of blue than Aunt Brenna's but sharp and canny. He was well dressed in a wool tunic and leather breeks. His weapon was costly, his speech less coarse than Owen's. But for all that, he was a fiend bent on abducting a beautiful woman.

"I'll fight you, man to man," Hunter growled.

Behind him, Owen laughed, the sound cold and ugly. "Cheeky lad. I say we run him through and get out of here."

"Nay." Brenna broke free of her captor and started forward, hands stretched out. "Run, Hunter! Get away from here!"

As if he could do that. But her bid for freedom caught their captors off guard. Wrenching the knife from his belt, Hunter spun and leaped for Owen's throat.

The man was big and bulky, with a barrel chest, long black hair and a blunt-featured face Hunter would never forget. "What the hell!" Owen put up a beefy arm to deflect the blow. With the other arm, he caught Hunter in the chest and sent him flying.

Hunter landed in the rocks. His head struck something hard. The night went bright, then dark. The last thing he heard before the inky blackness sucked him down was Aunt Brenna's scream…high, wild and anguished.

The scream still echoed in Hunter's brain when he clawed his way back to consciousness.

"Aunt Brenna?"

Only the burbling of the burn answered.

His head pounding, Hunter sat up. He was alone beside the creek, his sword and knife gone.

"Aunt Brenna?"

Nothing.

His stomach rolling, his vision blurry, he crawled to the creek and submerged his aching head in the icy water. It cleared his head but did not ease the guilt strangling his very soul.

He had to find her. Pulling himself up on a rock, he took two staggering steps, tripped and rolled down the hill. The rocks battered him all the way to the bottom. Vaguely he heard someone screaming and realized it was him. He landed in a heap against a huge boulder and lay there, too hurt to move. There was blood in his mouth, a sharp pain in his left leg.

"Hunter! Hunter, by all that's holy!" Uncle Jock materialized out of the woods, a dozen McKies at his back. "Bloody hell, what happened to ye?"

"Aunt Brenna…kidnapped," Hunter said weakly.

"The hell ye say." Jock roared the orders that sent his men crashing through the woods. "Do ye know who it was? Where they might have taken her?"

"Two men…Alex…tall…a nobleman, I think…red hair.

The other..." Hunter turned his head and spat out blood. His uncle's face was hazy, and he knew he was likely to faint again. "Black hair...ugly...Owen. Owen's his name."

Jock McKie cursed, leaped up and kicked a nearby rock. "'Tis Alex and Owen Murray. Bloody hell, I should have known, what with the way Alex was sniffing around my Brenna at the last Truce Day."

"She knows him?" That made an odd sort of sense to Hunter's battered brain. "Mayhap he won't hurt her."

Jock cursed again. "Faithless jade. I should have seen this coming." He seized hold of Hunter's shoulder. "Did she have anything with her? A ledger? Tally sticks?"

"Nay." Memories dipped dizzily in and out of focus. "Wait. She...she was in your counting room for a time. When she came out, she was carrying the basket."

"Dod! Where is it now?" Jock rose with a roar. He shouted for his men, and when they'd assembled, gave orders for some to carry Hunter back to Luncarty while the rest came with him. "Alex Murray'll rue this night's work."

"You'll get Aunt Brenna back, won't you?" Hunter whispered.

"Aye, that I'll surely do, then I'll make certain Alex Murray pays for taking what's mine."

Chapter One

Scottish Middle Marches
August, 1393

A thin crescent moon shed pale light on the Cheviots. Desolate and treeless, the hills stretched toward the horizon like a great rumpled quilt, pocked by narrow valleys and steep bluffs. Atop the most prominent sat Luncarty Tower, its stark stone walls blending with the hillside that plunged fifty feet to the Lune Water.

Stretched out on her belly in the coarse grass of a neighboring hillock, Allisun Murray scanned the fortress domain of her clan's most hated enemy. Jock McKie's ancestors had chosen the site well.

Small ravines guarded the approaches on either side of the tower, and the only entrance was a winding trail up the face of the bluff to a drawbridge spanning a deep ditch. On the other side stood the tall gatehouse, its stout door tightly shut, a pair of arrow slits staring out like giant, malevolent eyes. A single McKie manned the open battlements above, his round helmet and long spear gleaming in the moonlight as he paced to and fro.

"It'll no' be easy getting in and back out again with our stock," muttered Owen Murray.

Allisun sighed and shifted fractionally on the hard ground, her muscles cramped, her bones jarred by the hard ride from their hideaway at Tadlow. But she dared not let her fatigue show. Though the death of her brother, Daniel, had made her head of their small clan, no Scot would follow a woman into battle. She was here only because she'd insisted and Owen, Daniel's captain, had backed her. "We must find a way," she said.

"I'm for throwing our scaling hooks over the back wall, climbing in and fighting for what's ours," growled Black Gilbert, hunkered down behind a pile of rock to her left.

A murmur of agreement swept through the thirty Murrays sprawled along the hill's summit, clad in riding leathers and armed for battle, their faces bleak with fury and frustration.

Allisun understood both. For twelve years the feud between the Murrays and the McKies had raged. She'd lost first her father, then her home and finally, her two brothers, Sandie and Daniel to Jock McKie's punishing raids. Daniel's death had cut the deepest, for he'd been only twenty and a gentle soul. "Aye, let's give them a taste of Border justice," she muttered.

Owen caught her arm with a wide, scarred hand. "Easy, lass," he whispered. "I know how you feel, but 'twould be suicide. Getting ourselves killed will not bring Danny back."

"Have you forgotten how that foul, deceitful old man lured Danny into meeting him with promises of a truce, then tortured and killed him?" She shuddered, torn by the memory of her peace-loving brother, lying broken and bloody in a high meadow twenty miles from here.

"Nay, I've not forgotten a single one of Jock McKie's

crimes against us. Each death is carved into my heart. But young Danny withstood Jock's brutality for our sakes.''

Allisun nodded. She knew full well why Jock had tortured her brother—to learn the whereabouts of their camp so he might finish what he'd started so long ago.

"We cannot let his sacrifice be for naught," Owen added. "You'll be remembering Danny's last words ere he rode out."

She looked up at the weathered face of the man who'd been like a father to her since her own had been killed by the McKies five years ago. Before leaving to meet with Jock and, hopefully, forge a truce, Danny had ordered them not to avenge him if something went awry. "I cannot let it pass," she said.

"You must. You and your sister are all that's left of your family. What of her and the others waiting for us back at Tadlow Mountain?" Owen asked roughly. "Who will hunt for them, who will protect them, if aught happens to us?"

Duty dulled the hunger for revenge that clawed at her. Privately Danny had urged her to take Carina and leave the Borders if he was killed. That she could not do, but neither could she let Danny's death pass. "They do outnumber us."

"Pair of weak-willed women, ye are," Black Gil taunted, his scowl as black as his hair. Though five years younger than Owen's forty, he was as hard as the land, the wicked scar bisecting his cheek a memento of the feud. "I say we go in and kill as many McKies as we can."

"Aye," growled a chorus of Murrays.

"We've got to strike back," muttered Wee Harry, the giant who served as their blacksmith. "Else they'll keep picking us off one by one till there's not a Murray left alive."

That, Allisun knew, was Jock's goal, his obsession. And

Wee Harry was right. They had to do something to keep the McKies at bay. To do that, they needed food. Meat, preferably, to keep their fighters strong and their bairns alive through the long winter. They had no coin to buy sheep or cattle to replace those lost to McKie raids this year. Eighteen head, to be exact. Allisun was determined to get them back. "Where do you think he's got the stock penned?"

"In the barmkin beyond yon walls," snapped Black Gilbert. "Which is why we've got to go in."

"What of that shieling we skirted on the way here?" Allisun asked, recalling the large huts they'd bypassed to avoid having anyone sound the alarm and alert the countryside to their presence. "I heard cattle near there. We could relieve the crofter of eighteen head to replace ours."

"What of Jock McKie?" snarled Black Gil. "Does it not trouble yer conscience that he lives free and clear whilst yer father and brothers molder in the ground?"

"Of course it does." Allisun felt the tears gather behind her eyes but blinked them back. "And we'll have our revenge against the McKie. That I swear," she added, looking around the circle of hard-faced men. She'd known them all her life, lived with them from the good days at Keastwicke Tower before the feud began and the McKies burned them out. They'd been driven from one hovel to the next, forced to take shelter in burned-out towers and abandoned huts. How hard she and Carina had worked to turn them into some semblance of a home, only to be forced out into the hills each time Jock found them.

Tough living, it was, and it had scarred them all. Short rations turned their bodies thin and wiry. The constant threat of discovery bred children who seldom cried and never laughed. Allisun's heart bled for them. Somehow, someway, she was going to make Jock McKie pay for what he'd done.

Allisun glanced at Owen, drawing strength from the approval in his dark eyes. Throwing up her chin, she challenged Black Gil. "There must be a hundred McKies behind Luncarty's walls. To venture within would be tantamount to suicide, and we can ill afford to lose even one man. Nay, we will wait till we can lure Jock McKie out into the open where we stand a fair chance of winning." Seeing her men nod in agreement, she added, "Mayhap the raid on Jock's herds will do just that."

"Aye." Gibb's Martin, tall and lanky as his sire had been before he'd caught a McKie spear in the chest, turned to crawl back down the hill. "Allisun has the right of it. We'll attack the croft, lure the bastards from their tower, then cut them down as they did our kinfolk."

"Wait," Allisun said as the others made to follow. "We'll not succeed if we go crashing off through the woods. Let us ride to that hillock behind the croft. We will wait there while Owen and Mouse scout the area to judge where their guards are posted. When we're sure of success, we'll strike."

Owen smiled. "Exactly right. You've as canny a mind as your da, God asoul him."

Allisun flushed, warmed by his praise. Though her father and brothers had forbidden her to ride out with them, she'd spent many an hour listening while they talked strategy. Little did any of them realize she'd need those lessons.

Black Gilbert grunted. "I still say we should—"

A shout from Luncarty Tower sent the Murrays scrambling up the hill to observe a party of mounted men hailing the tower. Allisun counted twenty in the band. Even from this distance, their horses looked enormous, great black beasts draped in red blankets. Their riders were no less amazing, tall men clad entirely in metal that gleamed like fire in the moonlight.

"Who do you suppose they are?" she asked.

"Knights," Owen replied. "French, likely. Or English."

"English." Allisun savored the word. "If we could prove Jock is treating with the English, Andrew Kerr would be forced to investigate, wouldn't he?" The Warden of the Scots Middle March was charged with keeping the peace, but he had rejected the Murrays' complaints against the McKies because Jock paid Sir Andy a handsome quarterly bribe.

"But we know proof is hard to come by," said Owen.

"Aye." How different things might have been had that not been the case, Allisun thought.

The guards at Luncarty called out, no doubt asking the identity of the newcomers.

The foremost man, more richly dressed than the others, his armor covered by a sleeveless tabard, removed his helmet and shouted something back. His reply was inaudible to the Murrays, but it sent the guards scrambling to lower the drawbridge.

Allisun eyed the leader of this band. His hair gleamed bright as newly minted gold in the light of wind-whipped torches, but it was his bearing that impressed her. He sat taller in the saddle than any man she'd ever seen, his back straight as a pikestaff. Arrogance, she decided. Aye, he carried himself like a man who owned the world. "Do you think he is an Englishman?" she asked.

Owen shrugged. "Possible. Though I'd not have thought Jock so foolish as to trade openly with them."

"The standard they carry, the black lion on red, I've seen it before," said Black Gil.

"Where?"

"I do not know. 'Twas a long time ago, but I'll remember."

Owen scowled. "Mayhap we should stay and see what they do."

"I say we go after those cattle," Gilbert grumbled.

"Agreed," Allisun said, but as the Murrays began to creep down the hill, she looked back at the armored knights walking their mounts over the drawbridge. "Those metal suits look vastly heavy."

"Aye, and cumbersome. Ill suited to the sort of fighting that goes on hereabouts." Owen kept pace with her during the descent. At the base of the hillock, he spoke gravely. "Once we're back at Tadlow, I'm going to see about getting you and Carina away someplace safe."

"Nay." Allisun cursed and spun away from him.

Owen caught her arm. "Mind your tongue. Your poor lady mother is likely spinning in her grave to see how I've let you forget all she taught you about being a fine lady."

"Lady." Allisun spat the word. "What good are lessons in reading and playing the harp with my menfolk dead and the McKies hounding us? Better you teach me to wield a sword."

"Nay." Owen enclosed her icy, knotted fist with his warm, callused one. "I swore to Danny that I'd take you away to live in Edinburgh before I'd let aught happen to you."

Allisun shook her head so vigorously her thick red braid beat against her back. "Never. I—"

"This is no' the time, nor the place to discuss this." Owen rubbed a hand across his whiskered jaw. "But our time is running out. Clearly Danny did not tell Jock where we're hiding, but someday soon the old bastard will find us, and then—"

The McKie would not only kill them all, he'd discover

the secret her father, brothers and countless other Murrays had died to protect. "Before it comes to that, I'll take Will Bell up on his offer of *protection*," she teased.

Owen's eyes rounded in horror. "You cannot be serious, lass. Desperate we may be, but Ill Will Bell is—"

"A disgusting old reprobate." And leader of the most infamous reiving family on the Borders. It had been her bad luck to be spotted by Ill Will one day when she and Danny were in Kelso fetching supplies. The old coot had leered at her and offered to aid the Murrays in their little disagreement with the McKies. The price of that help had been patently obvious. Shuddering, Allisun thrust away the memory. "Come, if we're going to lift a few head of McKie stock, what better time than whilst Old Jock is busy entertaining these knights."

"Does it seem strange to be back here?" asked Gavin Sutherland as the party cantered over the wooden drawbridge.

"Aye. If Uncle Jock had not sent for me, I'd have been content never to set foot here again." Hunter Carmichael's mouth was held in a grim line, torchlight flickering on features as bleak as the land they'd traveled to reach this place.

Gavin knew full well what had caused his usually jovial cousin to look so dour. "Not since Aunt Brenna disappeared." Though Brenna Carmichael McKie, sister to Hunter's father, Ross, had not really been Gavin's blood kin, the Carmichael and Sutherland clans were as close-knit as the dark Highland plaids both men carried rolled behind their saddles.

"Not since she was kidnapped—" Hunter corrected him "—by those cursed Murrays."

"It has been a bloody feud."

"One I vow to end—permanently." Hunter's oath echoed hollowly off the stone passageway that led them under the gatehouse and thence to the barmkin.

It was no idle threat, Gavin mused as he followed his cousin through the open meadow, bounded by Luncarty's high walls and filled with grazing sheep. This second son born to Lady Megan and Ross, Laird of the Carmichaels, carried on the family tradition for valor and ferocity. While his older brother, Ewan, distinguished himself on the field of battle, Hunter was a warrior with words. Chief justice of King Richard's high court at the age of five and twenty, so fiercely did he defend the cause of justice that he was often called the King's Lion.

None outside the family knew that Hunter's obsession with justice stemmed from the guilt he felt over that fateful moment twelve years ago when his aunt had been taken by the Murrays while Hunter, a youth of three and ten, watched helplessly.

He was not helpless now, Gavin thought as they passed under the portcullis and into the tower's courtyard. Standing well over six feet tall, with muscles honed by hours of rigorous swordplay, and a razor-sharp mind, Hunter was a match for any man, be he statesman or swordsman. Almost, Gavin pitied the Murrays whom Hunter had come to punish for this latest outrage against poor Jock.

"Dieu, Luncarty's a dour-looking place." Gavin gazed up at three stories of sheer gray stone, broken only by a pair of tiny, shuttered windows on the uppermost floors.

"Aye, the peel towers are drear and poorly furnished," Hunter said, glad for the change of subject. "Especially after what we're used to at Carmichael Castle. And though you'll not believe it when we get inside, Luncarty is finer than most Border peels. Uncle Jock's a wealthy man. We've been riding on his land for nearly half the day, and those cattle herds we passed are his, too."

"Pity he has no son to inherit all this."

Hunter nodded. Walter, Jock's son by his first wife, had died the year before he wed Brenna. That union had been too brief to bear fruit, nor had any of his mistresses quickened. There were some who speculated that Jock's seed was dead.

"Why, 'tis wee Hunter, all grown-up," said the old man who'd come out of the tower to greet them.

"Hutcheson, isn't it?" Hunter swung down and handed the reins of his warhorse to his squire.

"'Tis Old Hutch, now, my lord. This is Young Hutch, my son. He'll be steward after me."

A skinny youth with his father's pale eyes and hooked nose stepped forward and nodded. "We've put ye in the new tower." He waved toward a two-story structure of gleaming gray stone.

Hunter smiled, grateful to be spared the room he'd stayed in the last time. "My uncle?" he asked anxiously.

"Ach, the old bird's too tough to kill," said Old Hutch. "But 'twas a near thing." He shook his head dolefully.

"They say he'll no' walk again," added Young Hutch. "The Murrays took a Jedburgh ax to him. Crushed his leg, it did."

"Aye. He's lucky to be alive," said Old Hutch.

"He does not see it that way." Young Hutch's features tightened. "Better dead than crippled, he says."

Hunter's belly cramped, recalling the big, energetic man who had taught him to fish and trap. If only he'd been stronger, quicker himself twelve years ago, none of this would have—

"Hutch!" bawled a coarse voice from an upstairs window. "Is that my nephie come at last?"

"Aye, my lord," the steward shouted back. "Just coming up."

"See ye're quick about it!"

Hunter smiled, the fear that had plagued him since receiving Jock's call for help easing. "He sounds the same."

"A bit testier is all." Old Hutch herded them through the tower's only entrance, a set of double doors, one of metal grating, the other made from thick oak planks banded with steel. "Go on up, ye know the way. Young Hutch'll see yer men settled in the barracks building across the way. Tell Jock I'll be along directly with ale and meat."

"Come with me, Gavin." Hunter led the way through a maze of kegs and oat sacks that filled the ground floor storage room to the turnpike stairs. The tightly coiled steps spiraled clockwise, so right-handed attackers would find their sword arms pinned against the wall as they tried to fight their way up.

"Practical folk, these Borderers," Gavin mused, his steel-clad shoulders clanging on the close walls.

"Oh, aye, you'll find they're a breed apart, fiercer even in some ways than you Highlanders."

"Ha, that I'd like to see."

"Likely you will if I cannot persuade Uncle Jock to handle this matter my way." *Though why should he, when I mishandled things so badly last time?* Hunter thought, sobered by the memory of his aunt's abduction and subsequent death.

"Aye, well, your Border reivers will find this Highlander battle-trained and well protected." Gavin thumbed his fist on the steel breastplate made in France of Spanish steel.

"Our armor is stronger than their quilted leather jacks, but they're a tough lot, hardened by a life spent constantly at war with reiving English and raiding Scots alike."

They crested the stairs and found themselves in an entryway the size of a horse stall. It was as dark as one, too,

the faint light of a single torch playing over walls whose
only decoration was a coat of soot from a long-ago fire.

"Charming." Gavin wrinkled his nose.

A muffled bellow turned both of them toward a heavy,
iron-banded door, the worse for a few ax cuts.

"Coming, Uncle." Hunter reached for the door latch and
took a deep, steadying breath. It did nothing to ease the
knot that had cramped his belly from the moment Jock
McKie's disheveled messenger had banged on the gates of
Carmichael Castle. It wasn't fear, it was the hunger for
revenge dueling with his inbred sense of justice.

"The Murrays have paid for what they did to my sister,"
his father had told him before he left. "Jock saw to that.
There's been enough blood spilled—on both sides," added
Ross Carmichael, a man of peace and reason. "Jock would
not listen to my pleas he end the feud, but now that he's
sent for you, use that golden tongue of yours to make him
see reason. More deaths will not bring our Brenna back."

Nay, nothing would do that, Hunter thought, his hand
tightening on the latch. But he would give all he owned—
coin, property—to be cast back twelve years and have a
chance to plunge his blade into Alex Murray's black heart.
He wrenched open the door and was driven back a step by
the harsh light, the stench of smoke and unwashed bodies.

"Dieu," Gavin whispered, goggle-eyed. "I've stayed in
taverns that were more…"

"Civilized? Luncarty was once." When his aunt was
alive. And yet, the great hall was much as Hunter remembered—narrow, dark and low ceilinged, a peat fire smol-
dering in the corner hearth, hard-looking men in rough
wool seated jowl to jowl at the scarred trestle tables, eating
and arguing fit to raise the dead. It was a world away from
Carmichael Castle with its linen-draped tables, tapestry-
covered walls and multicourse meals served by liveried

maids while a minstrel plucked at a harp and his parents spoke of books or his mother sang an ancient poem.

Hunter sighed. "When I came here to visit, I thought this the grandest place, so wild and free. Of course, with Aunt Brenna the lady here, things were much finer and cleaner."

"Hunter? Damn and blast, where is that lad?"

"Here, Uncle." Hunter squinted through the smoky pall to spy a big four-poster bed set square in the middle of the room.

"Does he not have a bedchamber?" Gavin whispered.

"Aye, he does, I expect, but Uncle Jock would have to be dead to stay away out of the thick of things."

The man propped up in the bed was nearly as unchanged as his tower. Oh, time had dulled Jock's black hair to steel gray and cut ragged lines in his square face, but the eyes staring from beneath beetled brows were as sharp as ever.

"Well, I'll be damned. Ye're bigger even than old Lionel Carmichael was. Come here, lad!" Jock waved an imperious arm.

Conscious of the grinning McKies, Hunter flushed and trailed across the room, feeling like a lad again.

"Aye, ye've your mama's coloring, but yer grandsire's size. Foul-tempered old bastard, he was. Always liked that about him. What of ye?" Jock grabbed hold of Hunter's forearm and squeezed hard enough to draw a wince. "Not bad...not bad. See," he shouted to the room at large. "I told ye he'd have been lifting something weightier than those bloody books of his da's."

"I—"

"Chief justice of the king's court, he is." Jock's whiskered jowls lifted in a huge grin. "Mighty proud of ye, lad. Mighty proud. Aren't we?"

The chorus of congratulation barely swelled when Jock

cut across it. "Still ye must have found a few quarrels ye couldn't settle with them fancy words yer da pounded into ye."

"Actually, it was the university in Paris that did the pounding," Hunter said dryly. His concerned parents had shipped him off to study only a few weeks after bringing him home from Luncarty—as much to prevent him from joining Jock's war against the Murrays as to educate him. Distance, time and exposure to the fundamentals of law had accomplished their goals. He'd returned to Scotland four years ago a cautious, educated man who weighed the outcome of a step before venturing to take it.

Belatedly recalling his manners, Hunter turned and beckoned Gavin over. "This is Gavin Sutherland of Kinduin. You may recall that Aunt Elspeth wed Lucais Sutherland. Gavin is my second cousin, the son of Uncle Lucais's—"

"Whatever. Welcome, Gavin. Robbie!" Jock bellowed, causing a young man to spring from those crowded around the bed. "See young Gavin has food and drink. And give my nephie and me a bit of privacy." While the space around them cleared, Jock waved Hunter onto a stool beside the bed.

"'Tis good to see you looking better than I'd expected," Hunter said.

"And glad I am to see ye." Jock's wide cheeks deflated. "Though I wish it'd been under better circumstances." He waved at his left leg, a huge mound under the coarse blanket. "Broke it in two places trying to get away from Mad Danny Murray."

Hunter sat forward on the stool. "He attacked you?"

"Aye, under a flag of truce." Jock's lids sagged. "I lost three men before we brought him down."

"Your message said Daniel Murray was dead."

Jock smiled. "Aye. The last of Alex Murray's sons is dead."

"So, it's over, then."

"Over!" Fire leaped into Jock's eyes. "It'll no' be over till I've wiped out every one of the murdering bastards who stole my—"

"But the man who took Aunt Brenna is dead, and his sons, too. You burned the Murrays out of their tower five years ago," Hunter added, summing up the facts as he did in many a case from the high bench. "So 'twould seem the feud is at an end."

"Nay!" Jock sat up straighter, cheeks puffing, face red. "There'll be no end to it till I've found and killed them all."

"But, Uncle, there can be little left of the Murrays except old men, women and children."

"Aye, what of it?"

"'Tis not Christian to make war on women and children."

"Was it Christian for that rutter, Murray, to take my Brenna away from her home and family? Was it Christian of them to send her bones back to me when he was done with her?"

"Bones?" Hunter's blood ran cold.

"Aye. Six years ago they sent her bones in a bag, her cross still around her neck, my ring on her finger." He waved his left hand under Hunter's nose, light glinting off the gold band on his little finger. "Dod, I wish I could kill Alex Murray again."

Hunter shivered. Twelve years he'd spent trying to forget, now the pain and the rage flooded back. "I did not know of this. My father never said—"

"Likely trying to prevent ye from riding down here and helping me and the lads deal with these bastards." Jock clapped Hunter on the knee. ''Narry fear, lad, ye're here now, and yer help's most welcome, what with me unable to sit a horse.''

''What would you have me do?''

''We need to find out where they are holed up. They're a wily lot, these Murrays, dodging and hiding from our patrols. Owen Murray will be leading them now we've finally gotten rid of Mad Danny, and Alex's oldest daughter may be riding with them.''

''A woman reiver?''

''Aye, that Allisun Murray's a hard bitch, and canny, too, they say, like her cursed sire.''

Hunter frowned, picturing an ugly crone dressed in riding leathers and wearing a sword.

''Rumor has it she was seen treating with Ill Will Bell.''

Air whistled between Hunter's teeth.

''Ye've heard of him, even in Edinburgh, I see. Dod, the man's a vicious beast. I dinna need to tell ye what'll become of the McKies if Allisun seduces Ill Will into making war on us.''

''Nay,'' Hunter said slowly. ''I've a warrant outstanding against the Bells for kidnapping, ransom, thievery…''

''Oh, aye, and that's only the evidence presented by folk who were brave enough to complain—or still alive to do it.''

''Why does Sir Andrew Kerr do nothing about this?''

Jock hawked and spat onto the rush-covered floor. ''Ill Will's got Andy by the short hairs. Took his youngest daughter in a raid on Kelso last year. Threatened to send her back in pieces if Andy moved against him. 'Course—'' Jock shrugged ''—if she's still alive, she's doubtless in a bad way. Will's got a taste for rape, they say.''

Disgust rose in Hunter, a bitter, choking wave. What kind of people lived like this?

"But—" Jock brightened "—we've set a wee trap for the Murrays. If they take the bait, ye can follow 'em home and wipe out every one of them," he added with relish.

Bloody hell. The thought of killing women and children went against everything Hunter believed in. "I'll take them and bring them to trial, Uncle."

"Trial?" Jock shrieked. "My Brenna died unshriven, and ye blather about niceties like trials and such." His eyes narrowed. "Or mayhap it's that ye're afeared to fight the Murrays. There were some who said that was why ye didn't stop Alex from carrying off my Brenna all those years ago. I told them ye were no coward, just a wee lad. But ye're a man grown, now, with strength aplenty to wield that sword ye wear."

"I'm no coward."

"Jock! Jock!" A flushed and sweaty clansman dashed into the room. "There's a party of raiders sniffing about the cattle."

"Murrays?" Jock demanded.

"Aye." The man seized a cup of ale and drained it, panting as he wiped the foam from his mouth. "There's twenty or so of them, dressed for reiving. I spotted Owen Murray and the one called Wee Harry, for sure."

Jock crowed and clapped Hunter on the back. "Go to it, lad. But mind ye let the Murrays lift what cattle they will so as ye can follow them. Then—" he grinned wolfishly "—ye'll get a chance to see how we Borderers deal with thieves."

The McKies clansmen roared their approval of the plan and swarmed from the hall like angry bees, shouting for their horses and buckling on their swords.

Hunter nodded grimly to his uncle, then he and Gavin trailed after the clattering McKies.

Jock looked up at the one man who'd remained at his

side. "Well, Cousin, has he not grown into a likely looking lad?"

"Humph." Red Rowy McKie was younger than Jock by a dozen years, but just as burly and ruthless looking, his muscular body straining the seams of his leather jack. "Dinna see why ye had to send for him. I'm yer heir, I should be the one—"

"I've told ye a hundred times, ye great ox, Hunter's here to lend a bit of respectability to our little venture."

Red Rowy spat a curse. "We dinna need him."

"Aye." Jock's smile turned calculating. "Aye, we do, if I'm right about what Alex Murray did with those tally sticks Brenna stole from me. Now go along with ye. I need ye to be there when they breach the Murrays' hidey-hole. Ye know what to do?"

"Aye. I know."

Chapter Two

The moon, which had guided the Murrays to the steep-sided ravine a quarter mile from the herders' croft, had disappeared behind a bank of clouds, draping the land in dark shadows.

Allisun shivered, hoping it was not an ill omen.

From the shelter of a copse of trees atop the ridge, she anxiously watched the plain below, a narrow valley that meandered between the rolling hills. All was still and quiet, not so much as a leaf or a blade of grass stirring.

Ominously quiet.

A half mile distant lay the shielings, squat stone huts where the herders lived during the summer while their beasts gorged on long sweet grass. No light shone from the huts, and the McKies' vast herd was bedded down for the night, hundreds of black dots sprawled across the valley floor. They made a tempting target, guarded only by four or five men who slept rolled in their cloaks around a tiny campfire.

Too tempting? she wondered, shivering again.

"I do not like it," Owen had said when they'd arrived. "Things are too quiet, too—"

"The McKies have grown careless in their arrogance,"

Black Gilbert had muttered. "We'll cut out what we need to replace the beasts they stole and be away before they're any the wiser."

Owen had grudgingly agreed, but he'd refused to let Allisun go down with them. "Bad enough I let you come this far. You'll not be lifting any cattle." He'd overruled her objections and ordered her to wait on the hill with Wee Harry as guardsman.

"Ach, there they are," Harry whispered.

Allisun looked where he pointed, down to the black slash of stone and brush that marked the ravine's entrance. A low-slung shape crept from the mouth of the gorge. In a quick blur of motion, it slipped into the long grass, leaving her wondering if she'd imagined it. Nay, there was another and another. The grass barely twitched as they crawled closer to their objective.

Her heart racing, her fingers clenched tight around her hobbler's reins, she watched as her men rose suddenly from the grass and fell upon the slumbering guards. The scuffle was brief and nearly soundless, a single muffled thud the only outward sign the herd was now at the Murrays' mercy.

Allisun breathed a sigh of relief when Owen stood and waved his arm, signaling the Murrays forward. They rode out from cover, leading the rest of the horses. As soon as they'd mounted, the men fanned out and moved slowly toward the herd. "They are going to do it," she whispered.

"Dinna count them ours, yet." Wee Harry frowned, dour as ever. "This is a chancy business. Cattle are queer things, like to take a fright over naught and run off or trample a man."

"You are right, of course." Sending up a silent prayer, Allisun rose in her stirrups, counting every step the men took. So absorbed was she in the drama unfolding below that she ignored the flicker of movement at the mouth of the ravine, thinking it must be a Murray left on guard.

The moon chose that moment to shake free of the encumbering clouds. Long, white fingers raced across the landscape, banishing the dark, lengthening the shadows, glinting briefly on something bright amongst the brush and bracken.

Allisun swung her head toward the gorge, saw moonlight sparkling off polished metal. Armor?

Lordy! It was armored knights…the same ones she'd seen enter Luncarty a few hours ago. And with them came smaller, darker shapes. *McKies!*

"Harry! Harry, it's a trap! Look there!" she cried.

Harry turned and cursed.

"We have to warn them." Allisun set her heels into her mare's ribs.

"Wait! Come back! Ye cannot go down there!"

Allisun knew there was no time to wait. Already the knights and the McKies were moving onto the plain. With the thick grass to muffle their hoofbeats, they'd take her kinsmen unaware.

"Owen!" Allisun shouted as she sent her stout hobbler clattering down the rocky slope. "Behind you! A trap!"

Her words, high and shrill with fear, shattered the still night, freezing men and turning heads across the narrow valley.

The Murrays paused in the act of rousting a score of prime beef, looked around and spied the knights. Over the hail of stones her horse kicked up, Allisun heard Owen roar the orders that set the Murrays to flight.

The knights looked up the hill toward her, cursed loudly and spurred their mounts to intercept her kinsmen.

The cattle, roused so rudely from sleep, snorted, heaved to their feet and stood, shivering with apprehension.

To Allisun, the outcome was as predictable as thunder following a bolt of lightning. The Murrays were badly outnumbered, the weary mounts that had brought them so far tonight no match for the sleek McKie horses. They'd be caught ere they reached the end of the valley. Unless…

Looking over her shoulder, she spied Wee Harry, his face white with dread, his teeth bared as he raced after her. "Stampede them," she shouted to him, motioning toward the herd.

Harry looked, weighed the moment with the canniness of a man who'd lived long on the Borders. "Aye. I'll see to it. Get yerself clear, lass. Head back up yon ravine and make for home."

Allisun nodded, but she had no intention of leaving, not when two figures streaking out of the dark would the sooner set the wary cattle to flight. Just as she reached the herd, she stood in the stirrups and whooped, "Hey! Hey!"

The call was taken up by Wee Harry as he plunged into the thick of things. The cattle started, eyes rolling, whites showing. With snorts of bovine fright, they turned and ran, crashing into the uncertain mob behind them, starting a ripple that pulsed through the whole throng. Backs humped, tails lashing, the beasts fled, filling the air with panicked bellows and clods of soft turf.

Allisun was swept along on the fringe of the tide yet felt no fear, only elation. Her horse bumped along in harmony with the cattle. Over their horned heads, she spotted Wee Harry, urging the beasts on. To her right and a bit ahead, the McKies and their knights bobbed about, struggling to extricate themselves from the jostling mass so they might pursue the Murrays who, having been in front of the herd when it bolted, were getting clean away with a small knot of beeves.

In that moment of triumph, with her heart singing and her kinsmen's escape all but a certainty, Allisun glimpsed something shiny out of the corner of her eye. Whipping her head around, she saw one of the knights had worked his way up alongside her.

The polished metal helm covered his face, but his eyes glowed like hellfire in the sockets. His breath steamed from the mouthpiece, misting like dragon's smoke in the cool air.

"I've got you, at least." He grabbed her arm.

Allisun screamed and tried to wrench away from the gloved fingers. The shift caused her horse to stumble. Clutching at the pommel, she fought gamely to keep her seat. But it was too late. She was going down into the churning mass of deadly hooves.

Hunter felt his captive slip, tightened his grip and yanked hard. A quick, expert twist and he had the Murray free of the saddle and anchored securely against his thigh, his arm around a surprisingly narrow waist.

Why, it was only a lad, Hunter thought. Then he noted the soft, unmistakable swell pressing into his arm and realized it was a woman he'd saved.

A woman reiver?

Dieu, what sort of people took a woman along on a raid? His opinion of the Murrays fell another notch. The woman was obviously too frightened to struggle. For which Hunter was thankful. He had his hands full trying to control his mount. Aggressive by nature, the warhorse had been taught to aid his master in battle by striking out at anything that came near. To Zeus, the roiling, grunting mass of cattle represented a terrible threat, one he tried to combat with teeth and hooves.

"Nay. Easy, easy," Hunter repeated, fighting to keep his voice calm. He had his legs clamped tight around Zeus's girth, but with only one hand on the reins, it was nearly impossible to direct the horse. "Damn, we'll never get free of this."

"Let go of me," said a slightly breathy voice.

Hunter looked down at the top of the woman's head, a

mass of curls burnished red in the moonlight. "I cannot drop you."

"Nor was I suggesting it," she replied dryly, legs milling above the cattle. "Swing me astride before you."

He eyed the jostling bovine backs. "Can you do it?"

"Oh, I've every incentive to try, I assure you."

Despite their dire circumstances, Hunter chuckled. "At the count, then. One...two...three."

In a move so smooth they might have practiced it, Hunter lifted her up. She swung her right leg over Zeus's neck and settled before Hunter, secure between the pommel and his body.

"There." Hunter grabbed the reins in both hands and drew sharply as Zeus gathered himself to strike. "None of that. Get us out of here, lad." Pulling hard on the right leather, he tried to make for the edge of the herd.

"Head at the diagonal instead of trying to turn this giant, and cut straight across the herd," commanded the woman.

Hunter raised his brows, surprised by her tone of authority, but he did as she suggested. It worked. Every step they took brought them closer and closer to the edge of the herd, till finally they burst free.

Zeus tossed his head and trumpeted a final challenge before obeying Hunter's command to slow. Sides heaving with exertion, the horse expelled great puffs of mist into the air.

"He's ill suited to herding," commented the woman.

"Aye. They're bred for strength, not racing." He looked ahead, seeing his Carmichaels and the McKies, gamely trying to turn the cattle. The Murrays were doubtless miles in front with their purloined beef.

All except this one.

A minute shift in her weight was all the warning Hunter had before his captive swung a leg over Zeus's neck and attempted to slide free.

"Nay!" Hunter caught her around the waist, plopped her back before him and anchored her there with his arm. "I've lost the others, but I'm keeping you. Who are you? What is your name?"

She stiffened and shook her head.

"You are a Murray."

She remained stubbornly silent.

Not that it mattered. He had a fair idea it was Allisun Murray he held before him. But he judged it would do more harm than good to confront her here and risk a struggle. "Whoever you are," he said, and looked toward the last of the cattle, just disappearing between the slim bottleneck created by two opposing hills, "you and yon men are thieves."

"We are no such thing," she said hotly. "We're but taking back the eighteen head the McKie have stolen from us."

"If that's true, and mind, I'm not saying it is," Hunter replied, rather enjoying the byplay, "you got rather more cattle than your due."

She sniffed. "My men will have taken only eighteen. If the McKies lose more than that, it'll be because they weren't skilled enough to find them in the bracken."

My men. "Is your husband a Murray?"

"I'm not wed."

"But those men are your kin. You'd not have taken such a fool chance to warn them if they weren't."

"Is a blood bond the only kind a Lowlander recognizes?"

"Nay." He was beginning to grow irritated by her evasions. "'Tis said that Borderers have no loyalty...even to their own."

She tensed but said evenly, "You just accused me of risking my neck for my kinsmen."

"So, they are your kin."

She shrugged. "I thought we'd agreed they must be, or I'd not have lifted a finger to save them from you."

"You're a Murray, then."

"Ah, but we've not established that they are Murrays."

Hunter ground his teeth in exasperation. Many's the time he'd fenced with words. He did not like finding them so expertly wielded by another. And by a woman, at that. A small woman, he thought as he urged Zeus toward the end of the valley. Her head came only to the center of his breastbone. How fragile she'd felt when he'd lifted her clear of her faltering horse. The memory merged with that of watching her race down the steep slope, calling a warning to her kinsmen.

A small, brave woman.

Hunter shook away the notion. He had no business admiring a woman who must surely be Allisun Murray.

The main body of the herd was gone by the time they entered the pass into the valley. A few head of cattle, the very young and the very old, had fallen by the wayside. Some stood about, horns lowered, puffing hard. Others had collapsed on the turf, mayhap never to rise again.

"We'll be all night rounding up the stock," Hunter muttered. "And I fear my uncle has lost a goodly num—"

"Uncle!" She jerked her head around, giving him a shadowed glimpse of a white face dominated by large, dark eyes. Her eyes were filled with horror. "Jock McKie is your uncle?"

"Aye. I'm—" His explanation ended in a curse as his prisoner erupted into a storm of flailing limbs. He wore full body armor, but only woolen hose on his legs and arms. It afforded little protection as her booted heel cracked down on his shin. "Ouch! Damn you!" His grip on her waist loosened fractionally. He felt rather than saw her go for the knife at her belt. "Nay!" Seizing her wrist in his rein hand, he wrapped the other around her throat.

"Damn you!" she wheezed, struggles ceasing.

"Drop the knife."

"Nay."

Her bones were so fragile he could break them with a flick of either hand. She knew it, too. The pulse in her throat beat a wild tattoo against his palm. The cadence of it jangled every nerve in his body. An unsettling awareness washed through him, a primitive urge to capture, to conquer. Dieu, he thought, shoving the notion away in disgust. Not even in the aftermath of battle, when blood lust drove some men to rape, had he felt this unholy stirring. It must be the violent Border air. "I do not want to hurt you," he growled as much to reaffirm his civility as to reassure her.

"Aye, you do." She swallowed, shivering slightly.

That small shudder awoke something else in him, something equally primitive. The urge to protect. "Nay. I came here to put a stop to this senseless bloodletting. To prove it, I will let you keep the knife." Doubtless a grave mistake, but he needed to atone for his rapacious thoughts. "Providing you sheathe it."

"This is some trick."

"It is not, I assure you I—"

Hoofbeats sounded on the trail behind them. Over his shoulder, Hunter saw riders, coming fast. Leading them was a great bear of a man with a distinctive white streak in his dark, shaggy mane. Not McKies. Likely more Murrays.

"We'll settle this later." Hunter let go of her and kicked Zeus into a ground-eating gallop.

"Faster," urged his prisoner, peering back behind them.

"Not your kin, then, I take it."

"Dod! Far from it. That's Ill Will Bell, next of kin to Old Cootie himself. He'll rape me, pry you out of your fancy steel suit and roast you over a slow fire till you give up your gold."

"Aye, I've heard of the man." Hunter concentrated on

the rough way ahead. They raced flat out over bleak moor-
land, following the trampled wake of the cattle. They
couldn't sustain this pace for long. In the distance, he saw
more of the straggling herd and hoped to come upon his
men and the McKies.

"Go to the left," ordered the woman. "There, between
those two boulders."

"The herd…"

"Too far. Your horse won't last." She grabbed the left
rein and tugged hard.

Conditioned to instant response, Zeus wheeled, slipped
between two black rocks and plunged down a steep trail.

The woman turned to look back. "They have gone by."

"Either they missed the turn in the dark…"

"Or they have decided to go after the cattle."

Hunter grunted and focused on controlling their descent.
The moon had disappeared again, and he had no idea what
lay ahead. The path—more of an animal trail, he guessed—
was rock strewn, the hillside covered with trees. Dewy
branches slapped at his helmet and tugged at his tabard.
"Where does this trail go?" he asked, sawing back on the
reins to slow their progress.

"I—I have no idea." Her words were punctuated by
groans as she absorbed the jolts. "I do not know the land
hereabouts."

"You knew where to turn off," he said, wary of a trap.

"I saw a break in the hillside and thought it might provide us with a way out."

"And into what?"

"I—I do not know."

The trail veered sharply to the right. Hunter eased Zeus
around the turn, then stopped.

"What is it?" She looked up over her shoulder at him.
Her features were indistinct in the gloom—a pale face, and

wide dark eyes surrounded by tangled hair. Was she beautiful, this fey creature with the stout heart and canny mind?

A sound scattered his musing. "Listen."

"I do not hear anything," she said, voice hushed.

The stallion did. His ears pricked forward, his great head swung to look back up the trail.

Far above them, Hunter heard the faint crunch of stone. He leaned down and murmured, "They are coming."

She nodded, her hair tickling his cheek, teasing his nostrils with the faint scent of woman and heather. "They are not many, I think. One…two, mayhap."

"Aye."

"Do we go or stay?"

Hunter looked around at the thick pines, the black rocks that lined the edge of the trail. "'Tis not a place I'd choose to make a stand." He edged the stallion into a walk. A few paces they went, each one filled with tension. It radiated from the slender body bolt upright before him. He saw the glint of steel in her hand and realized she'd drawn the dirk again. Oddly he didn't fear she meant to use it on him this time.

"They follow," she whispered.

Hunter nodded.

The trail dipped. The stallion's hooves flirted with the edge, sending a hail of stones into unseen darkness. Hunter counted the beats till they hit bottom. It seemed a far ways off. "Easy, lad." He nudged a toe into the stallion's ribs, moving him over.

In that instant, something broke from cover. A rabbit.

The stallion screamed and sidestepped.

Into nothingness…

As they went over the edge, Hunter cursed, grabbed hold of the woman and kicked his feet free of the stirrups.

He hit hard on his back, grunted as rock dented steel. He tried to brake with his heels, groaning as his foot caught

on a rock. Pain radiated up his leg. They bounced off the
rock and slid down, like rainwater off a slate roof. Gravel
clawed at his unarmored rump and rattled against his helmet. He spared a moment's thought for the woman, protected only by her woolen trews and tunic, and clutched
her tighter against his chest.

"Hang on," he growled.

"Where?" Her fingers groped at his chest, his waist.
"You're slick as a great metal pitcher."

Hunter chuckled. But the bit of mirth was short-lived.
His back slammed into something solid. The impact drove
the air from his body. The night exploded in a shower of
bright stars.

Allisun's head hit his metal chest with a resounding
clunk, jarring her teeth, addling her wits. A moment, maybe
two, she lay there collecting herself. Then the unnatural
stillness penetrated her stupor.

They'd stopped sliding, yet the massive arms that had
held her during the fall were still clamped around her.

"You can let me go now," she whispered, raising her
head.

A bit of light filtered in through the canopy of leaves,
gleaming softly on his armor. The visor of his helmet had
come up. In the shadows it cast, she glimpsed a square jaw,
aquiline nose and closed eyes.

"Sir knight?"

He neither moved nor opened his eyes.

"McKie?" She pushed his arms aside, alarmed they
moved so easily, crawled off his chest and shook him.
"McKie?"

Nothing.

Above them on the trail, however, she heard a sound that
made her panicked heart skip a beat.

"They came down this way," said a coarse voice.

"Aye, I heard 'em crashing about, but all's quiet now."

"Bloody hell. They got away, then. Curse the luck. I gave up my share of the cattle in hopes of getting his armor."

Armor!

Allisun looked down at the expanse of metal shimmering traitorously in the pale light.

Gasping softly, she whipped off her cloak and flung it over the knight's head and torso. His left side was still exposed. She threw herself down on it, praying her dark woolens would hide the rest.

Then she lay still, listening and praying.

Chapter Three

He could not be dead, Hunter thought, for he hurt everywhere. Still, he couldn't move. When he forced his eyes open, it was to suffocating darkness.

"Dieu," he groaned.

"Shh."

Something covered his mouth. The woman's voice came out of the black, "Be still. They are above us."

"Am...am I blind?" he mumbled.

"Nay. Only covered so they won't see us."

Coarse voices grumbled above them, arguing, he thought.

The woman whimpered softly, her breathing shallow and raspy. Her slender body, pressed more closely against his left side, shuddering convulsively.

Instinctively he put an arm around her, grateful that it moved to his command. Mayhap he was not paralyzed after all. As he lay there in the dark, his mind leaped back over the night's events: the cattle raid, the woman he'd rescued, the precipitous flight from a band of brigands and the fall that had ended here.

A voice intruded, loud and coarse. "That armor he was

wearing would be worth a fortune.'' Gravel crunched. ''Looks like they went over the edge here.''

''Curse the luck,'' said another harsh voice.

The Bells, Hunter thought. He should do something…get up, draw his sword and prepare to defend. But he could not marshal the strength to move. To a man of action, lying here totally defenseless, waiting for the enemy to strike, was pure torture. His body jerked as he tried to force it to move.

''Stay still.'' The woman stroked his cheek. ''I know it is hard to stay hidden here,'' she whispered. ''But we could not hope to prevail against so many armed, ruthless animals.''

Hunter wanted to scream. At the moment, he could not have fought a week-old kitten.

''They could be hurt,'' said one.

''Do ye think so?'' the other Bell asked eagerly.

''Aye. They was fools to try this in the dark. If they aren't dead, they'll be sore hurt.''

''Easy pickings. What say, should we go down and see?''

''Idiot, I'm not chancing this trail at night. Besides, if they're hurt, they won't be going anyplace. We can go and get our share of the cattle, then sneak back later when it's daylight and take what we want.''

Their footsteps faded away.

''They have gone.'' She sat up, flinging off the cloak with which she'd covered them.

''Well, at least I am not blind,'' Hunter grumbled, blinking against the moonlight filtering through the leaves.

''I am sorry, but I feared they'd spot that shiny armor of yours.'' She slung the cloak around her shoulders and shifted to her knees beside him. ''They will be back. We must leave as—''

''I cannot move.''

"What?" She leaned over him, frowning as she poked and prodded. "Small wonder, I'd say. You're wedged in between a rock and the tree that broke your fall."

"My back?"

"I do not think it's broken." She smiled faintly. "Your armor's caught fast in the rocks. Here, let's get this out of the way for a start." She tugged off his helmet.

He swore as his head thumped on the stony ground. "Have a care what you are—"

"Sorry. I've never done this before." She attacked the leather buckles holding the breastplate and back of his armor together. When they were loose, she cocked her head, grinning down at him. "You look a bit like a turtle I once trapped."

"This is not amusing."

"The turtle didna think so, either. He ended up in a soup."

"Just get on with it, will you?"

"Aye, since you asked so nicely." She approached the task with far more zeal than skill. It was no easy task for a small, inexperienced woman to extricate a prone man from a set of full battle plate. After much sweating and swearing on both their parts, she wrested the armor from his torso.

Freed of the encumbering weight, which had indeed been jammed between two rocks by the force of his fall, Hunter managed to sit up. "Damn." He gingerly flexed first his shoulders, then his back. "Argh." His hand went straight to the spot just above his waist where he'd met the tree.

"Hurt?" She circled around and lifted the hem of the padded gambeson he wore to protect against the chafing metal. "The skin's not cut, but you'll have a dandy bruise."

"You say that so cheerily because it's mine, not yours."

She chuckled and came around to sit beside him. "It

could have been much worse. Worthless as I find your armor, it did save you from greater injury.''

"Worthless?" Hunter bristled. "It will stop an arrow and even a slashing blow from a sword or lance."

"Aye, but it weighs down a man and his mount and makes him far less agile in battle."

Hunter grunted. He'd heard that argument from more than one Scot who preferred the traditional armaments to the armor popular in England and Europe. "This time, I'd say my plate was both blessing and potential curse. My thanks, for hiding me earlier and for getting me free." Bracing his hand on a huge boulder, he stood. Pain stabbed through his left ankle, sending him back down.

"What is it?"

"My ankle."

"Can you move it?"

Hunter warily rotated the foot, then nodded.

"Mayhap it is not broken, then." She tugged off his boot.

Gritting his teeth against the pain, Hunter endured her poking and prodding.

"A bad twist, I'd say."

"Bloody hell!" Hunter gazed angrily around at the stark, wild land. Then a new worry intruded. "The stallion?"

"I—I do not know. I think he slid on past us, but I have not heard a sound from below."

They both turned to look at the wall of trees and rocks that hid the rest of the descending slope, then at each other. The same thought was in both their faces. The horse was dead.

"I am sorry," she whispered.

"So am I. My sire raised him from a colt."

Tears glinted in her eyes. "I could go down and search."

"Nay." The tightness in Hunter's chest expanded to fill

his throat. "He must be dead. An injured horse is not quiet."

"We cannot stay here."

"I know." Hunter glared balefully at his swollen ankle. If worse came to worst, he'd walk on it and damn the agony.

"It may not hold you."

"It will," he snapped. "But there is no sense blundering about in the dark. Mayhap a few hours' rest will improve it."

"Hmm." Allisun doubted that but saw no reason to argue. A poultice might aid the healing, but the herbs she'd brought with her in case anyone was injured were lost with her horse. "I could walk up to the trailhead and—"

"Return with your kin." His face and voice were as fierce as they'd been when he'd rescued her.

"Nay, that is not what I meant." But she knew he didn't believe her. Why should he? Though they'd worked together to escape the stampede and the Bells, they were enemies.

"They will come looking for you?" he asked.

"Aye. Of a certainty they will." Providing they were alive and free. Sweet Mary, what if they weren't? What if—?

"Just as my men will search for me."

"Providing the Bells did not get them all."

He snorted. "My men are more than a match for that rabble."

"That rabble is the most ruthless fighting force about."

"My men will best them."

Arrogant ass. Allisun glared at him. "The Bells may be more interested in cattle stealing than fighting."

"Let's hope so, for all our sakes. But it may be some time before my men find us." He gazed up the mountain, then back at her. "We should get what rest we can."

Allisun glared right back at him. "I have no intention of sitting here, waiting on a bunch of McKies."

"Because of the feud."

"Of course."

"So, you are a Murray."

"I never said—"

"Allisun Murray?"

She gasped. "How can you know that?"

"My uncle said that with your brother gone, you would lead your kinsmen in their raids. I thought him wrong to accuse a woman of such heathenish ways, but I was mistaken."

"Aye, you were." Allisun leaped up. "About so much." She whirled to leave.

He grabbed her ankle, bringing her to the ground with a plop and a grunt of pain. "You are my prisoner, and so you'll stay."

"Nay." She lashed out at him with her free foot. He captured that, too.

Holding both her ankles in one wide hand, he whipped off his belt with the other. "You are my prisoner."

"I saved your life," she exclaimed. "I could have left you here, unconscious, for the Bells to find."

"And I could have let you fall to the stampede." He hauled her closer, looped one end of the belt around her right wrist, the other around his left. "I would say we are even."

Fury overcame her fear. "You McKies owe me for the deaths of my father and brothers." She reached for her knife.

Before the blade cleared the scabbard, he seized her hand and held it fast. My name is Carmichael, not McKie."

"Carmichael?" Her face turned whiter; her eyes widened.

"Hunter Carmichael," he said with relish.

"You were there that day."

"Aye," he snapped. "I saw your father take my aunt."

The color rushed back into her cheeks. "You saw, but you know nothing." Her eyes narrowed. "This feud was your fault. Had you not raised a hue and cry—"

"Your lecherous sire would have gotten away with my aunt and no one would have known whom to blame for the heinous deed."

She laughed, the sound choked, wild and bitter. "How little you know," she whispered.

"I know what I saw."

"Appearances can be deceiving."

Not to a man who had always dealt in facts. "I was there."

"So you were." Her shoulders slumped. She bent her head and repeated the phrase softly, sadly. "And because you were, my family has been hounded—"

"With good reason."

"So you say."

Hunter stared at her, trying to pierce the veil of hair that hung before her delicate profile. "What are *you* saying?"

She turned, tossing the hair from her face, her eyes intent, burning into his. "Nothing, except that you are completely wrong about what happened."

Hunter glared right back at her. He felt guilty for not having saved his aunt, but he'd not shoulder the blame for starting this feud. Alex Murray had done that when he had kidnapped his aunt. "You'd best try to sleep," he said tersely. "We must try to leave here before dawn."

Her head came up at that, like a fighter sensing a challenge. "Oh, I will be ready, sir knight."

He slept.

Allisun listened to the rhythmic rasp of the knight's

breathing and knew exhaustion had overridden his wariness.

Slowly, cautiously, she bent to slide her hand down the outside of her left leg. There, in the top of her boot, was the small knife no Borderer went without. One eye on her enemy, she eased the dirk free. If the past twelve years had taught her one thing, it was patience. She applied it now, pressing the sharp blade ever so gently to the leather that bound her to him.

Long minutes passed.

An owl called out from the branches above. Its mate answered, and the pair set out, gliding from the trees on silent wings, hunting in perfect accord.

Her parents had been like that, Allisun reflected as she worked at the bindings. Two bodies, one mind. One heart. Their love had been a thing of beauty, till her mother sickened and her father turned to Brenna for solace. Aye, the Murrays' miseries, past and present, could be laid at the feet of that sorceress, Brenna. But she was gone, and there was no way to make Hunter understand that without seeming to vilify the dead.

She sliced through the last bit of leather, then held her breath, watching, waiting to see if he'd rouse. He was a handsome man, she thought, staring at his sleep-softened features, the square, stubborn jaw and full, expressive mouth. It was his eyes, though, that had fascinated her. So deep a shade of brown they looked black by moonlight, and so intent they seemed to see clear through her.

When he did not move, Allisun crept from beneath the cloak he'd draped over them for warmth and stole away. It had originally been her plan to climb up to the trailhead and wait in concealment for her men to ride by. But the fate of Hunter's horse weighed heavily on her mind. What if it was alive but unable to cry out? The thought of so noble a beast in pain sent her toward the base of the gulch.

Keeping low to the ground, moving from tree to tree as Danny had taught her, she reached the base of the mountain. Here the woods were fed by a bubbling burn, the water sweet and cool to her parched throat. As she drank, she thought of Hunter Carmichael, who doubtless hungered and thirsted, too.

Bah. The McKies would find him come morn and carry him back to Luncarty, there to feed him and tend his ankle.

Rising, she turned away from the stream, and nearly fell over the body of the great stallion.

"Poor thing." She touched its forehead.

"What are you doing?"

Allisun whirled around, the knife clutched in her hand. Hunter Carmichael stood a few feet away, leaning heavily on a thick tree branch.

"How did you get here without my hearing?"

"Because I am as good at sneaking about as you are." Limping forward, he knelt on the stallion's other side and gently stroked the satiny shoulder. "Broken neck."

"Aye. He did not suffer," Allisun offered.

"That is something, I suppose." His hand stilled. "I have two colts and a filly from him, but..."

"It is hard to lose someone you love."

Hunter looked up at her, surprised by the understanding, the compassion in her face. Most people would have scoffed at the loss of a horse. Allisun Murray was different in a way that tugged at him. He couldn't let it matter. "Why did you come down here instead of going up the trail?"

"I thought he might be suffering."

The tug twisted deep in his gut. "He didn't."

"Nay. I am glad of that. Still..." A single tear glistened on her cheek. "'Tis a sad end to so magnificent a beast."

Hunter stared at her a moment, wondering how a man as heinous as Alexander Murray, the kidnapper he'd hated for years, could have raised so gentle a daughter. Dismissing the notion, he turned away and removed Zeus's trappings.

"You cannot carry the saddle, not with that ankle."

"I've no intention of trying. I'll hide it and the lance in yonder brush, then cover his body with branches."

"Why?"

"If the Bells come down here looking for us and find the horse, they'll know we are afoot."

"If they don't see him, they'll assume we rode on." Allisun nodded, her mind racing. A half hour's climb would put her at the top of the trail. She was fairly certain the rocks there would conceal her while she waited for her kin.

"Go, if you want," said Hunter. "I'll not stop you."

She looked at his foot, braced gingerly against a rock, then up at the strong, clean lines of his face. "What of you?"

"I will soak my ankle in the cold burn till daylight, then climb up to the trailhead and watch for my men."

"What if my kin come along first?"

He grinned, his teeth a white slash in his tanned face. "Then I'll have to hope you'll intercede with them on my behalf."

"Why should I?"

"Because you're a fair-minded wench."

Allisun scowled. "We are enemies."

"Whom fate has thrown together. You've two sound legs to walk about. I've a sword for defense and food." He dangled a pouch before her. "Oatcakes, dried beef and a flask of whiskey."

"I'm not hung—" Her stomach growled in disagreement. There was never enough to eat, and she was always hungry.

Hunter chuckled. "What say we declare a truce, Allisun Murray? Just till we're rescued."

"What happens then?" she asked warily.

"I swear that if my men find us first, we'll either leave you here unharmed or take you to wherever you want to go."

She sniffed. "Jock McKie'll not abide by that."

"My uncle is back home at Luncarty. His leg was badly smashed when your brother ambushed him."

"What?" Allisun exclaimed, torn between outrage at the accusation and joy that their nemesis was wounded. "If Danny fought, 'twas only after Old Jock attacked him. And them riding under a flag of truce."

"My uncle says differently."

"Then he lies," she snapped. "My brother is not here to defend himself, but I will tell you this—Danny was a gentle lad, only a year older than I am, who had hoped to become a priest. This damned feud shattered that dream, as it did our lives, but Danny still hated killing. He'd not have struck first."

Hunter hesitated, weighing her earnestness against his uncle's earlier impassioned tale. Jock was loud and crude, but he had a reputation for honesty. And this woman was a stranger, an enemy. "It matters little what happened in the past. Fate has trapped us here, afoot in an area teeming with rapacious Bells. Our best chance of survival lies in working together. My offer of a truce between us still holds."

She eyed him narrowly. "That is what Old Jock offered when he lured my brother to his doom."

"Dieu," Hunter exclaimed, raking his thick hair back with an exasperated hand. "You are a hard, suspicious thing."

"Thank you. I'd not have survived otherwise. Still, I suppose there is naught to be gained by squabbling. So, I agree to the truce. But just till we're rescued, mind."

With her chin tilted up, her jaw set, Hunter could see

there was much of the fighter in Allisun Murray, too. "I agree to your terms."

To his surprise, they worked well together. Still it took time for a small woman and a limping man to do what must be done. Dawn was lightening the sky above the trees by the time they'd gotten the horse covered and the armaments hidden.

Hunter ducked behind a bush to remove his hose, then limped to the bank of the stream wearing only his thigh-length quilted tunic. The ankle was bruised, swollen to twice its normal size and throbbed like a bad tooth. He hoped it was just twisted and not broken. Sitting down on a rock, he eased his foot into the swift-running water. Air hissed between his teeth. "Ach, 'tis cold as ice." He pulled his foot out again.

"Just what's needed to bring down the swelling." Allisun knelt beside him, grasped his calf and pushed the foot back in.

The feel of her hands on his bare skin sent a shiver up his leg, stirring something he had no right feeling for Alexander Murray's daughter. Desire. But the body cared little for grudges and feuds. She was young and beautiful, in a wild, untamed way he found oddly appealing. The baggy trews that had disgusted him the night before molded temptingly to a surprisingly shapely rump as she bent to examine his injury.

Hunter groaned softly and tried to pull away.

"Easy." Her grip on his leg tightened, and so did other, less discerning muscles farther up his leg. "I just want to see..." She rotated the ankle.

"Ach!" Hunter yelped as pain exploded.

"Does it hurt here?"

"Of course it does. Damn thing's likely broken." And then where would he be? Crippled, if it wasn't set properly.

"If only my Aunt Elspeth were here. She's a skilled herb woman."

"If I were wishing, it'd be for two horses."

"I suppose you are right." He leaned forward, peering at his dripping foot. "Do you think it's broken?"

"Nay, I think…" She turned, and suddenly their faces were only a scant inch apart. The heat from his body, the faint scent of his skin teased her senses and made her insides draw tight as a bowstring. Fear? Nay, nor was it the hatred she wanted to feel. An odd sort of excitement ruffled through her, quickening her pulse, raising the fine hairs on her arms and neck.

Hunter watched her blue eyes darken and knew she felt the same sensual tug he did. The spark that arced between them kindled an unexpected heat deep in his belly. Lust stirred, dulling his brain, heightening his senses.

Her hair had come loose from its thick braid and straggled down her back. He wanted to thrust his hands into the tangled mass and see if it was as soft as it looked. He yearned to press her tense little body to the aching length of his and cover her mouth with his own. He longed to kiss her till they were both mindless and breathless with desire.

"Allisun," he whispered, lowering his head.

"What?" She blinked and shook her head, then flinched back away from him. "What do you think you're doing?"

"This." He moved closer, a hairbreadth from her lips.

She gasped and dodged aside. "Is this the way you keep your truce, by…by attacking me the moment my guard is down?"

"I was merely giving us what we both want."

"Want?" She dropped his leg back into the water. "You are mad! This unholy lust must run in the Carmichael blood. But I am not as easy a mark as my poor father was."

"You will cease implying that my aunt was some sort of—"

"Whore!" Allisun sneered. "Adulteress. Is that not what they call a woman who steals another woman's hus—"

"Hello, there!" called a loud male voice.

Hunter whipped his head up, shocked to find a band of mounted men watching them from across the stream. There must be a score, at least, dressed in leather jacks and trews, swords at their sides, riding sleek horses.

Allisun cursed ripely under her breath and reached for the knife she'd set on the bank.

"Not Murrays, I take it?" Hunter whispered.

"Nay. Nor Bells, either, but they're not the only vermin hereabouts." She scrambled to her feet, her knife held before her. "Stay back."

Hunter grabbed his sword from the stony riverbank, for all the good he'd be on only one leg.

Chapter Four

"**W**ho are you?" Hunter demanded.

The foremost man, a stout fellow with graying hair and a wide, florid face, smiled and held both his hands up, palms out. "Easy…easy. We mean ye no harm."

"English," Allisun hissed.

Hunter scowled. "How can you tell? He sounds like a Scot."

"To you, mayhap, but a Borderer can hear the difference." Allisun glared at the newcomers. "Be on your way, Englishman."

"Derk Neville," the man replied, directing a puzzled glance at Allisun before returning his attention to Hunter. "And the lass is right, I was born across the Tweed. Like many men, I've land on both sides of the river. Last year, I bought a fine Scottish tower, and that's where I make my home at present. We are on our way back there from Kelso." He gestured at his troop, which included a few heavily laden packhorses. "Went there to fetch some goods my wife ordered."

"How many men have you got sneaking around behind us?" Allisun demanded.

"None." Derk looked affronted. "We came down to water our beasts and saw ye two, er, doing whatever ye're doing.''

Hunter flushed. ''I've twisted my—''

''He's washing his feet,'' Allisun said.

Derk grinned. ''Oh, aye. Well, we'll just give the beasts a wee sip and be on our way.''

''Don't come any clos—''

Hunter clamped a hand on her leg. ''You'll have to excuse her curtness. We were set upon by brigands.''

''Was it Bells?'' Derk exclaimed.

''Aye,'' Hunter said slowly, neither trusting nor distrusting. ''How did you know?''

''Well, most of the ill deeds done hereabouts can be laid at Ill Will's door, but,'' he said as he glanced around, ''truth to tell, we'd not be taking this trail through the glen if my scouts hadn't spotted Will and his bunch up on the moor.''

''What were they doing?'' Hunter and Allisun both asked.

''Roasting a haunch of beef.''

''You are certain 'twas not a man?'' Allisun asked.

''The lass knows Ill Will, I see. Nay, 'twas a steer. They had a good-size herd standing about nearby. Will's men looked right busy keeping an eye on them, but my lads and I decided we'd not take a chance the Bells had time to rob us.'' He grinned. ''My Morna'd have a fit if I lost that thick Turkish carpet before she's had a chance to walk on it.''

Hunter smiled back and laid his sword down. ''We understand. Come ahead and water your stock, Derk Neville.''

''Nay,'' Allisun softly cried. ''What if he's lying?''

''Shh.'' Hunter motioned her down beside him. ''The truth is, if Derk wanted to kill us, there is not a damn thing I could do to stop him,'' he whispered. It galled, for he was a man who prided himself on his ability to cope with any situation. ''I might take one or two with me,'' he added, watching out of the corner of his eye as the Nevilles dismounted and brought their mounts to drink at the stream. "But I'd not win."

"Us," she hissed back. "I know how to use this, and if I had a sword—"

"Allisun." He closed his hand over her clenched fist. "Even if we had two swords apiece, they'd best us."

She glared hatred at the Nevilles. "What do we do?"

Derk Neville hailed them from across the stream. "Couldn't help noticing ye've no horses about."

"They are grazing," Allisun replied.

Hunter squeezed her hand, then looked at Derk. "Actually, we lost both mounts getting away from the Bells."

"Ah. Ye're lucky to be alive. Ye hurt yer foot?" At Hunter's nod, Derk frowned. "If ye like, we could juggle our load and free up a horse for the pair of ye to ride."

"Aye," said Hunter.

"Nay," said Allisun.

"We must. No telling how long before our kinsmen can safely look for us," Hunter said through his teeth. No telling if they were even alive. Then louder he said, "Thanks. We accept."

Allisun spat a curse that would have made a trooper blush.

"Did your mother never tell you swearing isn't lady-like?"

"She died when I was six."

Hunter's anger leached away. "I am sorry." Recalling the gentle guidance and unswerving love of his own mother, Hunter felt a stab of pity for this prickly lass. With his free hand, he gently grazed her cheek.

She knocked his hand aside, her eyes flashing blue fire, her chin mutinously high. "I'm not going with you."

Beneath her defiance, Hunter saw a flicker of fear. It stabbed at his conscience, reminding him that he was responsible for her safety. Whether she liked it or not. "Aye, you are. I'll not leave you here alone and on foot with the Bells—"

"You are not responsible for me," she snapped.

"Lovers' quarrel?" Derk asked, grinning as he waded across the stream.

Allisun glared at Derk and tried vainly to wrench her hand from Hunter's grip. "We are not—"

"Of a sort," Hunter interjected, seeing an answer to the questions he knew Derk would pose about who they were. "We were running away." Beside him, he heard Allisun draw breath to protest. He stilled it by wrapping a loverlike arm around her waist and squeezing...hard.

"Humph," Allisun wheezed, exhaling noisily.

"Her family does not approve of me." Hunter grinned in response to her outraged expression. Under cover of dropping a kiss on her brow, he whispered, "If you do not go along with me, he may learn you're a Murray and decide to collect the reward Uncle Jock has offered for you."

Her eyes widened, and her mouth snapped shut.

"Truly?" Derk climbed the bank, water streaming from his knee-high boots. His sharp gaze moved from Hunter's equally fine boots and Spanish-made sword to Allisun's worn tunic.

Hunter's nimble mind seized a likely response. "I'm a Highlander," he confided. "Her kin feared I'd take her north, and they'd never see her again."

"Highlander, ye say. What clan?"

"Sutherland. I am Hunt Sutherland of Kinduin," he added, borrowing his Uncle Lucais's surname and estate.

Derk nodded his head in acknowledgment and turned to Allisun. "And ye, lass?"

"Allie...Allie Hall."

"Hall?" Derk rubbed his thick gray beard. "From where?"

"Over Moffat way," she said grudgingly, glaring at Hunter.

"Allie Sutherland, she is now." Hunter met her scowls with a wide grin. "We are handfasted," he added, to prevent her from being branded a loose woman.

Allie made a choking sound, her eyes wide with horror. *Do you realize what you have done?* they silently asked.

Hunter was a little shocked himself. The words had just slipped out before he'd had a chance to think...really think...about the consequences. In some places, merely declaring themselves wed before witnesses was enough to unite a couple for a year and a day. Then if the marriage did not suit them, the couple could separate. They'd be parting much sooner than that, Hunter thought. "'Tis just till we can find a priest and be properly wed," he added, and hoped Derk would think lack of a permanent ceremony the reason for Allie's outburst.

"Women set store by that," Derk said. "'Tis pleased I am to meet ye both. Ah, here come the lads with the horses."

While Derk went to meet his men, Hunter levered himself to his feet. "I am sorry for that," he whispered to Allisun. "But I could not have him think you were a...a—"

"Better a whore than your wife," she snapped.

"You are not the mate I'd choose, either," Hunter said through set teeth. "But 'tis only for a few days, till my ankle heals and we can go our separate ways."

"If they will let us." Fear shadowed her eyes, and her lips trembled slightly as she watched the Nevilles close in on them.

Hunter felt another unwelcome stab of sympathy. Poor thing, she'd been hunted and hounded most of her life. "Do not be afraid." He put an arm around her. "I will not abandon you."

Allisun threw off his arm and glared up at him. "Is that supposed to reassure me?"

"Aye." Twelve years ago he'd been unable to save his aunt. He would not fail another woman.

"We are enemies," she hissed as the Nevilles led forth a horse. "Why should you care what happens to me?"

"I do not know." Hunter studied her delicate profile, the high cheekbones, haughty nose and willful chin. She was a complex lass, her bravery unquenched by hardship, her beauty undimmed by poverty. But the years had marked her, he thought, recalling the lush mouth that was made to smile but seldom did, the eyes so often shuttered and unreadable.

What was it about her that moved him?

The storm that had threatened the night before began in earnest as they set out.

The cool drizzle suited Allisun's mood exactly. She wanted to feel as miserable on the outside as she did on the inside, torn by concern for her kinsmen and apprehension for herself.

"Here, this will keep off the rain." Hunter draped over them both an oiled cloth he'd had in his saddle roll.

"I am used to being wet." Allisun flung back the cloth.

"Allie, 'tis possible they are back home, safe and dry."

"Our roof leaks," she snapped.

"I am sorry for that."

"Jock is not. He burned us out of our tower." The memory of that chaotic night, filled with fire and screams of pain, bolstered her anger against Hunter.

"Getting sick yourself will not change that." He tucked the oiled cloth securely around her, then clamped an arm about her waist to keep it there.

Allisun fumed, trapped against the hard wall of his chest. It was like being enveloped by a furnace. She tried to maintain her stiff posture, but the heat from his body seeped in to banish the cold from hers. Lulled by the warmth and the horse's rolling gait, her tired muscles sagged and her weary mind drifted back over the night's events.

Damn Hunter for being so confounding. His words, his actions confused her. She did not like him, but her reasons for hating him were no longer as clear as they had been. When he'd first guessed her identity, she'd expected to be abused or even killed. After all, he'd spent the past twelve years believing her father had murdered his aunt. But instead of taking his anger out on her, he had treated her with gentleness and respect. Oh, his high-handedness grated on her independent spirit, but his dry wit tickled her latent sense of humor. And that hadn't happened in a long, long time. How could a man be infuriating and amusing at the same time?

Well, there was nothing humorous about the situation in which she now found herself. Handfasted to Hunter Carmichael.

Her parents and brothers were doubtless turning over in their graves. The only consolation she could offer to them, and to herself, was that it was temporary. As soon as they reached Derk Neville's tower, she'd find a way to escape.

"Allie?"

"Hmm?" Realizing she'd slumped into him, she stiffened.

"Nay. Lean back, rest. I but wanted to tell you—"

"I am not tired." She sat bolt upright.

The sudden movement overset their mount, who shied and sidestepped on the narrow trail.

"Easy." Hunter's arm tightened around Allisun's waist. His muscular thighs bunched beneath her rump as he brought the horse under control.

Allisun was abruptly, vividly aware of him in a way she hadn't been before. Through the layers of wool that separated them, she could feel the muscles of his chest supporting her back. It unsettled her to find the measured cadence of his heartbeat echoing hers. For some reason the heat radiating from his body made her skin feel too warm and a size too small. Restless, she tried to sit forward.

"Sit still, or you'll rile our horse," Hunter murmured. His breath stirred the hair at her temple, sending gooseflesh tingling down her cheek and neck.

Allisun shivered. Was she sickening?

"Are you cold?" He held her closer. The pressure of his arm on her waist scrambled her insides and made the quivering in her belly worse.

"Nay, I tremble with hatred for you." She wished it were true. Wished she did not like him. "You are my enemy," she added, as much to remind herself of that.

"I have never done you ill." He managed to sound hurt.

Allisun bypassed the obvious—that had he not raised the alarm, Jock would never have known whom to blame for Brenna's disappearance. "You snatched me from my horse, tumbled us down a ravine and tied me to you with this handfasting."

Hunter's temper flared, goaded as much by pain and lack of sleep as her accusations. "Ingrate! In all this, I have but tried to protect you. Would you rather I told Derk who you are?" he whispered. "I am not the one with a price on my head."

She sagged in his arms and shook her head.

Oddly, that small sign of defeat deflated Hunter's fury. Who could blame her for being prickly and defiant, given what she'd told him about her life. Orphaned. Driven from her home. Forced to dress in rags and live under a leaky roof. Once he might have thought such hardships no more than the Murrays' due, but that was before he'd met this rare, brave lass. Strangely, he wanted to make it up to her, but he knew she'd reject his sympathy even more vehemently than she did his offers of help. "I wanted to tell you," he said in a stern voice, parent to child, "that when we reach Derk's home, I will offer to buy this horse from him so we can leave immediately."

"You have coin?"

"Aye." His father had taught him to carry a bit of gold in his boot, just in case. "Not a fortune, but enough to buy—"

"Two horses. I do not like being hemmed in like this."

Hunter grinned ruefully, glad his thick tunic kept her from knowing how he felt about the forced intimacy. What was it about this grubby, rebellious lass that made him want to forget the feud? His desire for her was inappropriate and inconvenient. Clearing his throat, he tried to ignore it. "Two horses then."

"And once we've got them, we'll go our separate ways."

"After I take you home."

She swiveled her head, pinning him with wide blue eyes. "Nay, you cannot know where I live."

"Nor can I let you wander about the countryside alone. What if you chanced upon the Bells?"

"Better that than to lead Jock McKie to our hideaway."

I would not betray you. But Hunter knew she wouldn't believe him. "Let us take each step in turn."

Allisun snorted and faced front again. "You can take whatever steps you like, but I'll not be showing you our camp." Despite her brave words, she was shaking inside, her mind racing to find a way out of this damnable situation.

"I do not think Derk Neville will harm us," Hunter said after a few moments. "He seems a decent man."

"Looks can be deceiving, especially hereabouts."

"Aye," Hunter mused. "I've heard Borderers are a rough lot. Constant feuds. Raiding, arson, kidnapping. 'Tis said robbery and blackmail are so common they're considered callings.''

"That is not true."

"Nay? What of the Elliots and the Armstrongs?"

"They are riding families."

"Meaning?"

"They make their way by raiding and reiving."

"My point exactly."

"But not everyone is like them. Most folk tend to their herds and their hearths."

"Unless someone steals their stock," said Hunter. "In which case, they ride hard after the raiders."

"Aye. The hot trod, we call it."

"Legalized cattle rustling, more like."

"The hot trod is only to reclaim what was stolen. Would you deny folk the right to get back what was theirs?"

"And mayhap take a bit more into the bargain?"

"Some might, especially if they had kinfolk hurt or killed in the original raid, but my da never held with such things."

Hunter listened to the passion with which she spoke of her father. Again he wondered what sort of man Alexander Murray had been. His own memory of the one time they'd met was bitter. "You cannot convince me your father never took what was not his."

"Well, he never *took* your aunt. She came willingly."

"I do not believe you." Yet he vaguely recalled Jock saying something about Alex sniffing around Brenna at a Truce Day meet.

"I wish it were not true. I wish it had never happened."

"But why? She and Jock had not been married long." Through his mind drifted the sounds of their voices raised in argument. A quarrel, one they had made up. He remembered, too, the sounds of their lovemaking.

"They were in *love,*" Allie said nastily.

Lust, more likely. It had been leading couples astray since Adam and Eve. It struck Hunter that he could be falling into the same trap. "Can you prove he did not kidnap her?"

"No more than you can prove he did."

Hunter scowled.

"Foul weather, ain't it," said Derk, coming to ride alongside them.

"Aye," Hunter muttered.

"The raiding season'll soon be upon us." Derk wiped a drop of water from his bulbous nose. "Hard times then."

"Is the threat so constant?" Hunter asked idly.

"Oh, aye." Derk shrugged. "There's little chance a band of broken men would attack a tower as stout and well guarded as mine, but if the great riding families take it in their mind to come this way…well, then it'd be fight or pay blackmail."

"Because you're English?"

"Don't matter much. Does it, lass?" He winked at Allisun. "There's English reivers just as like to cross the Tweed and burn me out as attack my Scots neighbors."

What a revolting way to live. "The Border Wardens?"

"Do what they can. Last year Rob Croser and his band ravaged the land around Jedburgh. Killed ten, left another dozen bad hurt. Andy Kerr caught him driving a herd of stolen stock. Hanged thirty Crosers on the spot, the Warden did."

"Without a trial?"

"Well, Andy feared if they waited about for that, Rob's son would gather up his men and their Nixon kin and get Rob free."

Border justice, Hunter thought, gut tightening with revulsion. His father had said that in this wild land, men were both victim and conqueror. "Such constant strife breeds hard men and women," Ross Carmichael had added.

Thinking of the woman seated before him, Hunter could only agree. And yet he wondered what would become of Allisun when they parted company. Would she die? Would his uncle be the one to kill her or order her killed?

Much as he wanted to avenge his aunt's kidnapping, Hunter did not know if he could live with that. It had been much easier to hate the Murrays when they were a faceless foe.

"Dinna fret about yer safety," said Derk. "Ye're welcome to stay with us till yer ankle's healed, then I'll give ye a pair of horses and a guide to get ye where ye're going."

"My thanks. That is most generous, is it not, Allie?"

Suspiciously so. Allisun grunted and watched Derk closely.

"Not at all," Derk said expansively. "We've plenty of room now the repairs have finally been completed. The tower was in such deplorable shape my wife spoke against buying it. But it came cheap and is so well located I figured it would be worth the trouble and expense of fixing it. 'Tis situated on a bluff that commands a sweeping view of the valley. No chance of anyone sneaking up on my tower. The fields have not been grazed in several years, and provide rich feed for my stock. The river nearby is filled with salmon. What more could a man ask?"

"It sounds a veritable paradise," said Hunter.

Allisun was less charmed. As the two men chatted about defenses, she watched the Neville out of the corner of her eye, searching for some sign of evil in his manner. By the time Derk called a halt, she was jumpy and grumpy.

Hunter reined in their horse beside the meandering stream. Dismounting, he reached up for her. "You'll feel better once you've, er, stretched your legs."

"I am fine." Allisun ducked under his hands and slid to

the ground. Her legs wobbled, but she caught hold of the horse's stirrup to steady herself. "Just fine."

"I can see that." Humor danced in his eyes.

She whirled and stalked off into the trees. Taking care no Nevilles were about, she eliminated one problem that had added to her edginess. As she stepped out from behind her bush, she found Hunter a few feet away, leaning against a pine tree.

"Why did you follow me?"

"To make certain you were all right." Before she could reply, he took her arm and led her back, limping heavily.

"You should not have bothered. Your ankle…"

"Is no worse." He grinned. "Thanks for your concern."

"I was not worried." Exactly.

"Well, I was. Derk said we'd not be stopping long, and I was afraid you might become…lost."

"I gave you my word I'd not run away."

"Aye, but you trust the Nevilles less than you do me."

Allisun opened her mouth to answer and shut it again, for Derk awaited them by the stream.

"A bit of food?" The Neville held out oatcakes and cheese.

"I am not hungry." Allisun turned away and sat down on a rock at the water's edge. Leaning over, she drank deep and prayed her empty stomach wouldn't growl.

Behind her, she heard Hunter sigh. "She is tired."

"Aye, and a bit nervous, too, I'd wager. 'Tis hard on a lass to leave her home and kin. Even for the man she loves."

Love. Allisun ground her teeth together.

"Allie?" Hunter touched her shoulder.

She bolted upright, ready to flay them with her tongue. Derk was gone, and Hunter's soft smile blunted her weapon.

"What is it?" he asked gently. "Why do you hate Derk?"

"I do not know." She looked over to where Derk stood watering his horse. Chilled suddenly, she chafed her arms through the rough tunic.

"If he intended to harm us, he needn't have gone to the trouble of bringing us with him."

That made sense, more so than the sense of impending doom that skittered through her. "It is just a feeling."

"I understand. Having been brought up as you were by—"

"Do not say anything against my father!" she warned.

His expression cooled. "I was not going to." He put an oatcake and slab of dried meat into her hand. "Eat. We'll be a long time on the trail, and I'll not pick you up if you faint."

As Allisun watched him limp away, leaning heavily on the stout branch, she felt an odd sort of loss. Bah, it was just that she knew him better than she did the others. Still she felt even worse when they mounted again. This time Hunter's silence was cold as the rain.

She was drooping in the saddle by the time Derk once again halted the cavalcade.

"There it is...Hawkehill," he said proudly.

Allisun looked up, blinked and rubbed her eyes, scarcely able to believe what she saw.

Nay, it was not possible. God would not be so cruel.

But it was.

Derk Neville had apparently renamed the tower he'd bought and repaired. But there, clinging to the ridge, silhouetted against the setting sun, was Keastwicke.

The tower her family had called home for generations.

"I am going back out to look for Hunter," said Gavin Sutherland, his armor speckled with mud, his face grim.

"But ye just rode in," Jock grumbled. "My men and yers are nigh dead on their feet. And the horses—"

"I am going," snarled the black-haired Highlander.

Jock cursed silently and wondered how best to work around the irate knight. They were alone in the great hall, his clansmen having stumbled off to sleep in the watch-tower above, exhausted by hours of fruitless searching. "Ye'll not be able to follow a trail in the dark. Wait till morn and Red Rowy—"

"'Tis because of him we lost Hunter. I wanted to keep after those cursed Bells, but he forced us to retreat."

"Because Rowy knows better than to mess with Ill Will."

Gavin clapped a hand on his sword hilt. "I've twenty trained fighting men who'll soon teach Bell a lesson."

"Ye're a braw man, young Gavin," Jock said carefully. "But the Bells can put two hundred men in the saddle just that quick." He shifted, cursing the broken leg that kept him out of the fray just when he was needed most.

"I'll send word to Lord Ross. He can raise an army—"

"Dod!" Jock exclaimed. The last thing he needed was to have his peace-loving brother by marriage here, sticking his nose into matters. "Do ye want to start a war?" he cried, desperation tightening his voice. "Show up here in force, and the Bells'll call for Fyre and Sword through the Borders. They'll drag the Armstrongs, the Elliots and the Crosers into this, for they're distant kin to all three families."

Gavin's eyes widened. "Ach, I've heard of them."

"And naught good, I'll wager." Jock smothered a grin. "Doubtless yer Sutherland clan will feel obliged to join and first thing ye know—"

"Hmm." Gavin let go of his sword hilt and rubbed his chin. "I did not realize it could come to that, but neither can I just let Hunter disappear. What do you suggest we do?''

"Let me handle this, lad. I've experience in such matters. I've got men out looking and watching. They'll soon learn where Ill Will has taken my stock, and they'll find Hunter, too. It may be his horse foundered and he's trying to work his way back here. If the Bells have got him, we'll ransom him back.''

Gavin's shoulders slumped. "I cannot sit by and do naught.''

"Get some sleep, lad. That's the best ye can do for now. Come morn, ye can ride out with my scouts if ye like.''

Gavin clearly did not like it, but he went. No sooner had he gone up the stairwell to the second floor than the entry-way door opened and old Hutch stuck his head in.

"He's here.''

"Ah.'' Jock levered himself up against the pillows. "Tell him to come up, then bring us ale and meat.''

Moments later, a muddy trooper shouldered open the door and stomped in. "Damn cold out there.'' He went to the hearth, extending scarred hands to the burning peat. Firelight played over matted brown hair, a wide forehead and a nose that had been squashed flat when Lettie Robson dropped a chamber pot on his face during a raid. Unfortunately, Dickie Bell had survived to be known forever more as Nebless Dickie.

"What the hell is yer da about, stealing my stock?''

Dickie turned from the fire, lip curling. "We didn't lift the beasts. It just happened.'' He accepted the cup Hutch held out, drained it and wiped his mouth on his sleeve, smearing more mud across his grimy face. "We spotted the Murrays coming down out of the hills and was about to spring the trap on them like ye'd arranged, when all bloody hell broke loose. Someone stampeded the stock. We was nearly killed in the—''

"Who did it?"

"The Murrays. They got clean away with a bunch of cattle."

"And the rest of my two hundred head?"

Dickie's close-set eyes turned evasive. "Well, some was lost in the crush, ye ken. We rounded up what we could."

"And where are they right now?"

"The lads have them down at Epson Crossing. We couldn't bring them back here," Dickie added. "Da said as how no one was supposed to know we was working with ye to catch the Murrays."

"No one was supposed to get hurt, either, ye great dolt, but two of my men got their heads bashed in."

"Weren't our fault," Dickie whined. "Things got confused like. Yer lads thought we was trying to lift yer stock, and—"

"What of my nephew? Did yer da take advantage of the confusion to capture him?"

Dickie frowned. "We didna capture anyone."

"Or did ye kill him for his fancy armor without taking the trouble to find out who he was?"

"We didna take anyone. Wait." Dickie, not the most quick-witted of fellows, scowled. "Two of the lads said they chased a knight down the trail toward Deadman's Leap." He shrugged. "Could be lying at the bottom."

Jock cursed and sagged back against his pillows. "I'll send men to look at first light. Now, here's where I want ye to leave my stock. And if there's any missing, the worth of them will come out of what I promised yer da to do this job."

Dickie grumbled under his breath and headed for the door. One hand on the latch, he turned. "Da wanted to know if things was set for the Lammas swearing?"

"Aye. It'll take place at Hawkehill just as I said. And mind none of yer kin shows up to ruin things," Jock said sharply. *When ye danced with the devil, it was important to make certain he remembered who was leading.*

"Da's not sure we can trust yer cousin's English husband."

"I've vouched for him, haven't I?"

"Da wanted ye to know that if the deal goes sour, he'll be coming after ye and the Englishman."

Jock sat forward, fire in his eyes. "Tell yer da he'd best not forget who he's threatening. A word from me in Andy Kerr's ear and the Bells'll be hunted men. Dead men."

Dickie's lip curled beneath his mashed neb. "I'll tell him, but Da don't like being threatened."

"Neither do I. Remember that."

Chapter Five

Warm, dry and fed, his injured foot bandaged by Lady Morna, Hunter sat in a high-backed chair before a roaring fire and contemplated his surroundings. Hawkehill was modest compared to Carmichael Castle, but luxurious after Luncarty and surely one of the finer Border towers he'd seen. The great hall was furnished with sturdy tables, benches and even a few chairs. Two colorful tapestries brightened the whitewashed walls.

The Neville retainers diced and joked at one end of the long room, while the servants efficiently cleared away the remainder of an excellent meal—a haunch of roasted mutton, a pudding of milk and boiled barley. There had been bread, too, a staple Hunter was used to but which was a rarity here, for grain crops were so vulnerable to burning that few bothered to raise them.

"You have a fine place here," Hunter said.

"Aye." Sprawled in a chair beside him, Derk puffed out his chest. "You should have seen it when we first bought it. The keep had been burned and ransacked years ago and left vacant. But it's stout, the tower walls fourteen feet thick, the barmkin over five feet high and seven feet thick. Whoever built this, built it to last."

"What happened to the owners?" Hunt asked idly.

"I've no idea. A...friend of mine knew I was looking for an estate in Scotland, because my dear Morna desired to live in the land of her birth. He heard this place was available and arranged for me to buy it."

Lady Morna bustled into the hall, long gray braids flopping against her formidable bosom. She was near forty, pretty in a faded way and quiet where Derk was expansive. The lady had made them as welcome as had her husband. While her maids took a reluctant Allisun off to be tended, the lady had provided Hunter with hot water for washing, fresh clothes and supper. "Sir Hunt," she began, fleshy face wrinkled with concern. "I am most worried about your bride."

"Allie?" Hunter straightened, feeling guilty because he'd totally forgotten her after Lady Morna whisked her away. "I thought she had gone to sleep."

"As did I. Oh, I feel terrible. My maids said the lass insisted on seeing to herself, and I thought her modest and unused to servants, coming from a poor house and all. When I went to check on her, I found her still dressed in her trail clothes. She will not eat or drink or lie down. She just stands there looking lost."

Dieu, what now? "I'll see to it." Hunter slid his bad ankle off the stool and took up his walking stick. "Where is she?"

"Through that door, first room on the right. I've put you in what was our old solar. All the other bedchambers are above stairs, and I thought you'd have trouble with the steps."

"Ah." One room, one bed. Hunter thought he saw the problem, but he could hardly tell these people he'd lied and they weren't wed. "I'll speak with her."

It took several moments for him to limp to the door. He knocked softly on the oaken portal. Getting no response, he pushed it open. His heart clenched when he saw Allisun, so small and forlorn standing in the middle of the large chamber.

He came up behind her, put a tentative hand on her shoulder and squeezed gently. "Allie, what is wrong?"

She shook slightly. "I cannot stay here."

"Oh, Allie." Hunter forgot all about the feud. He saw not Alex Murray's daughter, but a wee, frightened lass. Careful to keep his touch light, he kneaded her shoulder. "I know you must be concerned that I might, er, force myself on you, but—"

She turned, her face gray and drawn, deep circles under her eyes. "I had not thought of that."

"Then why...?"

"Because this place is haunted."

"Haunted?" Hunter scowled. Had fatigue addled her wits? Best to humor her, he decided. "I'll vanquish any ghosts that try to frighten you, my lady."

"You cannot. They are my ghosts...inside me."

"What?" His nape prickled.

"They cry out to me." She covered her ears with her hands. "I cannot stand it. I cannot. I cannot." She shook violently, her eyes rolled back, she began to fall.

Hunter dropped his stick and caught her before she hit the floor. Swinging her into his arms, he crossed to the bed. Pain stabbed up from his ankle with each step, but he barely felt it, his attention focused on Allisun. She felt light as eiderdown and so fragile. He laid her on the bed as gently as he could, then sat on the edge of it.

Light from the candle on the bedside table flickered over her still features, emphasizing the hollows beneath her eyes.

"Allie?" He took her by the shoulders, struck again by the delicacy of her bones. "Allie?" He shook her ever so carefully.

Her eyes opened slowly, but their dazed expression increased his anxiety. "Gone...all lost."

"What have you lost?"

"Everything. All gone...burned...smashed. We never came back...couldn't bear to see..." She moaned softly, her lashes drifting down again. "Tired...so tired," she mumbled.

"Sleep," he urged.

"Can't..." Her head shifted restlessly on the pillow. "Have to get back...have to save Carina..."

Hunter started. That was his grandmother's name. "Who is Carina?" he asked softly. When she didn't answer, he sighed. "You will see her when you get home," he murmured, determined he would get her there. "Go to sleep, now."

"Can't. What if the Nevilles come?"

He doubted there was any danger from that quarter. If Derk had wished them ill, he could have killed them at the creek. "I will keep you safe, Allie. Sleep now, sleep."

"Shouldn't trust you, but I am so tired." Incredibly, her shoulders went lax in his grip, and her breathing deepened.

"Poor lass." Hunter stroked the tangled hair back from her cheeks. She was as badly in need of a wash as he'd been, but that would wait till she was rested. So exhausted was she that she didn't rouse when he pried off her boots. He eyed her dirty, bedraggled garments but decided against removing them.

For both their sakes.

The same reasoning prodded him to sleep in the tunic and hose Lady Morna had lent him. That, and the fact that though he did not fear the Nevilles, he was cautious by nature. Easing down onto the bed, he covered them both with a blanket. Exhausted though he was, the whoosh of her breathing teased his imagination, made him wonder about the woman who shared the bed.

His pretense of a handfasting had infuriated and frightened her. Because they were enemies, surely, but he had not stopped to consider there might be another reason. Because she already had a man.

The notion of someone else holding Allisun, caressing her, loving her, sat ill. Why? Why her, of all people?

Hunter shifted toward Allisun, his gaze flickering over her still features, delicate, yet proud and lovely in a fey sort of way. He'd met more beautiful women, and taken his share of them to bed. But none had affected him quite so profoundly as did this wild Border lass.

Lust?

Aye, desire was part of it, he silently admitted, his lower body drawing tight at the memory of holding her slender, surprisingly well-toned body. But there was more to it than that. He'd admired her courage in trying to save her kinsmen from the ambush. He'd been intrigued by her dry wit and humbled by her efforts to hide him from the Bells.

She is your enemy, whispered a small voice.

Was she? True she was Alexander Murray's daughter, but it was hard to think of her as a villain. Indeed, Allie was as much a victim in this twisted affair as his aunt had been.

As Hunter drifted off to sleep, his last conscious thought was that he'd somehow find a way to end the feud before Allisun and what was left of her family suffered more.

"What possessed you to bring them here?" Morna snapped, pacing before the hearth in the master chamber, her steps muffled by the thick new carpet.

Derk sighed and raked a hand through his hair. "I could hardly leave them there, afoot with Ill Will Bell about."

"Why not? Suppose Hunt has deceived us, and his ankle's not really hurt."

"Was it not swollen, purple and painful?"

"Still something about them does not ring true."

"He is a bit too smooth and polished for a vagabond Highlander," Derk allowed.

"Aye. A man dressed as fine as he would have a tail of mounted men." Her voice held the sharp edge of a pouncing cat.

"Mayhap his family did not approve of the match with young Allie and so he sneaked off on his own."

"Possible...possible." Morna paused to admire the pair of gold chalices Derk had brought back with him from Kelso. Once they, and the rug beneath her feet, had graced a bishop's chamber. How far they'd come from that puny farm Derk had inherited from his father. Proof that guts and canniness did pay off. But, by God, she could still remember the low, smoke-clogged central room, the stink of the beasts penned up in the other side of the house. She was not going back to that. "But the timing could not be worse, what with Lammas two days hence."

"We could send them on their way."

Morna set down the fine gold cup with its intricately carved pedestal and gem-studded sides. "'Twould seem odd if we asked them to leave before his ankle is sound enough to walk on. That could take several days...a week."

"So. Even if they are here on Lammas, what will they see? Just men coming to pay their rent to me."

"To us," Morna said tightly, lest he forget that if not for her cleverness, they'd still be raising a few paltry sheep.

"Us. Of course." He threw an arm around her shoulder and kissed her forehead. "All will be well," he murmured.

Morna was not so easily soothed. "What if our young couple should chance to meet our guests?"

"That hardly seems likely to happen, what with his bad ankle. But it would not be good. Ian Maxwell, especially, is vocal in his displeasure over the rents."

"Ingrate. He should be thanking us for seeing to it his tower is not attacked again and his stock lifted."

"If it makes you feel easier, we can conduct our business in the long barn instead of the hall."

Morna sighed. "It might be best. And, too, I think we should set someone to watch them. Just to make certain they really are the innocent victims they claim to be."

Allisun awoke slowly, groggy and disoriented. Habit, refined from years of being hunted, kept her still, her eyes shut, her other senses alert, searching for hints of danger.

She was not at Tadlow, that much she knew. The air lacked the mustiness of the old caverns where her family had sought refuge. The pallet beneath her was not lumpy, nor the blanket over her coarse and scratchy.

Straining her ears, she heard slow, measured breathing. She was not alone. What had happened? Where was she?

Skin crawling, she slowly lifted her lashes.

Soft light from a nearby candle washed across the four-poster bed in which she lay. Turning her head confirmed her worst fears. A man's head occupied the other pillow.

Hunter Carmichael.

As though she'd spoken his name aloud, he moved suddenly, head jerking up, eyes opening.

"Allie." A smile curved his lips, lighting his whole face. "How do you feel?"

Sore. Confused. "I..." Then she looked beyond him to the narrow corner hearth where a bed of coals glowed. She remembered when the workmen had put it in to replace the old central fire pit that used to fill the room with smoke. How proud her papa had been of the improvement. The memory twisted deep inside her, sharp and cutting as a blade. "This was my parents' solar."

"What?"

"I lived here till I was ten and three, till Jock McKie forced us to flee into the hills and set the place ablaze."

"Allie, I am so sorry."

"Papa died making certain we got away safely." Her eyes were dry but haunted. "I wished I had died with him."

"Nay." Torn by her silent suffering, Hunter shifted to put his arms loosely around her. She came willingly, which worried him, her head falling onto his shoulder. Holding her like this felt so good, so right. He gently kneaded the tense muscles in her back and was rewarded by a shivery sigh that turned his mind from offering comfort. He was abruptly reminded of the desire that had flared between them on the creek bank. A hot flame that might have turned into a wildfire if Derk Neville had not come along when he did.

Hunter longed to pull her closer, but would not take advantage of her weakness. When she came to him, he wanted her strong and willing, aware of what they did, not dazed by grief and exhaustion. So he eased back, putting more space between their bodies. "'Tis all right," he crooned, stroking her back through the grimy tunic she still wore.

"Nay. Nor will it ever be. So many lost… They will kill me, too, when they find out who I am."

"Who will?"

"The Nevilles. They are in league with old Jock."

Hunter doubted that, but said, "I will keep you safe."

"It doesn't matter."

"Of course it does," he growled, alarmed by her hopeless tone. Where was the little warrior who'd faced him down two nights ago? "What of your kin? What of Carina?"

She gasped and jerked, her head coming up, shocked blue eyes locking on his. "How do you know that name?"

"You mentioned her last night."

"What did I say?" Her hands were clenched in his tunic.

"Only her name. Who is she?"

She let go of him and scuttled over to the very edge of the bed. "Carina is my younger sister. She and I have had our differences, but she is all that is left of my family."

Hunter tried to imagine what it would be like to lose his parents, his older brother and the passel of orphans his parents had adopted. Painful beyond bearing. And empty. God, how he ached for her, ached to help her. Hunter did not open himself to many people, partly because of his work, he supposed. Those he met in the course of a day were either villains or victims, and he'd found it best to hold himself aloof from both.

Yet he wanted to be close to Allisun, wanted to help her. Mayhap to make up for failing his aunt. How strange, he mused, that he should feel compelled to aid the daughter of the man who had taken his aunt. Why? Why did he not hate her?

Because she was innocent. An innocent victim.

Pity stirred in his chest. Pity and a good deal more. "Come here and lie down," he coaxed, levering himself up on one elbow and patting the blankets.

Allisun glared at him across the bed, her insides churning. In the wash of candlelight, he looked more handsome than she'd remembered, his rugged face clean shaven, his tawny hair hanging in gleaming tendrils to his shoulders. She should hate him. She wanted to, but he kept doing things that made hating hard. "I do not want to share this bed with you."

"I know." His midnight brown eyes glowed with sympathy.

"Get out," she commanded.

He shook his head. "There's only the one, and my ankle—"

"I'll sleep on the floor." She made to bolt from the bed,

but he was quicker, one hand snagging her wrist. She tried to wrench free. "You're hurting me."

"Nay, you are hurting yourself by struggling."

Allisun stilled, but her pulse beat wildly as she stared at her enemy. His eyes bored into hers with an intensity that stripped away everything but this moment. She was vividly conscious of his superior strength, held in check by the force of his will. Inside her, a primitive fear stirred. He could do with her whatever he wanted. None of the defensive tactics her father and brothers had taught her would help her now. She was utterly powerless. But she would not beg. Lifting her chin, she said, "Attack me and have done with it."

He had the gall to look hurt. "Allie, what have I done to make you think I would stoop so low?"

"You are holding me here against my will."

He arched one brow but did not release her. "'Tis the middle of the night, and you are still tired. Lie down and go back to sleep."

"I will not share this bed with you."

"You had no trouble before."

"I—"

"Allie." His thumb whisked across her wrist, making the flesh tingle. "We will be here for a few days. Though I do not think the Nevilles mean us any harm, 'tis important that we maintain this pretense that we are wed. That means sharing a bed and appearing to be deeply in love with each other."

Her lip curled. "As if I could love a McKie."

"A Carmichael, posing as a Sutherland, remember? Remember, too, not a drop of Jock McKie's blood flows in my veins."

"'Tis no consolation. You were riding with the McKies when they ambushed my men."

"They were stealing my uncle's cattle."

"We were taking back what was ours."

"Enough," he said wearily. "This is old ground, and we solve nothing by covering it again. Suffice to say we are stuck here together and must make the best of it."

"I would rather die," she said contemptuously.

Hunter gazed at her mutinous expression and knew her hatred ran as deep as his uncle's. What a waste of a beautiful, bright woman, he thought. She should have been a wife and mother, worried about raising her children, not plotting cattle raids. The futility of it all weighed on his soul. Had he not glimpsed the vulnerability beneath her icy glare, he'd have given up, let her sneak away and to hell with what happened. But that small ripple of fear in her eyes moved him more profoundly than if she'd gotten down on her knees and begged for his help.

Perhaps because he knew she'd never beg.

"I'd not thought you foolish," he said coldly.

She straightened, and he marked her rising temper in the flush that crept up her throat and cheeks. "I am not."

"Only a fool would risk her life to escape simply because she does not like me. Especially since I've done you no harm."

"You tried to kiss me."

Hunter sighed. "It will not happen again. I prefer my bedmates willing and—" he cast a scathing glance over her tangled hair and grimy tunic "—clean." Her flinch brought him no triumph, but neither would he beg her pardon. Strength seemed the only thing she respected. If he softened toward her, she'd run roughshod over him and his plans.

"I want your promise you will not try to leave without me."

Her eyes narrowed, and he could almost hear the gears in her quick mind grinding away. "I do not need your protection."

"Nay?" The thought of her wandering alone through the countryside terrified him. "I've no doubt my uncle has every McKie in the saddle looking for me. What if they find you?"

She gasped softly. "I'd not thought of that."

"Well, I have. When we leave, I will see you safely home."

"Why would you do that?"

"Because, I do not make war on women and children."

"And if your uncle should find us?"

"I'd not let him harm you."

"I am supposed to believe that from a Mc—"

"Allie, I am a Carmichael, pretending to be a Sutherland. Remember that. Remember, too, that I have had ample chances to hurt you if that was my aim."

She exhaled. "I suppose."

"Good. I am counting on you to play the part of my wife. We are simple folk, bound for my Highland home," he added for *his* protection. Before he'd left for Luncarty, his father had warned him that there were many men in the godforsaken land who made their living from blackmail and ransom. The fewer who knew he was a man of wealth and importance, the better. "I do not want them to think we lied. Nor do I want them to brand you a whore."

Her cheeks pinked again. "I will try."

Grudging acceptance, but he'd take what he could get. "Lie down, then. We both need a few hours more sleep." As a show of faith, he let go of her wrist and patted the blankets.

Instead of accepting his invitation, she curled up in a tight ball on the very edge of the bed, eyes open and wary.

Hunter gave her his most winning, guileless smile. She responded with a glare. Sighing, he lay down himself, closed his eyes and willed his ankle to heal.

* * *

Thin fingers of moonlight peeked through the heavy pine boughs. It was all Owen needed to follow the tracks along the floor of the gorge beneath Deadman's Leap.

"How can ye be sure our Allisun's with them?" Harry asked.

"I cannot be, but it seems likely. Ye saw the knight take her up before him." Owen had despaired when, having evaded the Bells and the McKies, the Murrays had met up at their rendezvous spot and discovered Allisun was missing. Wee Harry's tale had caused Owen to split their force. Dale Murray had taken the cattle to Tadlow while ten Murrays went back over the hills to search for Allisun. "And we saw the marks of a single, heavy horse coming down this trail."

"I should have gone after her when I saw the knight turn down that trail," Harry muttered.

"How could ye, trapped in the middle of a cattle stampede with a pack of Bells hard after ye?"

"What if she died in that rock slide on the cliff?"

"She didn't or we'd have found her body." Along the bank of the river, Owen *had* found two sets of boot prints. One small enough to be Allisun's. The other made by a one-legged man. The knight, though Owen thought it odd a cripple could control a warhorse. If Owen read the signs correctly, and he was very good at it, a party of twenty mounted men had come along. Allisun and the knight must have ridden off with them, for there were no footprints leading away from the river.

By daybreak, Owen and the search party had left the gorge and were traveling over the moors. He'd decided that several of the horses were either carrying heavy goods or big men, for their prints were unusually deep. It aided in the tracking, but the stony ground sometimes hid the hoofprints for long stretches. "At least we can thank God they're not headed toward Luncarty," Owen said as the trail turned north.

"Aye, but she could still be in the hands of someone who'd turn her over to Jock for the reward," grumbled Black Gilbert. "What if that happens? Or if we dinna find her?"

"We will." Owen had to believe that.

"'Tis possible we might not. What if she's dead and we just haven't found her body?"

"Shut up," Owen growled.

Black Gil's expression hardened. "I ken ye favor her, but if Allisun is gone, then Carina is our chief."

Owen gave him a sharp look. What the hell was Gil up to? He knew good and well that was not true. "Carina's too young."

"She is Alex Murray's last child," Black Gil said silkily, drawing murmurs of agreement from the others.

Owen glared at Gil, well aware that since Danny's death, he'd been filling Carina's ears with talk of revenge. Poor girl, she reveled in the attention. Only eleven and awkward, she lacked her half sister's strength of will. Too young to help with much but cooking or sewing, Carina often felt ignored and unloved. Small wonder, for many of the Murrays had transferred to her the resentment they'd felt for Brenna.

Allisun, God love her, had tried to be both sister and mother to Carina after Brenna died birthing her. And this in spite of the fact Allisun blamed Brenna for her own mother's death. But there was friction between the two lasses, boiling just beneath the surface. An ugly mix of guilt, resentment and pain that was one day bound to explode and hurt them both.

"Carina's a bairn," Owen grumbled.

"She could learn to lead, same as Allisun did. I'd be willing to help her," added Gil.

So, Gil thought to lead the clan through Carina. This was certainly an unforeseen complication. One that needed to be stomped out quickly. "Allisun is the eldest. We follow her."

"But she's not here." Black Gilbert looked around at the men who had grown old and tired fighting a defensive war that had cost them their homes and loved ones. "It felt damned good to get back our cattle and a few more besides," he said.

"Aye, it did," said Gibb's Martin, a skinny lad who clung to Gilbert like a shadow. "We ain't had meat for so long I forgot what it tastes like." The others nodded in agreement.

"I say 'tis time we were going after Jock McKie instead of sitting back waiting for him to pick us off," Black Gil added.

"And how do ye propose we do that?" Owen sneered.

"By joining forces with the Bells."

A collective gasp swept the group.

"'Twould be safer to sleep with the devil," someone said.

Black Gil scowled them into silence. "Will Bell makes a fearsome enemy, I'll grant, but he's loyal to his people. He'd give us the men we need to fight Old Jock and win."

"At what price?"

Gil's eyes darted away from Owen's searching gaze. "We'd not know that till we talked with him," Gil said.

Owen had a sneaking suspicion that Gil had already talked with Ill Will Bell. "We do not have anything the Bells want in exchange for this help," he observed. Except Allisun. Into Owen's mind popped her jest about becoming Will's mistress. The notion chilled his blood. "We'll not be joining up with Ill Will, and that's final."

Black Gil grunted and closed his mouth, but Owen knew from the set of the man's jaw that the subject was not forgotten.

Chapter Six

Sleep, Hunter had commanded, and apparently done just that himself. The wretch.

Allisun glared balefully at his relaxed features, listened resentfully to the even breathing that mocked her rapid, panicky pulse. She lay with her rump half off the bed, her nerves wound so tight with dread she'd never relax. But as the moments stretched out and he made no move to attack, fear gradually lost its grip on her mind.

As it ebbed, other feelings intruded, chiefly hunger and thirst. The grumbling in her belly was familiar, for there never seemed to be enough to eat at Tadlow. But just now she felt especially hollow, and her mouth was so dry. She'd had little to eat in days, except for the few morsels Hunter had shared with her this morn. Dod, that seemed a lifetime ago. Vaguely she recalled one of the servants bringing a tray of food. Then she'd been too consumed by the horror of being here to take a bite. Now she felt ravenous.

Keeping one eye on Hunter, Allisun raised her head and scanned the room. It was dark, except for the golden pool cast by the candle and the faint glow of fading embers. There, on a stool by the hearth, she spotted what looked like a tray.

Should she get up?

Her stomach grumbled encouragement. Ever so slowly, she sat and slipped one leg out of bed.

"Going somewhere?" asked a silky voice.

Allisun jumped and looked over her shoulder, stunned to find Hunter staring at her. "I thought you were asleep."

"How could I with your stomach rumbling like a war drum?"

"So, I am hungry." Allisun tossed her head and leaped out of bed. Just let him try to stop her. All the way to the hearth she expected to be seized and dragged back, but when she reached her objective and turned, he was sitting up in bed, arms folded over his chest, smiling warmly.

She spun around, rejecting him and his idiotic smile. Kneeling, she whisked the linen cover off the tray. A veritable feast stared back at her—chunks of cold meat, a wedge of yellow cheese and thick slices of bread. Bread! Her hand shook as she reached out and touched it.

Real! She'd seen bread in her dreams, but this bread was real! Her fingers trailed over it, savoring the springy texture.

"Is anything wrong?" Hunter asked from close behind her. Too close.

Allisun snatched up a hunk of bread and fled. Or tried to. The angle of the wall blocked her retreat. She huddled in the corner, the bread clutched to her chest. "Leave me alone."

"Easy." Hunter limped to a chair several feet away, lowered himself into it and leaned his stick against the seat. His ankle throbbed, but he ignored it, all his energy focused on soothing Allie. "The bread is good," he said blandly. "Fresh and yeasty. I also recommend the mutton."

It was painful to watch her watch him with the haunted eyes of a cornered animal. A starving animal. How long had it been since she'd had a decent meal?

"Go ahead, eat," he coaxed.

She raised the bread to her lips and took a small bite. Her eyes closed as she chewed, her expression turned blissful.

Dieu. He'd seen suffering in his time, but this... Tears prickled behind his lids, and he had to turn away. When he looked back again, she was hunched over the tray, stuffing meat and cheese into her mouth with both hands.

"Allie, I do not think 'tis wise to eat so much so fast."

She muttered something uncomplimentary around a huge bite of mutton and reached for an apple tart. Her stomach chose that moment to rebel. He knew it by the way she suddenly dropped the tart and covered her mouth. Her eyes went round with horror.

Hunter swore, grabbed her under the arms and hauled her the few, painful steps to the window beside the fireplace. The shutters were open, thank God. He lifted her up so her head cleared the stone sill and held her there while nature prevailed. When the shuddering stopped, he gently set her on her feet and handed her the linen cloth that had covered the tray. It touched him that she leaned against him for support while she wiped her mouth.

"Better?" he asked, putting an arm around her waist.

She nodded, her head averted, her shoulders slumped. Another tremor shook her, then she straightened away from him. "Thank you." The words were raspy and grudging.

They warmed him anyway, because he guessed what it cost her to say them. He guessed, too, that she was perilously close to collapse. He ached to take her in his arms, to coddle her and care for her as she so obviously needed. But the fire in her eyes warned she'd fight him. Out of fear, pride and habit. "Behind yonder screen, you'll find the garderobe and water with which to rinse out your mouth."

She nodded and walked to the screen without looking at him. Her steps were slow and deliberate, as though each taxed what little strength she had, but her head was high, her back as stiff as an iron poker, evidence of her unbowed spirit.

Hunter sighed and bowed his head, humbled by her quiet dignity. Damn, how did he breach that protective shell of hers? How did he convince her to accept his help?

Filling her belly was the first priority. It must be done slowly and carefully, tiny meals taken often. He knew that, because she was not the first victim of starvation he'd rescued. That she was a woman and the others had been men, soldiers imprisoned by their enemies, made *him* sick.

Steeling himself for a long, drawn-out struggle, Hunter limped to the cupboard on the wall opposite the fire. He gathered up two cups and a flagon of ale and made his way back to the chair. The ale eased his parched throat but not the tightness in his chest. Pity? Nay, his concern for her went beyond that. He'd not rest till he had her healthy and safe.

Seizing a slice of bread, he tore it into small pieces. Though how he'd get her to eat it was another matter, for she was bound to fear getting sick and disgracing herself again.

Long minutes passed. So long he grew worried. "Are you coming out?" he called.

"Nay," came the muffled reply.

Hunter smiled. "Not ever?"

"Nay."

"Not even for a sip of this very fine ale?"

A stubborn silence followed.

"Allie, are you not thirsty?"

"Oh, all right." She stomped back around the screen, her shoulders square, her surly expression back in place.

Hunter fought to keep from smiling as he offered her a cup and the other chair.

She took the cup, but remained standing as she sipped

cautiously. When she raised her head, her eyes were somber. "How did you know the food was poisoned?"

"'Twas not poisoned," he said gently. "You ate too much, too fast. The same thing happened to the prisoners my men and I freed from Berwick Castle. They'd been so long without food, they could not hold much down for—"

"That's an English stronghold. How did you get in?" Curiosity had replaced her wary contempt.

Seeing a way to reach her, he smiled. "Ah, now there's a tale. If you'll refill my cup and bring that stool closer so I can rest my foot on it, I'll tell you what happened." He was tired, and moving around had worsened the ache in his ankle, but he could not let this opportunity pass.

At first, she perched on the edge of her chair, like a bird about to take flight at any sign of danger. But soon she was caught up in the story and forgot to be afraid. She settled in and listened intently as he told of the English supply train his troop had waylaid, the soldiers they'd stripped of clothes and identification so they might take their places.

As he talked, Hunter moved the pile of bread to his knee. He ate one and handed one to her. Mesmerized, she popped it into her mouth and chewed absently. Another followed and another, till she'd slowly consumed both the gist of his story and a slice of the bread.

"Once inside the castle, we waited till everyone slept, then disabled the dungeon guards, freed ten Scots and escaped."

"But how did you get away without getting caught?"

"Drink your ale, and I'll tell you."

She obediently drained what remained in her cup.

Hunter fought to keep his triumph from showing. Meat was what she needed, but not yet. "I cut through the ropes holding the drawbridge, down it came and out we rode."

"But, what of the English?"

"They were busy…putting out the fire." He chuckled,

though at the time the escape had been a close thing. "You see, we had brought with us wagons of grain. We rolled them in front of the doors to the barracks and set them ablaze."

She laughed, the sound pure and magical as sunlight. Joy transformed her face, easing the strain from around her lips, lifting the shadows from her eyes. He glimpsed the lively, carefree lass she might have become if not for the feud.

Fascinated, he caught up one of her hands and squeezed it. "You've a lovely laugh, like bells on a clear morn."

She blushed, looking even younger and more innocent. He knew, then, that there'd been no man in Allisun Murray's life. No one to hold her, to touch her, to teach her the ways of men and women.

Inside him, something stirred, something even older and more powerful than the urge to protect. But passion had never before built this swiftly. Like a hot tide rushing through him, it tore at his reason, made a mockery of logic and patience. He had to touch her. Now.

"Allie." He slid his hand along her soft cheek. Cradling her jaw, he lifted her face and saw his passion-hazed features reflected in her widening eyes. "I will not hurt you." He breathed the words an instant before he brushed her mouth with his, half expecting her to bolt. Instead, her lips trembled on a sigh. The sound, half surprise, half acceptance, was all the encouragement he needed to kiss her. It took all his willpower to keep from crushing her to him and kissing her with all the longing pent up inside him.

So, this was a kiss. Vaguely Allisun realized she should be afraid or repulsed, but she felt neither. His mouth was firm yet gentle, his hands warming her as they slid around to her back, enveloping her with their strength. She felt sheltered, secure. His tongue traced a featherlight path across her lower lip, making it tingle. The heat spread, like ripples on water, like candlelight banishing the dark. Deep inside her, something bloomed, a tiny flame where there'd been only cold.

Hunter felt her shiver and raised his head. "Allie?"

She shivered again, passion and wariness mingling in her eyes when they opened. "You should not have done that."

"'Twas time."

"I do not understand. Time for what?"

"For us to find out the nature of this thing between us."

"There is no us." She leaned away, and he let her retreat back into her chair. "There can be no us."

"The wanting was there from the moment we met."

"Nay," she whispered, but he knew she lied, knew she'd felt the pull between them. "Our families are feuding."

"'Tis high time the feud was stopped. We can do it."

"How?"

Hunter considered the dozen half-formed plans rattling around in his brain and decided that now was not the time to argue their merits. They were both tired, his ankle pounded like a bad tooth and she was far from strong. "We will find a way."

"There can be no peace till Jock is dead."

Or all the Murrays are, he thought. He was not going to let that happen. "We will find a way," he repeated. "But not tonight, or what is left of tonight. Go back to bed, Allie."

She stood, wary as a cornered deer. "What of you?"

"I'll sit here awhile."

Lips pursed, she looked from him to the bed and back again. "Your ankle would be more comfortable if you stretched out."

"But you'd sleep better if I was not in that bed."

"Doubtless." She drew in a ragged breath. "But I feel I owe you for that." Cheeks pink with shame, she waved toward the window where she'd lost her supper.

Normally he did not like people to feel beholden to him.

In fact, gratitude of that sort made him uncomfortable. God knows that a lifetime of good deeds would not outweigh the one time Hunter had failed. But with Allie, he needed whatever advantage he could get. "A truce, then," he proposed, struggling up from the chair and reaching for his walking stick.

"What sort of truce?"

"The usual sort. No hostilities."

"And no kisses."

Hmm, if ever there was a lass in need of kissing and cuddling, it was Allie, but he shrugged. "Unless you ask."

"As if I would ever do that." She marched ahead of him to the bed and climbed in.

Hunter followed more slowly. He had not stated any conditions for this truce. That was best left for tomorrow, because he suspected she'd like his terms no better than he liked hers. The difference was, he intended to see she stuck to his terms, while hers...

Well, he'd find a way around them, for both their sakes.

"Yer bath is ready, my lady," chirped the maid, peering out around the screen in the corner of the room.

Allisun glared at Hunter. Seated before a roaring fire, his bad foot on a stool, he looked as unmovable as stone. "Why do you not go out to the hall?"

"My ankle pains me," he said, feigning a whine. He picked up a bun from the tray the maids had brought for their breakfast. "You might want to chew on this while you wash."

"Eat in the bath?"

"Why not? A bath can be pleasurable."

"The hot water will be pleasure enough after all the cold streams I've bathed in."

Hunter shook his head and nodded toward the screen.

So? Allisun shrugged. Let the maid think she was dirt

poor. It was not far from the truth. She stalked around the wooden screen to examine the bathing prospects. A small tub, cleverly fashioned of leather stretched over a metal frame, sat in the corner. Nearby were three buckets of cold water, a linen cloth and dish of soft soap.

"Shall I help ye out of yer, er, clothes?" the maid asked, clearly scandalized by Allisun's male garb.

"Nay, I'm used to seeing to myself." Nor did she want an audience. She waited till the maid had left before picking up the soap and sniffing. It would be Rosemary. Her favorite, and her mother's. Tears welled in her eyes. She swayed, momentarily weakened by the loss.

"Is something wrong?" Hunter called.

"Nay." *Aye, everything.* It should have been her parents instead of the Nevilles in the master chamber above. And she should have been fast asleep with Carina in the room they'd shared on the third floor. Or more like, being now eight and ten, she'd have been wed with babes and a home of her own.

"Do you need help with the water?"

"Nay. I can do it myself." Allisun dashed away her tears and put down the soap. "You'd only spill it, limping about as you—" The words ended in an "oof" as she rounded the corner of the screen and bumped into Hunter.

"Easy." He steadied her with one hand and still hung on to the kettle he had in the other.

"So, this is how you keep your word. Hoping to catch me in the tub, were you?"

He grinned, eyes rounding in mock hurt. "Never. You'd not had enough time to undress, and you're not so scatter witted as to get into a tub of cold water and leave the hot—"

"Oh, give me that." Allisun made a grab for the iron pot.

He moved it out of reach. "'Tis hot and heavy. Let me set it beside the tub, then you can ladle out what you need."

Damn. Why did he have to be nice to her? "Oh, do what you will," she growled, turning back toward the tub.

Hunter set the pot down and handed her the garments he'd had slung over his shoulder. "Lady Morna sent these, too, a gown, chemise, hose—"

"I'd prefer my own clothes."

"They're a trifle worse for wear." He lowered his voice. "And I do not want anyone connecting Allie Hall Sutherland with Allisun Murray, reiver."

"I am not a reiver."

"But," he prodded.

She sighed. "I can see your point."

"I am glad." His smile drew her gaze to his mouth, made her remember the kiss.

That damned, captivating kiss. Her first. Her last. She could not afford to be captivated by him. "Aye, well." She cleared her throat, but the fullness remained. The memory lingered. Despite inbred caution and ingrained logic, she was drawn to this man. And he to her. It was wrong of her to want him. And yet, she could not help thinking how right it had felt when he'd kissed her. How safe she'd felt, how secure, as though nothing could harm her.

"Take your bath, Allie, before the water gets cold." His smile was friendly, nothing more.

She felt an intense sense of loss as he disappeared around the screen. Come back! she nearly cried. Nearly. Grabbing a lungful of air, she steadied herself. She did not need him.

Hunter turned toward the screen. Was that a cry he'd heard? He cocked his head, listening, but all was silent. After a moment, water splashed into the tub. Sighing, he limped to the chair and tried not to think about Allie in her bath.

He looked at the plate of bread and cheese the maids had

brought for their breakfast. It had nearly broken his heart
to watch Allie pick at the food when he'd known she
wanted to stuff herself. She'd only eaten half of what he
thought she should have. But he'd make it his business to
see she ate often.

How exactly he was going to explain that to the Nevilles
was another question. And then there was Allisun's hostil-
ity toward them. He supposed he could use his ankle as an
excuse to remain in their room till he was well enough to
leave, but would they not think it strange if he kept Allie
here, too?

Chapter Seven

The horn sounded, calling them to the noon meal. Still Allie did not emerge from behind the screen.

"Allie, do you need help?"

"Nay," came the quick reply. "My hair will not dry in time to eat. Go on without me."

And leave her here alone to brood? Or plot her escape? Nay. Besides, Hunter suspected wet hair was only a small part of the problem. Having to eat a meal in her former hall was what really troubled her. "Come here and dry it by the fire."

"I am not dressed."

"Then get dressed and come here where it's warm before you catch a chill."

"I'll come when I am ready."

Hunter swore and moved to go after her. The pain that shot up his leg when it touched the floor made him yelp.

"What? What is it?" Allie stuck her towel-covered head around the screen.

"My ankle. I tried to stand."

"Well, do not." She bustled out wearing the bed robe Lady Morna had lent her last night. It was a becoming shade of green, but way too big and so long she had to kick the skirts out of her way with each step. "Idiot. The more you walk on it the longer 'twill take to heal."

"Why should you care?" he grumbled, frustrated and furious to be incapacitated at a time like this.

"Because, the sooner you are healed, the sooner we can go." She stopped beside his foot, hands on hips, eyes flashing.

"Ah." Some of his anger faded. "I am glad you see the wisdom of waiting till we can go together."

"I am not a complete fool. Much as I wish I could steal a horse and ride out of here this very moment, I do not think I could get past the guards. To say nothing of Jock's patrols."

"I am sorry. I know how hard it must be for you to stay."

"You cannot possibly." She turned away to pace before the hearth. "'Tis like being thrust into purgatory to see the Nevilles holding sway in my family home. Almost worse is knowing Derk is in league with Jock."

"Why would you say that? Neville is an Englishman, newly come to the area because his wife has relatives here."

"So he says. But I say Jock gave or sold my tower to Derk. He'd not have parted with such a trophy unless he was in the Neville's debt."

"Derk told me he bought the tower through a friend and does not know the former owner. But whatever, I will not let anyone hurt you. Not Derk Neville. Not even my uncle. After all we've been through, can you not trust me a little?"

She hesitated, her eyes narrowed, locked on his with searing intensity. "I should not."

"Come now. I'm more to be pitied than feared, poor injured man that I am." He slanted her his most dazzling smile.

"Humph." Her lips twitched with what might have been the beginnings of a smile.

"I do need your help," he added, doing his best to look guileless and helpless.

She drew in a deep breath, seemingly unaware that her breasts strained against the fabric of the robe, tempting him. The longer he was with her, the more difficult it became to ignore the fact that he desired her. "I will do what I can." As she bent to examine his foot, the neck of the robe gaped open, giving him a glimpse of the pale upper swells.

Hunter groaned and looked away, his palms tingling, his pulse scrambling.

"I have not touched you, yet."

Innocent though they were, her words sparked images of her hands on needier places. "I was merely anticipating."

"I'll be gentle." She was, unwrapping the bandages slowly, then carefully prodding the bruised ankle. The pain that caused was the perfect antidote to his impure urges.

"Ouch!"

She rocked back on her heels, smiling faintly. "I thought knights were supposed to be brave and stalwart."

"I am, usually, but I feel so—"

"Frustrated?"

"Oh, aye." In more ways than one.

"I know exactly how you feel."

He doubted that. "'Tis agony to sit about when I would be up and gone. I do not expect you to believe me, but I want to get you away from here and safely home."

"Why would you care?" she asked, mimicking his words.

"Because that is what I do. I help people." This time, his quest went beyond righting a wrong. He admired and respected her. He feared for her. He desired her. The combination was a heady one, indeed.

"Some sort of knightly oath?" she asked warily.

"Aye," he hedged. Now he did not entirely trust her. Not when it came to this. There were many on the Borders who would love to get their hands on the king's justicular. Why, they could ransom him back for a fortune in gold or mayhap a pardon for their past crimes. "'Tis more than a little lowering to find myself in need of aid."

"I can understand that." Shame tightened her features. "I did not want your help last night when I took sick."

Hunter nodded. They were much alike, he mused—proud, loyal and canny—though he doubted she'd welcome being told she had anything in common with one she considered an enemy. "I would call us more than even if you could heal this cursed ankle."

As he'd hoped, she relaxed fractionally. "I will try." She stood, absently drawing closed the neck of her robe. "I will ask if Lady Morna has any ragwort. You should soak your ankle in it twice daily to bring down the swelling. Between times, it should have a poultice of pennyroyal to counter the bruising."

"So you're an accomplished healer," he said, starved for more information about her.

"I know a little about a great many things. 'Tis necessary when you are so few."

There was a knock at the door and Edna, the brown mouse of a maid, peered in. "Lady Morna asks if ye're coming out to sup?"

Hunter opened his mouth to say aye.

"Nay, my hair is not dry and my—my husband's foot is worse." Allie was clearly back in command.

"She said as how ye might be...weary. From the trip and all." Edna cast a sly glance at the rumpled bed. "I'll bring a tray."

Allie sniffed. "Very well," she said as regally as though she were lady of the manor. "And I'll need some medicines." She rattled off what she wanted. The moment the door closed behind the maid, she turned on Hunter. "Did you see how she looked at us? She thinks we've been in here all this time, er..."

"Making love?"

The memory of his kiss rose to haunt her. If just one kiss could scramble her insides and turn her whole world upside down, what would it be like to lie with him? To lie naked with him? To feel his hands on her bare skin? To have him cover her, fill her? Just thinking of it made her body warm and ache.

"'Tis what newly wedded people do, I'm told." Hunter chuckled. "You needn't look so alarmed. I will not try to take advantage of you or our temporary marriage."

She was alarmed. Not because she feared he'd attack her. It was herself she did not trust. His kisses made her forget all propriety, all the many reasons why she must hold herself aloof from him. "Mayhap we should go out to the hall after all."

"Nay. 'Twould be painful for you, and I could not sit there knowing you were hurting."

His compassion moved her, yet she could not afford to soften toward him. "More to the point, walking would make your ankle worse."

"There is that," he said blandly, but she suspected his sharp brown eyes saw clear through her excuse to the heart of the matter. They saw, but they did not condemn. They offered support, not pity.

Allisun was suddenly aware of how easy it would be to open herself to this unusual man. Clutching the robe high around her throat, she began her retreat. "I had best dress and see if I can get a comb through my hair."

"I will be here if you need me."

That was what she feared. Needing him. Allisun fled behind the screen. She tore off the robe and unwound the towel from her head. Her hands were trembling so badly she could barely get the chemise on. It hung loose on her, but the blue wool gown she donned over it was a perfect fit.

She smoothed the skirt over her hips, noted it hugged her far better than did her own clothes, and was made of far finer stuff. The low, square neck and tight sleeves were banded with an intricate floral design in red and yellow thread. Curiously the hose Lady Morna had provided was so large it bagged about her ankles, and the shoes...well, she could not even get them on.

"Allie? Are you all right?"

"Aye. Stay where you are. I'm coming." She grabbed up the comb and rounded the screen, still frowning.

"What is it? What's wrong?"

"This gown." She spun in a circle before him.

"'Tis vastly becoming." His eyes moved over her in frank approval. He did not leer as she'd seen some men do, even her own, but by the time his gaze moved back up to her face, she felt warm and wriggling inside. "What is wrong?" he asked again.

"Wrong?" She shook herself. "I am only puzzled as to whose clothes I am wearing. The gown fits as though it had been made for me. The chemise is too big, the shoes way too small."

"So, Lady Morna borrowed from her maids for you."

"Nay. The only thing I have on that is poor enough to belong to a maid is the hose. This gown is costly, the chemise, even more so. 'Tis silk." Lifting the skirt, she showed him the hem of the knee-length undergarment. "See."

"Aye." Scowling, he rubbed the fabric between thumb and forefinger. "Fit for a wealthy lady. Why is that a problem?"

"Because the lady who owned this chemise would wear a gown of silk or velvet, not wool." Allisun dropped the skirts. "I think that these things are stolen."

"Stolen?" His eyebrows rose in disbelief.

"From several different people. I think Derk Neville is a reiver, and this is part of his plunder."

She expected him to argue. Instead, he shook his head and chuckled. "I know you hate Derk because he has your tower, but to make him out a thief—"

"Laugh if you like," she muttered. "But I am right."

He sobered. "I am sorry. I should not have laughed at you. 'Tis just that Derk is so soft and pleasure loving I can scarce cast him in the role of raider."

Allisun sniffed and tossed her head, the effect ruined when a damp hank of hair slapped across her face. "Oh, drat. I've got to get this combed or it will look like a bird's nest." She set to work, grumbling and swearing when the comb's wide wooden teeth caught on the tangles.

"Easy, you'll snatch yourself bald." He seized the comb before she could stop him. "Sit." He patted his knee.

"I'd rather do it myself."

"I would rather tend my own ankle, but we agreed to aid each other while we're here."

"You will pull."

"Nay. I've often done the same for my sisters. Sit." He took her hand and gently tugged her down onto his knee. He was just as deft and careful moments later in pulling the comb through her waist-length hair. His brow furrowed in concentration as he patiently worked on each tangle. "You have beautiful hair."

"'Tis too curly, too red."

He slid one hand into her hair, sifting the strands between his fingers. "Like fire, silken fire."

Allisun's scalp grew tight and tingly. Gooseflesh rippled down her neck, and her stomach fluttered. Carina had combed her hair a hundred times, but never had she felt so shivery, so aware of another's touch.

"Did I pull?"

"Nay. I grow chilled." Snatching back the comb, she retreated to a stool by the hearth. "Thank you. I can finish."

"I understand," he said quietly, his eyes locked on hers. Once again she was very afraid he did see.

What if he guessed she desired him?

Shame and fear warred inside her. She did not want to desire any man, least of all one who might use her passion to bring down her family.

"Why would anyone steal clothing?" he asked after a moment.

"To use. To sell."

"Hmm." He rubbed his chin thoughtfully. "'Tis true that during the war between France and England many an Englishman made his fortune by selling the possessions of the nobles they captured. But those clothes were encrusted with precious gems. These are plain. Who would buy them?"

"Papa used to say the goods went to merchants in large cities like Edinburgh or Carlisle. Sometimes, they are even ransomed back to their owners."

"Jesu, the gall."

Allisun shrugged and set the comb aside. "To true riding families, like the Armstrongs and the Elliots, thievery is a business. One they've prospered at for generations. A man who'd kill for a few sheep would not quibble over selling someone back their clothes and bed linens."

"I'd no idea. Someone should do something about it."

Allisun snorted. "People have been trying for years. For generations, but 'tis a complicated situation."

"How so?" he asked sharply.

Before Allisun could reply, a knock sounded at the door.

"'Tis Lady Morna," said a muffled, hesitant voice. "Are you, er, unoccupied."

Hunter waggled his brows at Allisun. "Come in."

Lady Morna stepped slowly into the room carrying a small chest. "When Edna said you needed my medicines, I thought I'd come see how you were getting on." Her eyes darted warily about.

Small wonder she was suspicious, Hunter thought. Her husband had brought home two bedraggled strangers. Two people who could, for all the Nevilles knew, be spies or murderers. "Fine, except for the pain in my ankle," he said amiably. "We much appreciate your hospitality, do we not, love?"

Allisun sniffed, took the medicine chest and set it on the floor at his feet. Though she busied herself rummaging through the jars and pouches, he could feel the hatred seething beneath her stony mask. He prayed she did not erupt ere Lady Morna left.

"I hope you don't feel we're neglecting you," Morna said haltingly. "We've guests coming tomorrow for Lammas, and there are dozens of arrangements to oversee."

"Not at all," Hunter said. "If you need this chamber for your guests, we can sleep in the hall."

"Or the stables," Allie added with suspicious eagerness.

"Nay," Morna said quickly. "Our guests live within easy ride of Hawkehill Tower, and—"

Allisun slammed down the lid of the herb chest.

Morna jumped, one hand fluttering to her ample bosom. "Oh, my. Guess I'm a mite overset, what with all that's going on. As I was saying, no one will expect to stay the night, so you are fine here. Just fine."

Hunter could tell that Allie was anything but fine. There were tears in her eyes, and her lips were pressed into a thin line. To keep from blurting out that she'd once lived here?

Damn, he had to get rid of Morna at once. If he'd had two good legs, he'd have hustled her from the room. "Well, thank you again, Lady Morna. Sorry to put your maids to the trouble of waiting on us, but my ankle—"

"Quite right. Best to stay off it. If you need anything, you've only to ask." She bustled toward the door. "But—" she spun around and looked at Allisun "—there's no reason you need stay cooped up in here, my dear. I could have one of the maids sit with Hunt if you'd like to walk in the garden or dine in the—"

"Nay! I'd see to him myself," Allie exclaimed.

"Well..." Morna frowned, then shrugged. "I'll send Edna along with your dinner presently."

Hunter watched the door close and let out the breath he'd been holding. "Allie."

"Did you see the way she looked at us when she came in?" Allie whispered. "I told you they meant to harm me."

"It could be they fear we will harm them." Used to trying to see all sides in a dispute, Hunter told her how the Nevilles might view them as a threat.

Allisun listened, admiring the cool way he set out the facts on both halves of the ledger. She even allowed that he could be right. But privately she still thought the Nevilles were up to something. She meant to find out what it was, and if her suspicions about them were correct, she'd gather what evidence she could against them. If she'd learned one thing, it was that you needed proof to bring down your enemies.

"I thought her wariness had eased by the time she left," Hunter went on, chuckling. "Though after the way you insisted on staying to care for me, she doubtless thinks I'm holding you here so I can have my way with you."

Allisun flushed and went back to rooting through the medicine chest.

Derk was waiting in the corridor when Morna emerged. "Well, what do you think?" he asked.

She glared at him and motioned for him to follow her down the hall. When they were well away from the chamber, she stopped and faced him. "'Tis as Edna said. The lass is cold and curt to the point of rudeness. He fusses over her like a hen with only one chick."

"So, she *is* sick," Derk whispered. Edna had shown them the soiled napkin found in the garderobe, proof one of them had been ill. "Dod, what if I've brought the plague here?"

"I do not think she has that sort of sickness," Morna said slowly. "She's up and about and shows plenty of fire, but she is too skinny and too pale. I'd guess she is breeding."

"Of course." Derk brightened instantly. "We should have thought of that. It explains so much—running away from her kin, the hasty handfasting."

"Poor lamb. Torn from her mother's arms, attacked by brigands and sick to boot." Morna sighed heavily. "I remember how I felt when I was carrying our wee Richie."

"'Tis not an easy time for either party," Derk said with feeling. Morna had been sick the whole while and as cantankerous as a wolf with a sore paw. "We should do something for them."

"Aye. I shall prepare one of my nourishing custards. That'll rest easy on the stomach."

"An excellent suggestion, my dear." Derk kissed his wife's wrinkled cheek. "You are the soul of generosity."

That might be, but her primary concern was for her family fortunes. Still Morna smiled and slipped her arm through Derk's. Together they walked along the gloomy corridor. "I hope we are not being too trusting. What if they discover what we're about?"

Derk shrugged. "If they did, they'd take the tale to the Scots Warden. Andy Kerr is in Old Jock's pocket and can be counted on to do nothing."

"Aye, but Jock would not like it if our business became public." She cocked her head. "Odd, is it not, my cousin has spent the past dozen years hounding the Murrays into extinction, yet he wants other folk to have a good opinion of him.''

''Mayhap 'tis because of that.''

''Hmm.'' Morna nodded thoughtfully.

''Jock must have loved his Brenna well, for his vengeance burns bright after all these years.''

''Love? I am not so sure I'd call it that. Even as a lad, Jock was not one to cross. If ye took what was his, ye could expect he'd make ye pay…and pay…and pay.''

Derk shivered, despite the warmth of the corridor. ''We must make certain to stay on his good side, then.'' He nervously fingered the neck of his tunic. ''Once the rent is paid, do ye think we should take it and the ledgers to him?''

''Nay. He was most definite about sending his own men to fetch it and sufficient guard to see it back to Luncarty. And as for the ledgers, well he'd not want them under his roof.''

''Nay.'' Sweat broke out on Derk's forehead, and he tugged again at his neckline. '''Tis dangerous work.''

''Which is why it pays so well.'' Morna straightened his tunic with a wifely twitch. ''I wonder if young Hunt has a home for his wife and new family?''

''I do not know.'' Derk glanced at her. ''Why?''

''He's a likely looking lad, is all. Broad shoulders, deep chest and the muscular arms of a swordsman. We might have use of such a man.''

''What are ye plotting?''

''Naught. Only Jock will not live forever. When he's gone, I'd hate to see this fine business we've helped build fall into other hands…say Ill Will Bell's.''

''Dod. Ye're not thinking of challenging Ill Will?''

''Not at present. But it pays a body to be prepared.'' When her husband continued to stare at her as though she'd lost her mind, Morna sighed inwardly. Derk was a good husband who seldom crossed her, and a fine father to the two of their five children who'd survived infancy. But he could be annoyingly short on guts at times. On the other hand, Hunt Sutherland had the cold, calculating eye and muscular body of a warrior. Just the sort of man she might use.

Providing they could trust him.

"We will need to keep a watch on Sir Hunt and his wife while the men are here for the Lammas swearing."

Derk nodded. "But I cannot imagine he is a spy. For my part, I think we have more to fear from Ill Will Bell." He shuddered. "Dod, whatever was yer cousin thinking when he joined forces with that devil?"

"Large profits at very little risk to himself," Morna said with asperity. "And we shall have a share in it."

"Hmm. So long as the devil does not turn on us."

Chapter Eight

It was every man's dream to be locked up in a room with a woman he greatly desired.

Unfortunately, it was not a fantasy Hunter could act on. Not in good conscience.

As Allisun busied herself tending his ankle, Hunter reminded himself of all the reasons why she was forbidden.

Her father had abducted his aunt.

But Allisun was not her father, and she had suffered greatly for Alex Murray's crime.

She was an innocent.

But she had responded to his kisses. The memory curled through his body, warm and seductive.

He had promised not to touch her.

But she was touching him, her hands sliding gently under his heel, lifting his foot.

Hunter yelped as she plunged it into a basin of hot water.

"None of that now." She held his foot in the water and sprinkled herbs into the basin. The room filled with the pungent scent of earth and pine.

"Torturer," Hunter grumbled.

"'Tis for your own good."

"My mother used to say the same thing before she dosed me with some particularly vile potion."

"Your mother is a healer?"

That she should ask him a question pleased him and distracted him from the pain. He desperately hoped it was an overture of peace. If he could not be her lover, he'd be her friend, for she needed one. "Aye, among other things. Before she wed my father, she was *seanachaidh* of her clan, the Sutherlands."

"A woman bard? Is that not unusual?" She released his leg but remained seated on the floor.

"Aye, but her father recognized her gift for retelling the old myths." His foot having grown used to the water, he settled back in the chair. He was proud to claim Megan and Ross as parents, for they were fine people whose many good deeds he much admired. "Mama had ample time to learn them, for she broke her leg when she was young and spent months abed while it healed."

When she did not respond, Hunter sighed. To one whose mother had died early, a broken leg must not seem like much, yet he could not drop the subject. If he could make her see that he came of honorable stock, maybe she'd begin to trust him. "They did not think she would walk again or bear children, but—"

"Obviously, she proved them wrong." She rose to put away the herb packets.

"Aye. Mama endured much pain and humiliation before she managed to walk again. She still limps, especially when she's tired. My parents were wed ten years before she had my older brother, Ewan. They had given up hope of having any children of their own and adopted six orphaned bairns."

He expected Allisun to smile or at least commend his parents for their open hearts. Instead, she said, "My mother died of a broken heart when Da brought Brenna to live with us.''

Hunter could feel her pain. ''Dieu, Allie, I am so sorry.''

''It was long ago.'' She crossed to the wooden cupboard that occupied the wall opposite the hearth.

But she had not forgotten or forgiven. Oh, Aunt Brenna, did you love so unwisely? So cruelly?

''Clan Murray has orphans aplenty,'' Allisun said. ''I worry what will happen if I cannot care for them.''

The knowledge that she expected to die struck him hard. Till this moment, he'd not known how much he cared for her. The pain grew to a grinding ache in his chest. He could not, would not let that happen. He'd saved others, men, women and bairns who were strangers to him. He could do no less for Allisun.

''I have an estate, Renfrew Tower,'' Hunter said. ''Three or four days' journey from here, I would guess.''

''Oh.'' Allisun opened the cupboard and rummaged through the odds and ends stored there—spare bed linens, an assortment of wooden cups, dice and two gaming boards Hunter had found in there yestereve. She returned with an old, tattered sheet.

''Did you hear what I said?'' Hunter asked.

''Aye. You've an estate. Doubtless you're anxious to return to it.'' She plopped down onto the stool beside his footrest and began tearing the sheet into strips.

''I suppose.'' He actually spent little time at Renfrew, being busy ministering justice. But over the years, he'd sent several homeless waifs there to live. ''I mentioned it because I would like to take you to Renfrew.''

Her head snapped up. ''You said that when we left here, we'd go our separate ways.''

''Aye, but that was before I knew how bad things were for you and your family.''

''We are fine.''

"You are like to starve to death if my uncle does not kill you all first."

"We do not need any help from you," she growled.

She was wrong. And that mistake in judgment might cost her her life. "'Tis not charity I offer, but work. I raise horses at Renfrew. Large warhorses like Zeus. My castellan is always in need of men to help care for them and train them."

Some of the resentment left her eyes, but they were still cool. "Our place is here on the Borders."

"Allisun." Leaning forward, he captured her hands. "If you will not go to Renfrew, let me at least try to negotiate a truce between you and Uncle—"

"Nay." She snatched her hands free. "You do not know what he really is. Jock is not to be trusted."

"I would stand surety for his pledge. I would—"

"You could not watch us every minute, and that is what it would take, because Jock McKie cannot afford to let us live."

An odd turn of phrase. "Why do you say that?"

"Because 'tis true." She took up the sheet again and began tearing it into strips.

"Allisun..."

"Let it go, as you must let *me* go when we leave here." She bent over her work, her jaw set, her lips thinned.

Staring at her mutinous expression, Hunter wanted to shout and rant, but he knew that would only drive her further into the shell from which he'd begun to coax her. Damn, damn, damn, he had never felt so frustrated. He was used to being trusted by those he sought to aid. It hurt that this girl whom he wanted so desperately to save would take nothing from him.

Hunter was not, however, a man to give up. His tenacity was partly what had made him the King's Lion of Justice, for when he set his sights on a goal, he pursued it as ruthlessly as a lion on the hunt. He would just have to try harder to convince Allie to let him help end this feud.

So Hunter leaned back and set himself to charm. As he watched her fussing with the herbs and unguents, he realized that one thing she'd responded to was his injury. Used as he was to being stoic and self-reliant, it was the only card he had to play. So play it, he would.

Allisun breathed a sigh of relief when Hunter stopped glaring at her and settled into the chair. She tried to immerse herself in the routine of preparing the poultice, but she was keenly aware of him. All her life, it seemed, she'd lived in close proximity to men, yet none had affected her the way he did. None had seemed as overwhelmingly male. His presence filled the room. The unique scent of his skin teased her nostrils; the sound of his voice made her heart skip faster.

Do not think. Do not feel. Just work.

By rote, she lifted his foot from the water, dried it and inspected the purple and yellow bruising.

"It looks less swollen," he murmured. Was it her imagination, or did his voice seem huskier than usual?

Allisun kept her head down. If she did not look at him, she would not be drawn in by those compelling eyes. She gently rotated his ankle. "Still sore?"

"A bit." Huge sigh. "Mostly I weary of sitting here."

"Well, sit you must," she said briskly, healer to patient. On familiar ground, she applied the pennyroyal paste and bound his ankle in a strip of sheeting.

"'Tis too tight," he said mournfully.

"So it must be." She bustled about, emptying the basin down the garderobe shaft and putting Lady Morna's medicines away. When all was tidy, there was nothing to do. Edgy, she paced to the window and stared down at the courtyard.

"Come play with me."

"What?" Allisun spun about.

Her nemesis, all six feet and three or so inches, managed to look like a small, truculent lad. "I am bored," he grumbled.

"That makes two of us."

"We must find something to do. You know what they say." His eyes danced briefly. "An idle mind is the devil's playground."

Into her mind leaped the memory of that damned kiss.

"Draughts," he exclaimed.

Allisun blinked. "What?"

"Or Nine Men's Morris. There are boards for both games in the cupboard. Fetch them."

"I've not played in years, and I have no intention—"

"Then sing."

"I am not some minstrel to perform at the snap of your—"

"A story, then."

"I do not know any."

"Well," he said with a casual shrug. "There are only so many amusements that can be pursued by a man and a woman locked up together. If we do not keep each other occupied—"

"Draughts, it is." Her face hot, she hurried to the cupboard and took out the game boards. When she returned, Hunter had cleared off the small table beside his chair and awaited her with the bright smile.

"You are spoiled, do you know that?" she grumbled. "Too used to getting your own way."

"My way is usually best."

"Humph." Allisun sank into the other chair and glowered at him, but he was busy poking through the bowl of game pieces.

"The counters are hopelessly mixed together. Help me sort them out, will you?"

Before she could object, he seized her hand and cradled it in his massive one. The feel of his warm, callused palm enveloping her hand rocked her clear to her toes. Never had she felt so safe or so threatened. Shocked, she sat immobile while he dropped the round counters into her hand.

"Damn," he muttered.

"What?" She looked up and immediately regretted it. Their gazes met, locked. The faint irritation in his eyes suddenly shifted to something darker, earthier.

"We are missing a few." His voice was barely a whisper, his eyes hot and glittering beneath lowered lids.

That heat kindled a tiny flame inside her. "A few?"

"Counters." His thumb whisked across her wrist, making her pulse scramble. "There are only twenty. We need four more."

"Well..." Nervously she wet her lips. "We could borrow some of the Morris men."

"Aye." His eyes turned hungry as they watched her tongue. "An excellent suggestion." He squeezed her hand, then sighed and released it. "We had best get at it." He centered the checkered draughts board on the table.

Allisun hurried to set the pieces on the board. She should be glad he was a man of honor. Instead, she brooded that he had not liked kissing her while she had liked it far too well. Bah, this idleness was driving her mad. To combat it, she focused on the game with ruthless intensity. He had graciously allowed her to take the black, thus she made the first move, shifting one of her twelve counters on the diagonal to the next white square.

The opening gambits tended to be dull and predictable, each player sliding ahead on their color blocks. It was only when the men reached the middle and encountered each other face-to-face, so to speak, that the excitement began.

Allisun drew first blood, jumping over one of Hunter's men. She chuckled as she removed it from the board.

"Feeling smug, are you?" He reached across the table to tuck a lock of hair behind her ear. His fingers lingered on her cheek, making it burn. There was no leer in his expression, no hint that it had been anything other than a friendly gesture. Nor did he give any quarter where the game was concerned. His moves were quick and clever.

She had to concentrate, not only on her current move, but on those upcoming, just to stay even. Her blood heated and hummed with a different sort of passion, one she understood better than the sensual battle going on beneath the surface. Strike. Counterstrike. He took three of her men, she two of his. He maneuvered one marker to her side of the board, and she was forced to crown it. Now she had to be doubly on her guard because the king could move backward as well as forward.

"Well done, lass," he said when she got a second piece to his side. He crowned it and filled two cups with ale.

She drank absently, studying the battlefield, planning her moves and trying to predict his. When she looked up, he grinned at her across the checkered board, eyes alight with good-humored rivalry. A day ago, she'd not have dreamed of playing at draughts with Jock McKie's nephew.

Oh, but it was hard to think of Hunter as her enemy. Not only was he the most handsome man she'd ever met, he'd thus far proved himself to be honorable. A commodity that was in short supply here on the Borders. Another man might have taken advantage of their unusual circumstances. Instead, he'd offered to take her family in and give them work.

Part of her ached to accept.

A permanent place to live. Food. Shelter. Freedom from fear. And best of all, hope for a future. Her spirits soared, then sank. What if it was all a ruse?

Allisun watched him through her lashes, looking for some hint of corruption in his ruggedly chiseled features, some sign he hungered for revenge.

"There." He advanced one counter. "That's the best I can do, but I think you've got me at your mercy." He rested his arm alongside hers on the table. The warmth of his flesh seemed to seep into her body.

The heat curled through her, making her heart race, making her long for his touch. To be held and kissed by him again. She wanted those things more than she'd dreamed possible.

"Allie?" His voice was barely a whisper.

Jerking her gaze to the board, she fought for control. *Do not let him guess.* "Hmm." She saw her move, the one that would spell his downfall. Picking up her marker, she began to jump, zigzagging across the board, taking all three of his remaining men. "I've won."

"So you have."

"You should pay a forfeit."

"What would you like?" Sensual light gleamed in his eyes.

Her heart slid into her throat. Till that moment, she'd not fully understood how dangerous he was. Everything about this mercurial man—his canniness, his humor, his rugged good looks—drew her. When she was with him, she forgot about the past and thought only of the present, of how good it felt to be with him. And she longed, God help her, for a future.

That, she could never have. She stood quickly. "I need to get out of here."

"Allie? What is it? What's wrong?"

His compassion turned her knees to jelly. She fought for the strength to resist. "I am sick of being cooped up here. I am going for a walk."

"I thought you did not want to see the Nevilles here."

"'Tis preferable to being with you.'' She put into the words as much sting as she could, yet when the hurt flashed through his eyes, she felt the pain.

"I am sorry you feel that way." His expression was grave, yet gentle. "Be careful, Allie. I will be here if you need me."

Terrified she'd give in and stay, she fled. Outside the door, she paused, trapped like a rat in a maze. She could not have braved the hall for anything. The need for privacy and solitude made her think of the battlements. She hurried up the tightly spiraling staircase she'd traveled hundreds of times, through a heavy door and into the open. After the darkness of the stairs, the sunlight was blinding. She shielded her eyes and drew in a great gulp of fresh air. With it came the tang of rich earth and ripening grasses. *Home.* No matter what name they called it by, this was her home. One day, she'd live here again.

"What are ye doing here?" called a coarse voice.

Allisun forced her eyes open, dismayed to find herself surrounded by six armed men. "I am Allie, er, Sutherland."

The oldest guard, a scar-faced man, grunted. "The one Lord Derk found at the bottom of Deadman's Leap?"

"Aye." She retreated a step. If they wished to, they could have her on her back with her skirts tossed up ere she screamed.

"Ease up, Lorn," said a skinny youth with greasy blond hair. "Ye're scaring her with that ugly face of yers." He grinned, displaying broken teeth. "John's my name, my lady. Did ye take a wrong turn on the stairs?"

She shook her head and forced out a few words. "I've been tending my husband and came up for a bit of air."

Lorn grunted and shoved his sword into the scabbard. "Get back to yer posts, lads." He swaggered toward the chest-high stone wall rimming the battlements. The other men, with the exception of John, drifted away.

"How is he doing, then?" John asked.

"F-fine."

"That's good news," John said earnestly.

"John!" Lorn bellowed. "His lordship's not paying ye to chat up the guests."

The young guardsman sighed. "I'd best be getting back. His lordship's a stickler for his protection." He strolled away.

Allisun considered going inside, but the prospect of being cooped up with Hunter was more daunting. She walked to the wall that surrounded the battlements. Looking out, she scanned the hills she'd explored as a lass. They stretched toward the horizon like a great green blanket, dotted here and there by stands of trees, pines, rowan and oak.

Cutting through the land from left to right like the furrow left by some giant's plow, was a rocky gray ravine. The maze, her family had called it, for the ravine was filled with giant boulders and seemed to end in a boxed canyon. She could still recall the day Danny had found the way out, a slender passage from the ravine to the fringe of trees atop the distant knoll.

Battling tears, Allisun pressed her body against the sun-warmed stone. How rich their lives had been; how far they had fallen. She wondered if her father regretted the act that had started them on this downward spiral? The resentment she had felt toward her father and Brenna had dulled over the years. She could not forgive or forget, but she had been forced to accept their affair as fact. How could she not when there was such tangible proof.

Carina. Her skinny half sister with Brenna's black hair and solemn blue eyes. Over time, Allisun had grudgingly accepted Carina's presence in their lives. What she had never been able to understand was why her father had betrayed his wife. Till now, that is. Now she knew that passion was a dark, insidious force that could not be driven out by will or reason. So must it have been for her father, bound by duty to a sick, dying woman and drawn to a beautiful, vibrant one.

"Do not blame your father," her mother had urged.

The pity was, Allisun still did.

As she bowed her head, her gaze swept over the courtyard three stories below. It looked much the same as it had, the wooden building burned by Jock having been replaced by new ones. Derk had even added another stable building. It was a monstrous affair, fully twice the size of the old stable.

John stepped up beside her and cleared his throat. "Lorn said as how ye'd need to be going back in, my lady."

She nodded. "Does Sir Derk raise horses."

"Nope. Don't raise much of anything."

Then how does he support the estate? Allisun had her own answers to that question.

"I tell ye, it was our Allisun," Owen muttered, still looking at the battlements. They had reached the tower midafternoon and taken up positions in the trees on the next hillock. "There's no mistaking that hair."

Black Gil grunted. "What's she doing back home?"

"She must be a prisoner of whoever holds it now."

"How'll we ever get her back?" Martin asked.

"Oh, we will do it somehow." Owen's jaw tightened. "'Tis only a matter of how and when. I want ye to spread out, lads, watch the road and the tower. See if ye can find some way we might get in and rescue our lass."

Chapter Nine

The chamber seemed hollow and empty with Allisun gone.

Odd, Hunter thought, staring at the closed door, how important she'd become to him in a few short days. Nor was she as immune to him as she tried to pretend. He'd seen the desire and the longing in her eyes before she'd fled the room. But he was not such a fool as to believe she'd be weakened by either.

So how the hell was he going to help her?

Force her?

Ha! Corner his little fox and she was likely to either bite him or run from him. Or both.

Seduce her?

Now that idea was far more appealing, for she drew him as no other woman had. But she was an innocent, and to lure her into his bed went against his sense of honor. Still he brightened as a mitigating factor leaped to mind. By strict interpretation of Scots custom, they were handfasted, having declared themselves wed before witnesses. It was no sin to bed his own wife. And it was a husband's right, nay, his duty, to protect what was his.

Hunter snorted. Therein lay the problem. How to coerce

her into doing what he knew was best for her, and for her family, without turning her completely against him.

Cursing under his breath, Hunter eased out of the chair and gingerly tested his ankle. It bore his weight with a minimum of pain, but he knew from experience that it would take several more days of rest ere he could walk easily, to say nothing of riding or fighting.

"What are you doing?" demanded the very vixen he'd been pondering. Eyes aflame, she shut the door and advanced on him. "The minute my back is turned, you undo all my efforts to heal—"

"Easy. I've not taken a step." Hunter held up his hands. "I was but seeing if it had improved."

She stopped and cocked her head. "And?"

"'Tis on the mend. Thanks to you. We should be able to leave in another day or so."

"We will see. No sense in pushing it."

"What is this? I thought you were anxious to go."

"Oh, I am." She walked to the window and rested her arms on the sill, her gaze slanted toward the courtyard.

"What has happened?"

"Nothing."

Liar. Hunter took up the walking stick and hobbled over to her side. "Where did you go?"

"To the battlements."

"And what did you see from there?"

"Noth—"

"Do not lie to me." Hunter seized her arm and turned her to face him. "Whether you like it or not, we are in this together. I cannot help you if you keep secrets from me."

"I suppose it is useless to say I do not want your help?"

"Totally."

She glared at him, but he caught a hint of relief in her gaze. "Do you see that building, the large wooden one?"

"Aye."

"I think Derk Neville is storing his plunder inside."

Hunter groaned. "Not that again."

"John, one of the guards, says they do not raise horses. What else could so large a barn be used for?"

"Barracks?"

"No windows. And why would a barracks have those big double doors if not so that a wagon filled with ill-gotten booty could be driven inside? I think Derk is a reiver."

Hunter sighed, leaning his hip against the wall to ease the weight from his foot. "'Tis none of our business."

"I suppose." She left the window and began to pace. Her brooding expression boded ill.

"We are in no position to stop him, if that is what you have in mind."

"'Tis not."

"Allie." Hunter took an incautious step, winced and swore.

"Idiot," Allisun grumbled, taking him by the arm and herding him back into the chair.

Not so much of an idiot that he didn't know she was up to no good. Hunter tugged her onto his lap, quelling her struggles to escape with a firm arm around her middle. "I'll not release you till you tell me what you are scheming."

She stilled instantly, her mutinous gaze locking on his implacable one. "If I can get proof that Derk is a raider, I could take it to the warden and—"

"Have him arrested and, mayhap, get back your tower."

"Aye." She raised her chin. "Do not try and stop me."

"Allie." Hunter rubbed her stiff spine with one hand. "What sort of proof could you find?"

"The stolen goods. There must be jewelry or other things that would lead me to the folk from whom Derk stole."

"How could you get the goods out of here?"

"I am very good at sneaking about."

That, he did not doubt. "Derk does not have the men

for the large-scale raids it would take to fill that barn. Nor does he conduct himself like a ruthless reiver.''

"Looks can be deceiving.''

"Aye, they can,'' Hunter muttered, thinking how Allisun's fragility hid a will of iron. "But I've dealt with criminals for years and have found that the bent toward evil is not something a man can turn off and on like an ale spigot. If Derk were the sort who robbed and murdered for a living, he'd not have befriended two vulnerable travelers. Nay, he'd have taken one look at my fine clothes and imprisoned me till I paid a fat ransom.'' He did not add that men like that were no respecters of women and would likely have raped Allie.

"He is an outlaw. I intend to prove it.''

She was stubborn, but so was he. "A few days ago, you told me the warden was not an honest man. What if Derk bribes him to overlook your charges?''

"Then…then I will take my case to the king.''

She would try it, too, Hunter thought. Despite the terrible odds, the grave danger. "Allie, I will make a bargain with you. Leave here with me, and I will look into Derk's activities.''

"You?''

"Bringing criminals to justice is my business. I've a cadre of men trained in gathering evidence. If Derk Neville is up to something, I will find out what and see him punished.''

The hope that flickered in her eyes was almost painful to watch. "What of my family's property?''

That was trickier. "How many men do you have?''

Allisun stiffened. "I'd not tell you.''

"Easy.'' He stroked her back. "I merely wondered if you had the men to hold the tower.''

She shivered, and her shoulders slumped briefly, then she rallied to lift her chin. "We would manage.''

They would try, and likely die in a McKie raid. "Let us take this a step at a time," he urged, skilled at working around stubborn people. "While we are here, I will keep my eyes peeled for anything that smacks of illegal activities."

"What could you see cooped up in this room?"

"Not much, that's true," he said. "But I could move my chair closer to the window and watch the courtyard."

"It would be better if I took a look around. Mayhap I can find an excuse to get inside that build—"

"Nay." He put a protective arm around her.

"Aye. 'Tis the only way." She attempted to wriggle free.

Hunter tightened his grip on her. "Allie. Be reasonable. If you are right about the Nevilles, and they catch you snooping about…" Fear choked off his words.

"I'd be careful."

"Not careful enough." He took her by the shoulders and stared deep into her mutinous eyes. "'Tis too dangerous."

Confusion clouded her gaze. "I am not your concern."

Hunter sighed. It made no sense for him to be so obsessed with the safety of a lass whose family was at war with his uncle. So he told her what he did know. "I am responsible for you being here. Had you not stayed with me when I was hurt, you would never have met the Nevilles or been forced back here."

She nodded. "Actually, I am not sorry things turned out as they did, for this may be our only chance to regain Keastwicke."

"Even if it has meant living in close quarters with me?"

She blushed. "It has not been too horrible."

"Far from horrible." He put all the tenderness he felt into a slow grin. "I have enjoyed getting to know you."

The pink in her cheeks intensified, and she gifted him with a shy smile. "I, too. You are not what I expected."

As declarations went, it fell far short of his goals, but

he'd have to cultivate patience where she was concerned. "You have also been a surprise. A delightful one." He ran his hands down her supple back, pleased by the way she shivered and moved slightly closer, her own hands resting on his chest. "I care for you, Allie, and I want to help you."

Allisun stared into his face, stunned by his words. The dimness of the chamber could not hide the tenderness there. His empathy affected her nearly as much as the feel of his strong hands stroking her. She was swept by the most ridiculous urge to throw her arms around his neck and cling there. "Hunter, I...I do not know what to say."

"Just that you trust me. That you know I would never hurt you." He lowered his head and sealed the pledge by brushing his mouth over hers.

Good. So good, Allisun thought. She whimpered when he ended the gentle kiss. "Please." She lifted her head, wanting more.

Whispering her name, he gathered her close and traced her lower lip with his tongue.

Allisun's eyes closed on a moan of pure pleasure. Of its own accord, her tongue came out to touch his. A growl reverberated through Hunter's body and into hers as his mouth slanted firmly over hers, exploring her with a thoroughness that made her blood pound. Deep inside her something broke loose, something wild and sweet and wonderful. It surged and built with the fury of a summer storm. For once in her life, she didn't pause to think or analyze. She reveled in the storm, craved this fierce sensual whirlwind.

Twining her arms around Hunter's neck, she followed where he led, matching his movements as he devoured her. Her whole body ached and pounded to some strange yet exhilarating rhythm. She arched against him, straining to get closer, needing to reach the center of the storm. He must have known, for one of his big hands slid up to envelop her breast. The heat of his palm burned through her gown...so good. So right.

Allisun moaned and pushed herself more fully into his hand. He rewarded her by taking her tingling nipple between thumb and forefinger and rubbing. The prickle shot through her, like lightning across a summer sky, tightening the coil in her lower belly. "Oh!" She wrenched her mouth free, gasping for air.

"You like that." His eyes dark, his smile supremely male, he toyed with first one, then the other nipple, tugging sensuously till her moans became throaty purrs.

"Hunter...oh, Hunter." Allisun shoved her hands in his hair and drew his head down, kissing him with all the hunger clawing inside her.

The feel of Allisun coming apart in his arms tore at Hunter's control. He ran his hands over her, stroking and caressing, memorizing every hollow and curve.

"Allie." He wrenched his mouth free and buried it in the shell of her ear. "Dieu, but I want you. I do not know if I can make it to the bed." He tugged up the hem of her gown.

The loss of his kisses, the shock of cool air pouring over her heated legs tore aside the sensual haze. "Wh-what?" Allisun stammered, pushing his hands away and drawing down the gown.

"I want you." Hunter's eyes burned with raw intensity. His breathing was raspy, his nostrils flared like a stallion scenting its mate. "And you want me."

That Allisun could not deny, not with the blood surging hot as fire in her veins and her heart rapping against her ribs. "This is wrong, all wrong."

His features tightened. "We are handfasted."

So they were. For an instant—one mad instant—Allisun thought about surrendering to the desire they'd kindled in each other. Then duty reared its ugly head. Duty and the ills of the past. "I—I cannot."

Air hissed out through his clenched teeth. The hand still resting on her knee tightened. Possessively. "You need me."

Aye. The pity of it was she did need him, in more ways than just this one. But she could not let him know that. For if he did, he'd never let her go. Tossing her head, she fixed him with her coolest gaze. "'Tis long since I've, er, lain with a man, and you are not unhandsome, but—" she said as pain flickered in his dark eyes "—there is too much bad blood between us." She shook her head again. "If I coupled with you, I'd hate us both."

"You do not really believe that." His voice was low and as tight as the anguish in her chest.

"I do." Allisun pushed free of his grip, surprised he let her go, more surprised her legs held her when she stood. Wrapping her arms around her body to still its trembling, she walked stiffly to the window. "I am sorry I misled—"

The sight of two Nevilles entering the storage building dried up her apology. Between them, they carried a heavy chest, but the door shut behind them before she could see more.

"What is it?" Hunter called. "What did you see?"

Turning, Allisun described the men and the chest.

Hunter nodded, the lips that had driven her wild a few moments ago pursed in thought. "It might be well if I, at least, took dinner in the great hall tonight," he said after a moment. "A few casual questions may tell us what is going on here."

Allisun crossed to him. "You would do that for me after...?" Her cheeks heated, and she dropped her gaze from his.

"I did not offer you my aid on condition that you sleep with me," he said crisply.

She almost wished he had. It would make resisting him easier if he were mean and cruel. "I will sup in the hall and see what I can—"

"You will not," he growled. "If he is a reiver, one incautious word, and Derk will have you locked up...or worse."

"I will be circumspect," she snapped.

"You could not be, for you are far too close to this."

Allisun did not bother to deny it. "You cannot prevent me from going where I will."

"Nay, but I can go with you and keep you from harm."

She glared at him, but deep inside she was secretly glad she did not have to go alone into the hall that had once rung with the Murrays' laughter.

She was good at hiding her feelings, Hunter thought, one eye on Allisun's profile as he listened to Derk rattle on about the stag hunt he was planning. But the strain of sitting in the room where her family had held sway was there in the taut lines around her mouth and the stiffness of her back. While the Neville retainers stuffed themselves on roast venison and rabbit pies, Allisun picked at the food Hunter had heaped onto the trencher they shared. Her eyes leaped about the long, well-appointed room as though she were cataloging the furnishings for a sale. Her ears were pricked forward like a hunting hound's. He could only hope that their hosts were too busy trying to impress him to notice Allisun's odd nervousness.

Thus far, the visit to the hall had been uneventful. Derk and Morna had expressed surprise and delight when Hunter and Allisun had entered the hall that evening.

"You are a quick mender," Lady Morna had exclaimed, shouting orders to set two additional places at the head table and fetch chairs for their guests.

Hunter had smiled and leaned more heavily on his cane

than was really necessary, faking a few winces as he settled into the chair set beside Derk's. It was gut instinct, he supposed, that made him want them to think he was still incapacitated. Force of habit had him taking stock of his surroundings. The Neville men were quiet as saints when compared to his McKie kin…more like his father's retainers.

They ate with relish yet drank sparingly of the ale. They laughed and teased one another, but the jests were friendly. Their speech and clothing both bespoke more refinement than he'd thus far found on the Borders. All and all, he had a very hard time picturing these men in the role of murderous raiders.

And yet, he could not dismiss the small things Allisun had told him about the clothing and the large barn.

"Do you think I might buy from you another set of clothing for Allie and myself?" Hunter asked when Derk paused for breath.

"Clothing? But of course, only there is no need for you to pay. Save your money for the balance of your trip," Derk said. "We have spare clothes aplenty. On the morrow Morna can show them to your wife, and she can take her pick."

Spare clothing. Hunter's neck prickled. Clothes were costly. The only people he knew who had enough to give away were the king's courtiers, who were wealthy enough and vain enough to wear a garment only once or twice. "Thank you," he replied, forcing a smile. "That is most kind, is it not, my love?"

His love grunted.

"Not at all, not at all," Derk said genially. He motioned a passing servant to refresh their ale cups.

"Do you have a position waiting for you at home?" Morna leaned around her husband to ask.

"Well, my sire raises horses, and I suppose he will let me work with him," Hunter said vaguely.

"Raising horses?" The lady frowned. "It seems tame work for so big and hale a man as you. And 'twould take your wee wife a long way from her kin."

"Mmm," Hunter said noncommittally.

"Our estate here is growing rapidly," Morna added. "We could use a strong, able man."

"In what capacity?" Hunter asked.

"Oh..." The lady looked to her husband.

"I do a bit of trade with the merchants in Kelso and Jedburgh," Derk said. "But the land hereabouts is wild and dangerous. Bandits. Thugs." He shuddered. "Even armed men are not safe, so I've decided to hire and train a larger force to guard my shipments. As their captain, you could command a good wage and a house inside Hawkehill's walls."

"That is most generous." Indeed, it was, considering Derk knew little about him. Hunter searched for a way to avoid making a commitment he'd later have to break. "But I had best wait to see how well my ankle heals. I'd not hire myself out for such work if I could not give you fair service."

"Ah, I knew you were an honest lad." Derk beamed as proudly as though he'd raised Hunter himself.

"I am certain you will recover fully," Allisun said. "He'd not admit it, but my Hunt is the best swordsman in the world."

Stunned, Hunter turned to gape at her. The steely glint in her eyes made his skin prickle with foreboding. The little witch wanted them to stay here. She wanted him to work for Derk and gather evidence against the Nevilles. Actually, he thought, eyes narrowing on her false smile, it was not a bad idea. Providing he could persuade her to leave.

"I have no doubt you are a fierce fighter," said Lady

Morna. "And your ankle seems better already. Say you'll stay."

Hunter looked from Allisun's pleading gaze to those of the Nevilles. "I will sleep on it," he said slowly, unwilling to agree till he had figured out how to guarantee her safety.

"But, Hunt," Allisun protested.

He turned on her, eyes flashing a silent warning. "Let me handle this," he muttered.

"We are in this together," she reminded him.

For the moment. Hunter hesitated, torn between the desire to get her away from Hawkehill in case things went sour and the knowledge that if she did go, she could potentially be in even greater danger from the McKies. "We will talk it over later."

The mouth that had driven him wild a few hours earlier turned down into a sulky pout. "I will retire now." She stood, spun on her heel and stepped down off the dais without bidding any of them good-night or thanking their hosts.

Hunter watched her stalk from the hall, marveling at the contrast between her stiff spine and sensuously swaying hips. The memory of holding her, of kissing her and touching her, rose up to haunt him. Dieu, he wanted her, bad temper and all. When she swished out the door, he looked over to find Derk and Morna studying him with a hint of pity. "I am sorry, she is not normally so rude, but..."

"No need to apologize," Morna said gently. "Breeding women are entitled to their moods."

"Breeding?" Hunter felt his jaw drop.

Derk chuckled and poked him in the ribs. "Edna told us your lass had been sick. That is the reason, is it not?"

"Mayhap she does not yet realize she's carrying a babe." Morna's usually sharp eyes softened. "Poor lamb. Torn from her mama, carted about the countryside by an unfeeling man."

"I..." Hunter mumbled, his mind blank.

Morna sniffed. "All the more reason to stay here a spell."

"Hmm." Hunter's brain clicked back into action. They were awfully anxious to hire him. "We will talk it over this evening and let you know on the morrow. If that is acceptable."

It was. After bidding them good sleep, Hunter limped from the hall and braced himself for the confrontation with Allisun.

"I think that went well," Derk said when they were alone on the dais. "But I still don't see why you were so insistent on having him when Jock will supply us with plenty of men."

"We need to amass a fighting force of our own."

"Why?"

Morna sighed. Derk's lack of vision was sometimes a trial. "Because things are less stable here than they were in England." She let it go at that. To speak again of taking Jock's place would only have worried Derk. But it had been much on her mind that they no longer needed Jock. They could act as reeves for Will Bell without a go-between.

"He's an honest lad," Derk said.

"Aye. 'Tis both comfort and concern. What if he's too honest? What if he balks at what we ask him to do?"

Derk looked affronted. "Why would he? What we do is not so terrible. We are like bailiffs, keeping the records and collecting the rents for our overlord."

In a way, she supposed that was true, but a scrupulously honest man might draw the line at collecting black rent. And he certainly would not want to be party to some of her future schemes. "Speaking of the rents, my dear," Morna said. "I feel that we are not being paid enough for the risks we take."

Derk frowned. "Oh, I hardly think we can ask Jock for a bigger slice of his pie."

"I was not meaning to do so, but…" She tapped her lips thoughtfully. "Maxwell and the others do not know what price has been set. If we added a bit to what we ask…"

"Jock would kill us."

"How would he find out? The whole purpose of our being in this is so that the Maxwells, the Humes and the others do not know Jock is involved. He is unlikely to speak with them about the amount of the blackmail."

"I do not think this is a good idea."

"It will work. Trust me." Morna smiled slyly.

Chapter Ten

They argued till they were both hoarse and red faced. Two stubborn people, both determined to have their own way.

"Fine, stay then!" Hunter snarled. "Throw yourself in harm's way. See if I care."

But he did care. It was clear in the way his big body trembled as he limped from hearth to window, stomping with his right foot, using the cane to protect the left.

"You'll make your ankle worse," Allisun said.

Grumbling something pithy, and physically impossible to do with an ankle, he stopped in front of the window. Hands braced on the sill, he stared down into the courtyard.

"I know you are only trying to help," Allisun began. When he did not reply, she sighed and went to him. She touched his arm. The muscles were hard as stone but warm, so warm. She lingered as the heat seeped through the woolen sleeve and into her icy hand. It had been like that earlier when he'd held her, his heat chasing the chill from her body. She thought about how good it had felt. She thought, longingly, of pressing up against him, of letting him warm her, hold her.

Nay. It would be cruel to torture them with what could not be. Could not last. Shaking away the yearning, she removed her hand and repeated, "I know you are only trying to help."

"Then why will you not let me?" He turned on her, eyes glittering beneath lowered lids, sculpted features stark in the moonlight. "Damn you." He seized her, wrapped both arms around her and held her tight. "Why must you fight me?"

Allisun's mind emptied of everything but the pleasure of being caught fast in an embrace so ardent it nearly drove the air from her lungs. His heart thundered in concert with hers; his breath stirred the hair at her temple, tickling her imagination. What would it be like to cling to him, to touch and be touched? To surrender to the needs building inside her?

This is mad, dangerously mad, whispered the voice of reason.

For once in her life, Allisun did not listen.

"I am not fighting you now," she whispered, sliding her arms around his neck. She smiled at his shocked expression, tugged his head down and kissed him. A moment was all she had to savor the surprise on his lips before he groaned and his mouth opened over hers, hot and satisfyingly greedy. A heady sense of power swept through her, scattering any lingering doubts. Tonight might be all they would have, but she would have this much, at least. A perfect memory of a perfect moment to carry with her for as long as she lived.

How long would that be?

Do not think about that. Think about this and him.

Tunneling her fingers into his thick hair, she wriggled closer, glorying in the growl that rumbled in his chest an instant before he lifted her, fitting them together. Male to female. Hard to soft. It was not nearly enough. Whimpering, she twisted in his embrace, struggling to ease the ache that throbbed to life in secret, heretofore unknown, places.

Joy raced through Hunter as he took what she so eagerly offered. He tempered her untutored haste with a gentleness he'd not known he possessed till now. Till her. Her passion, unfettered for the first time, drove him wild. He wanted to rip off the clothes that separated them and drive himself into the sweet haven of her body. And yet, he wanted more than that. He wanted her very essence, her soul, everything she was. He wanted to absorb her into himself, to possess her.

And protect her.

Dimly Hunter remembered her innocence. That alone kept him from taking her here, where they stood. He lifted his head, dragging in air to try to steady his pulse. "Wait," he gasped.

"I cannot," she whispered, looking up at him with passion-hazed eyes, her lips slick, her cheeks flushed.

"The bed."

"Too far."

Aye, it was, but somehow he found the strength to turn her toward it. Locked in each other's arms, they stumbled the few necessary feet and tumbled onto the bed, limbs tangling. He made certain she came out on top.

"Ah, now you have me at your mercy," he teased.

She giggled, the sound so wholly enchanting Hunter knew he would do anything to make her laugh again. But already her smile was fading. "What now?" she whispered.

"Are you afraid of me?" The thought was intolerable.

"Nay, of my inexperience." She ducked her head into his shoulder. "I want this, but I lied about there being others."

"Shh." Hunter rolled, laid her back against the pillows and stretched out beside her. His hand trembled as he stroked the hair from her face. "You have kept yourself pure all these years. Why give yourself to me?"

"Because I want to," she replied, meeting his intent

stare evenly and praying he could not see beyond her carefully maintained barriers. "I want you."

An odd light flared deep in those dark eyes. Arousal? Triumph? "Do you care for me, at least a little?"

The totally unexpected question moved her. *More than a little,* she thought. Yet she could not admit, even to herself, how much he'd come to mean to her, how greatly she dreaded the time when they must part. It could not be love—never that—but respect and admire him, she did. "I'd not be here with you if I did not care."

"Allie, I—"

She pressed her fingers to his lips, afraid he'd say more than she had the strength to hear. "I need you, Hunter. Can that not be enough for tonight?"

After a moment he nodded, but his gaze still probed hers, looking for a weakness, an admission she dared not make.

"Good." She moved her hands to his cheeks. They were darkly stubbled and gave him a threatening look. Appropriate, for he endangered everything she was, this man with the sharp wit and gentle eyes. If only she were someone else...but she was not. "Lie with me," she whispered. *Make me forget what cannot be.*

Hunter watched the ghosts flicker in her lovely eyes and thought he'd give all he owned to know how she really felt about him. Patience, he told himself. Patience and tenderness. "I do not lie with women," said the man who had had scores of affairs. "I make love with them."

Panic drained the color from her cheeks. "I cannot love you." Something he swore was regret tightened her voice.

"'Tis an expression, not a declaration," he said. And yet, if things had been different, it might have been.

"Oh." Her lower lip wobbled. She caught it between her teeth, then released it. "I see. As long as we understand each other," she added in a small voice.

He did not yet, but he was coming to. Whether she would

admit it or not, Allie loved him, at least a little. She was only frightened, that was all, but after tonight, she'd trust him with her love and her safety.

Instead of answering her with words, Hunter kissed her, devouring her with devastating thoroughness. By the time he raised his head, she was clinging to him, her nails digging into his shoulders, her breathing ragged.

"You are so beautiful." His callused finger grazed her cheek, then trailed down her neck, making her skin tingle, bringing her senses alive. His hand moved lower to hover over the topmost lace of her gown. "Shall I loosen them for you?" he asked softly.

"Aye." Her heart began to pound as his big, warm hands deftly worked the narrow ribbons. Beneath the fine wool, her nipples peaked in anticipation of the moment when he'd touch her. She gasped when he slipped a finger between the laces and into the valley between her breasts.

"I want to touch you here. Do you want that, too?" He whispered the question into her ear, then nibbled on the lobe.

Allisun shivered, hot and cold at the same time, her belly tightening, her breasts swelling. "Aye." The word ended on a moan as he parted the cloth and cupped her aching flesh. Fire shot through her as he rubbed the nipple into a hard nub, stroking, tugging till her gasps became throaty sighs.

"Allie...my sweet Allie." He kissed her cheeks, the hollow of her throat, and then his mouth closed over her nipple. Hot, wet, hungry, it drew down on her.

Allisun cried out as the sucking rhythm cascaded through her body. She tunneled her hands into his hair, arching off the bed, offering herself, demanding more. He obliged, transferring his ministration to her other breast. The fiery spirals spread lower and lower, gathering at the juncture of her thighs. Dimly she was aware of a rush of cool air as he shucked off her clothes, but it did nothing to ease the fire inside her.

With his hands and mouth he roused a passion in her she'd not known existed. Desire came in waves, each one carrying her higher. She'd never felt so vividly alive as she did at this moment with her senses spinning out of control, her body straining to reach some unknown goal. But he knew, her guide, her lover. He coaxed her along the sensual path with dark promises and lush words. Still she tensed when he touched the downy thatch that guarded her secrets.

"Easy, love, let me show you how it can be." A husky growl rumbled in his chest as his fingers slipped inside her. "Ah, you are dewy as a spring morn," he whispered, nipping at her lower lip. "I've dreamed of this, of holding you, of watching passion steal over your face." His long, clever fingers sent her flying off the precipice to which he'd led her.

Allisun sobbed his name and clung to him, twisting with the force of her release.

The sight of Allie coming apart in his arms shattered Hunter's control. When the last of her shudders had died away, he stripped off his clothes and rose over her, parting her thighs with trembling hands. "Allie, look at me."

She forced her eyes open and saw him poised above her in the moonlit chamber, corded muscles taut, expression fierce yet so tender he stole her heart. "Hunter." She raised her arms in welcome. A moan of pure pleasure passed her lips as he fitted them together and slowly filled her, body and soul. The momentary twinge of pain was washed away by a jolt of wonder. "Hunter...oh, Hunter," she gasped.

"Now we are one," he murmured.

"Aye." She felt it, too, the awesome sense of having found the other half of herself. Wonderful as it was, it frightened her to realize how easily she could lose herself in him. Stiffening, she tried to pull away.

"Nay. No dark thoughts. Tonight is ours, remember?" He kissed her until she could think of nothing beyond the lushness of his mouth and the sensual tug of his fingers on her breasts. Of their own accord, her hips began to match the rhythm he set. "Aye, take me deeper," he whispered. "Take all I have to give." Cradling her rump in his hands, he lifted her into the swift, sure strokes that carried them higher and higher.

Allisun gasped as he set her afire from within, melting her very bones. With each thrust of their bodies, she burned hotter and hotter until suddenly the molten core inside her shattered. Swept along on a wave of pure ecstasy, she cried his name.

"Allie!" Hunter buried himself in the depths of her release, consumed by the force that shook them both, by the feel of her body closing around his. He poured into her the love he dared not voice, the love she would not acknowledge...yet.

But after this miracle that had passed between them, how could she deny it?

Lammas Day dawned gray and ugly. A perfect match for Allisun's mood. Standing atop the tower's battlements, she contemplated the dark horizon and pondered her next move.

Running seemed the best option.

Especially after last night.

Shivering, she pulled the cloak tighter about the gown she'd donned before creeping from the room. She'd left Hunter still asleep, his big body sprawled across the rumpled bed, the sheets riding low on his hips. It had taken tremendous willpower not to hop back into bed and waken him with light touches and stinging kisses, as he had twice roused her during the night. In truth, they'd slept little, and she had learned a great deal about the pleasure a man and a woman could give each other.

Her cheeks burned at the memory of her wanton behavior. But shame did not prevent a swift rush of lust from assailing her. Nor did it dampen the longing that followed. Weak creature that she was, she yearned to return to bed.

That was why she'd left him.

That was why she was seriously contemplating running away.

Where Hunter was concerned, she simply could not trust herself. How could she have been so stupid as to think she could couple with him and remain unaffected? Was it the same for all women? she wondered. Did this sensual thrall men held over women explain why well-bred ladies sometimes ran off with unsuitable rogues?

If it had been like this between her father and Brenna, she understood why they'd been powerless to resist.

"Allie?" growled a deep, horribly familiar voice.

Allisun stiffened but did not turn. She heard his halting footsteps scrape across the floor, drawing nearer. Her insides fluttered like leaves in a high wind, and her heart raced.

"Allie, what are you doing out here?" He put his hands on her shoulders. The warm, strong hands that had held her and pleasured her through the night.

She jerked away like a scalded cat and fled to the far corner of the battlements. "I am…getting some air."

"I was worried when I woke and found you gone," he said from close behind her. Too close.

Her skin prickled with a mix of dread and anticipation. "You need not concern yourself." She gazed blankly at the fog that shrouded the land outside the wall and struggled to marshal her will. If he touched her again, she had to stay strong.

"You've been my concern from the moment we met." His hands closed around her upper arms.

A shaft of pure longing lanced her. Oh, how desperately she wanted to lean back, to let him enfold her in his heat, his strength. But giving in would only prolong the agony. She stiffened away from him. "Must you paw me?"

He drew in a sharp breath as her barb struck. "Aye." He wrapped his arms around her and pulled her into his embrace. "I am like a man addicted to drug," he said lightly. "One taste, and I cannot live without you."

"Do not say that." Panicky, she tried to wrench free, but his grip, though painless, was unbreakable.

"'Tis the truth, Allie, and I'd have no less between us."

The truth. Ah, what a tangled mess that was. If she told him even a bit, the whole thing would unravel like a ball of yarn. Once he heard Brenna had a daughter, Hunter would demand to see her. He would be even more determined to end this cursed feud. He might even get himself killed. Nay, she could not bear to lose someone else she cared for. Better to end this now.

She glanced over her shoulder, the sight of his haggard face cutting deep. Knowing she'd caused him such pain left her torn and bleeding inside. But she could not relent. "We had agreed that last night would be all we had."

"Those were your words, not mine."

"You said you understood why."

"I do not." A tremor shook him as he turned her in his arms, so she had no choice but to face him. "It meant something, our joining. Our lovemaking," he added fiercely.

"It was…" Wonderful. "Pleasurable."

"Pleasurable!" He spat the word, his arms tightening. "That is all it meant to you, a few moments of mindless pleasure."

''More than a few moments,'' she said, her tone teasing, her heart breaking.

His face went red, and his eyes narrowed. ''I know why you are doing this,'' he growled. ''You are too stubborn to admit that you love me.''

''Love you?'' Fear made her ruthless enough to laugh in his face. ''You confuse lust with love. I would be lying if I said I did not enjoy you.'' She managed to flutter her lashes as she'd seen other lasses do when they flirted. ''You are a most skilled bed partner, but love...'' She laughed again, coldly. ''I could never love any of Jock McKie's kin.''

The color drained from his face, the light from his eyes as his arms slowly dropped away from her. ''You slept with me,'' he said in a tight, raspy voice.

Allisun felt nearly as empty and hollow inside as she had when she'd buried her family. ''It will not happen again.''

He cocked his head, measuring her with that sharp gaze of his. ''Aye. It will, again and again, till I convince you—''

She gasped and backed up a step, bumping against the cold battlement wall. ''You would force me?''

''I will not have to.'' He was all menace now, harsh and dangerous as when they'd first met.

''Aye, you will.'' She lifted her chin to say more, but the clatter of hooves on the hard-packed earth below interrupted. Turning, she looked down to see a band of men riding in through the bailey gates.

Their leader was tall and rawboned, a mane of reddish gray hair falling to his shoulders. As he swung down from the saddle, his face came into view.

''Oh,'' Allisun exclaimed. '''Tis Ian Maxwell.''

''Who?'' Hunter stepped up beside her and looked down just as Derk Neville hurried out and greeted the men.

"The Maxwells have a tower and lands east of here," Allisun said. "I cannot think he is one of Derk's retainers."

"Would Maxwell recognize you?" Hunter demanded.

"Aye, he and my father—" She squeaked as Hunter whipped her away from the wall.

"Come," he ordered, tugging her toward the door. "We have to get you inside before Maxwell sees you and tells Derk that his guest is none other than Allisun Murray."

Chapter Eleven

Hunter peered through the crack in the window shutters and watched another party ride into the courtyard. More men dressed in sturdy woolen garments, swords slung over their backs, their faces as grim and watchful as condemned felons.

"Come see if you recognize any of this lot," he said.

Allisun stirred from her broody contemplation of the hearth and approached the window. She looked even more ill at ease than the men below, if that was possible. And she took great care not to brush against him as she stood on tiptoe and glanced out.

Though hours had passed since they'd returned to their chamber, the pain of her rejection still burned. Hunter closed his eyes, fighting it and the grinding need to seize her, to hold her—against her will if necessary—till she recanted her lies. Anger and frustration boiled inside him like hot acid. He wanted to hit something, hurt something as he'd been hurt.

God give me strength, he prayed. Strength and patience.

"The men in black wearing the blue tartans are Humes," Allisun said. "The big fat man leads them—Rank Rolly, by name."

Hunter opened his eyes on a shuddering breath, reached blindly for the windowsill instead of Allie and gripped it so hard his knuckles hurt. He had to concentrate on Derk's visitors. Blinking away the red mist that had clouded his mind and his reason, he growled, "Doesn't believe in bathing?"

She looked at him for the first time since they'd come down from the battlements hours ago and smiled faintly, eyes shimmering with gratitude and regret. "That and he has breath so bad it would stop a boar at twenty paces."

Hunter nodded and fought to keep his expression impersonal. He could do this. He must. "The others?"

She looked down again. "I think the others are Nixons. That spindly man who has yet to dismount is Tommy Nixon."

"Reivers?"

"Nay. At least they weren't when my da knew them."

Hunter rubbed his whiskered jaw. Lammas was the traditional time for renewing contracts and paying rents. "Could they be retainers of Derk's come to settle with him?"

"It seems unlikely unless they have all fallen on hard times and I've not heard of it. Both families are wealthy by Border standards. The Humes raise sheep and run the village of Ester a half day's ride from here. The Nixons live nearer to Kelso and control a dozen crofts and the gristmill."

"Mayhap they are just come to celebrate with Derk."

"I'd say they do not look best pleased to be here."

"That is true."

The fog had thickened, eddying around the courtyard like gray cream, lapping at the calves of the men clumped together in close-knit groups. Another in a string of oddities, that. Though the Kerrs and Turnbulls, who had arrived after the Maxwells, looked miserable standing about in the chilly damp, they had all refused Derk's invitation to come inside and warm themselves.

Morna had bustled out some time ago, followed by a horde of servants who had set up trestle tables and spread upon them food and drink. The offerings had remained untouched, though Hunter reasoned the Borderers must be hungry and thirsty after the long hours in the saddle.

"None of this makes any sense," Hunter muttered. "What the hell could be going on here?"

"They are up to something." Allisun crossed her arms and glared at him. "I am going down to find out wh—"

"And take the chance that one of them will recognize you?"

She shivered, but met him glare for glare. "It has been years since I've seen them. I am willing to take the risk."

"Fool. Stubborn little fool." Though he'd promised himself he'd not touch her again, Hunter grabbed her by the arms and shook her once. "Do you want to be killed?"

"Nay, but I have to prove Derk is a criminal. Don't you see, this could be my only chance to regain my family's home."

The air hissed out between Hunter's teeth and with it some of his anger. Much as he hated to admit it, she was right about this being the ideal time to learn what Derk was doing. "You cannot show yourself. It's too dangerous, but…"

Hope eased the lines in her face. "You have a plan?"

The start of one. "Derk and Morna said they wanted me to work for them. Mayhap I will go down, accept their offer and meet their guests."

Her eyes rounded. "What if they do not want you there? What if they fear you'll betray them and so attack you?"

"That's unlikely. Too many witnesses. At best, they'll welcome me. At worst, they'll tell me to go away." Later, if they feared he'd learned too much, the Nevilles might act against him, but he'd shoulder that worry alone.

Allisun bowed her head for a moment. When she looked up, a single tear slid down her cheek. "Oh, Hunter."

"Do not cry." He pulled her into his arms, ready, nay, eager to comfort her. And mayhap heal the breach she'd forged.

She wedged her hands between them, keeping him at bay. Tears shimmered in her eyes, but not a one fell. Why had he ever admired strong-willed women? "There is no way I can repay you for risking your life in my cause," she said.

He could think of a few but kept silent. "I tell you again that I would do anything to help you, Allie. Anything."

"I know. I wish…I am sorry I hurt you." The words were barely a whisper, ripe with pain and longing.

Hope flared in Hunter's heart, easing the cold lump that had settled there when she'd refused to acknowledge what was between them. In time, she would come around. It was up to him to insure they had that time. "I'll go down and see what I can learn. I want your promise you'll stay here."

She nodded. "I will take no unnecessary risks."

"Allie," Hunter warned.

"If there is trouble, you cannot expect me to remain in this room, because I will not."

Short of tying her up, he supposed that was the best he could hope for, but he hated leaving her.

Aided by the damned cane, Hunter limped through the deserted hall and into the narrow stone entryway decorated with banners bearing Neville's crest. The display grated on his sense of justice and stiffened his resolve to see the Murrays' colors there again. Stepping out onto the wooden steps, he surveyed the courtyard with a jaundiced eye. Nothing had changed. The people below still resembled actors in some strange play, the black stone walls behind them and the wisps of fog adding a touch of mystery or a hint of danger to the drama.

Shoving his personal anguish to the back of his mind, Hunter started down the stairs. He kept his gaze moving over the assembly, capturing every detail. It was a gift he had for gathering bits of information and fitting them together to solve a puzzle or, more often, a crime. Thus he marked the moment when the Nevilles looked up and saw him.

Both fleshy faces registered surprise. Derk's was mild and quickly turned to pleasure. Morna unexpectedly looked furious and, aye, afraid. That was when he truly knew there was something going on, for she had no reason to fear him.

Hunter kept his own expression bland as he reached the bottom of the steps and was pounced upon by the pair.

"Whatever are you doing up and about?" Derk asked.

"Aye...what?" Morna grumbled.

"Well, I saw your guests and thought 'twould be good to speak of fighting and hunting for a bit," Hunter said wistfully. "Not," he added, contriving to look a bit ashamed, "that I am bored with Allie's company, but..."

Derk clapped him on the back and winked. "I'm sure not, still men belong in the company of men. Most times." Another suggestive wink.

Morna scowled. "We have business to conduct here today."

Which she clearly did not want him to witness. Hunter wondered if he should try to use their offer of a post.

Derk did it for him. "If he's to work for us, there is no harm in young Hunt being there when the rents are—"

"He is not yet our man," Morna said curtly. "Till he is, he cannot be privy to our...affairs."

Hunter was taken aback by her commanding tone.

Derk appeared unaffected. "Aye, but..."

"It will not sit well with our *guests* to have an outsider present for this," Morna said with cold finality.

Derk shrugged and sent Hunter an apologetic smile. "My lady is ever concerned with others' feelings."

More likely, her own welfare. Nonetheless, Hunter smiled and allowed Derk to herd him toward the refreshments. He had learned two things. Firstly, these men were here to pay rent. Doubtless they resented handing it over to an Englishman, which might account for their sullenness. Secondly, Morna, not Derk, held sway in this marriage.

Hunter tucked both bits away and studied the crowd over the rim of his ale cup, wondering whom he might approach. No one looked interested in speaking with him, much less sharing information. After casting speculative glances his way, the men had returned to whispering amongst themselves. All except Ian Maxwell, who glared at him with hostile eyes.

"Er, how is your ankle?" Derk asked.

"Mending." Hunter saw Morna bustle off to speak with a servant and decided to take the offensive. "Could you introduce me to a few of these men?"

Derk started. "Whatever for?" he exclaimed.

"I thought someone might have news from the north," Hunter said casually. "I've been long from home and wondered if there has been trouble while I was away."

"Were you expecting problems?"

"Always. The Highlands are nigh as unsettled as the Borders. There's ever a feud spilling over to involve innocent bystanders. If such is the case, it would make your offer to stay here all the more attractive."

Derk smiled. "Ian Maxwell has kin up there, we could ask—"

"What are you two up to?" Morna demanded.

They both jumped like lads caught filching apples. Derk

gulped. "Er, Hunt was wanting to meet some of the men so—"

"Not now," his wife snapped. "'Tis past time we were getting started, else we'll not finish before dusk."

Derk nodded and gave Hunter another sheepish smile. "I'll put your question to Ian and let you know at dinner."

Hunter sighed and mentally consigned Morna to whatever hell was reserved for loud, managing females. He did not, however, let his pique show as he bowed to her. "I nearly forgot to ask if I might have more of that magical custard for Allie."

Morna's frown vanished. "It helped settle her belly?"

"Aye, she was sleeping peacefully when I left her. Part of why I felt so restless," he added.

"Humph," she replied. "She'd recover more swiftly if you gave her a few nights' respite from your amorous advances."

"Oh, you can be sure I will," he said. More like a permanent one, unfortunately. Hunter turned and set the cup down on the table. His ankle throbbed, protesting the strain he'd put on it, and he had nothing to show for the effort.

"Who the bloody hell are ye?" demanded a low voice.

Hunter whirled, dropping his cane and reaching for the hilt of his sword. He hesitated when he saw it was Ian Maxwell who confronted him. "Hunt Sutherland," he replied slowly.

"Are ye Jock McKie's new man, then?"

Hunter was so shocked to hear his uncle's name that his mouth gaped open. "Wh-who?" he stammered.

"Never mind. I've got my answer." Ian whirled and stomped off after the men filing into the huge barn.

"Wait!" Hunter leaped in pursuit. White-hot pain lanced up his leg, driving him onto his knees in the dirt.

Lady Morna materialized beside him. "Lorn! John! Help Sir Hunt to yon bench." She tisked and fixed him with a hard, suspicious glare. "Have a caution, lad, or your leg will never heal well enough for you to leave Hawkehill."

Medical advice had never sounded more like a threat.

Allisun gasped and went up on her toes as Hunter pitched forward in the foggy courtyard. That he did not seem to be in horrible distress did little to ease her conscience.

No matter how desperate her need to trap Derk, she should not have let Hunter walk about on his half-healed ankle. Her qualms settled a bit when she saw Morna rush over to him, accompanied by two guards. The men lifted Hunter and staggered over to deposit him on a bench directly below her window.

Hunter's voice drifted up. "I am fine. If someone could find my cane, I'll go upstairs and Allie can—"

"Let her rest," Lady Morna commanded. "My lasses can bind up your ankle, and the men will see you settled in the hall."

"But I want—"

Hunter's wants were buried under an avalanche of orders from Lady Morna. Barely had she finished speaking than a bevy of maids converged on him, medicine chest and bandages in hand.

"See you bind it tightly," Lady Morna admonished. She stepped back and scowled at him, as though he were at fault for something. "I must join the others, but I'll see you at dinner."

Allisun watched the older woman cross the courtyard and disappear inside. The double doors slammed shut with dreadful finality. Their metal bands glowed softly in the gray light, tempting her to see what lay behind them. She could not boldly walk up and open those doors, but there might be windows on the far side, or cracks in the building through which she could peek. The risks were nearly nonexistent, she reasoned. The men who might know her were all confined within.

She looked down at Hunter, his sun-streaked hair surrounded by the tousled heads of the maids attending him. He was doubtless receiving excellent care.

Spinning from the window, Allisun snatched up the tunic and hose she'd arrived in. They'd been washed by Lady Morna's maids, and in them, she might stand an even better chance of passing undetected. It took but a moment to shuck off her borrowed gown and pull on the male garb she was far more used to wearing. After tucking her braid up under a woolen cap, she raced for the chamber door.

Because she knew the tower so well, it was easy to slip down the back stairs, through the deserted pantry and out past the kitchen building. The scent of roasting meat and clatter of pans reassured her that most of the staff was occupied with dinner preparations. Still she grabbed up an empty bucket from beside the kitchen door and clasped it to her chest. If anyone asked, she'd say she'd been sent to gather eggs for the cook.

Allisun walked boldly, for there was nothing more suspicious than someone who crept about. She rounded the corner of the stables and stopped. The area between the back of the building and the inner bailey wall was filled with horses. The visitors' mounts, all still saddled but hobbled to prevent them from wandering about.

How convenient, she thought as she edged along the stables, taking care not to alarm the beasts. If she needed a way out of Keastwicke, here were rides aplenty. But first she had to find out what Derk was up to. She paused at the corner of the building and gazed across the open space to the storage barn.

It hovered in a sea of fog, silent, waiting.

Just as she stepped away from the stables, someone caught her from behind. A steely arm banded her middle, a wide hand covered her mouth. Allisun instinctively fought back, kicking her captor in the shin. The blow sent pain slicing up her leg, but his grip on her just tightened.

"Hold, dammit. It's me."

Hunter! Did he think to stop her? Allisun began to struggle in earnest.

"Shh. Do you want to alert the guards?"

"Guards?" She mumbled into his palm.

"Aye." The word was a whisper, tickling her ear. "There are two men behind yon building walking this way."

Allisun groaned softly as she picked out the dark figures barely visible in the mist. Another few moments and she'd have run right into them. As it was, the guards would likely spot her and Hunter when they reached the corner.

"I'm going to lift my hand," Hunter whispered. "Don't scream." Before she could do more than nod, he removed his hand, spun her around and lifted her off her feet. "I'm sorry about this, but it's too late to run." His mouth covered hers.

Allisun jerked, her whimper of protest trapped between them. His lips were as firm and warm as she'd remembered, his arms as strong and protective. But where before he'd kissed her with an intensity that had heated her blood and numbed her mind, this time his mouth barely touched hers.

"They'd seen us," he murmured.

Allisun looked up, saw that Hunter's eyes were open to narrow, watchful slits. "Are they coming toward us?"

"They are talking it over. We'll have to be a bit more convincing. Put your arms around me and act as though you enjoy the hell out of kissing me."

Shivering, she wrapped her arms around his neck and arched into his embrace. The feel of his hard, muscular body pressing against her soft one was as seductive as before. It took no effort to throw herself into the task, her mouth opening, her tongue searching for his. The groan that shook him when they met, meshed, sent waves of the most exquisite heat through her.

The familiar fever gripped her, melting her bones, making her body ache and tingle where it touched his. He seemed to know, for his hands moved up and down her back, drawing her closer still as he took control of the kiss. The rhythm he set echoed deep inside her, a hot, splintering tension that built and built until she thought she'd go mad with the wanting.

From a great distance, she heard a man speak.

Hunter raised his head, breaking the kiss. "What?" he asked, in an odd, raspy voice.

"I said ye should take yer wife inside, sir."

"Aye. Just…just give us a moment." Hunter licked his lips and looked down at her, his eyes dark, dazed.

Embarrassed to know she must appear even more befuddled, Allisun buried her face in his tunic. It was somewhat reassuring to hear his heart galloping as unsteadily as her own.

"They've gone, but we dare not linger," Hunter said after a few moments.

"Aye." Allisun nodded but couldn't meet his gaze.

"What is it?" He cupped her chin and lifted it.

"I—I do not know what came over me."

"I do," Hunter said gently.

"Do not make more of this than there is."

"Oh, I do not think I am." He grazed her lips with his thumb, eyes filled with wonder. "I've never known the like."

His words moved her almost as much as his kisses had. Angry at her weakness, Allisun shoved his hand aside and stepped back. "Bah. 'Twas only an act."

"For you, mayhap, but not for me."

Allisun sniffed and looked away from his faint yet captivating smile. "Why are you walking about on that ankle?"

"Because when I went to our room and found you gone, I feared you were off getting into trouble." He leaned against the stables, wincing a bit as he took the weight from his foot. "Seems I was right. Did you not promise to stay in—"

"When I saw that you were hurt, I had to do something."

"What?"

"I am going to sneak around the back and see if there is a window or another door where I can listen."

"The guards…"

"Will be gone awhile." Slipping from his grasp, she darted across the open area to the storehouse.

Hunter cursed and hobbled after her. He'd come without the crutches, foolishly thinking his ankle healed. It was better than it had been, but pained if he didn't move slowly and carefully. He caught her kneeling on the ground, peering through a crack in the wall. "What do you see?"

She put a finger to her lips and motioned him down beside her. "Derk is on the other side of this wall."

Hunter put his eye to the space between the slabs of rough-hewn lumber used in the building. Neville sat at a table with his back to them, writing in a ledger of some sort.

"Ian Maxwell of Teatley," Derk called.

Maxwell stepped forward. Reaching inside his tunic, he withdrew a small pouch and dropped it onto the table with a clank.

Derk grunted, opened the pouch and counted the silver coins within. "Five pounds."

"Just as agreed." Maxwell crossed his arms over his barrel chest. "Ye said as how ye'd bought back the goods them damned Bells stole from my son and his wife."

"Aye." Derk consulted the ledger. "Two sheep, five chickens, an iron pot, a pair of leather breeches and—"

"The sheets off their bed," Maxwell growled.

"Good thing they were not in it at the time, else Ill Will might have taken yer daughter-in-law, too."

Maxwell nodded, grim faced. "Aye, we were grateful they got away unhurt, but I want their things back."

"Hmm. None of this need have happened."

"I know." Maxwell's jaw flexed and his next words seemed dragged from him. "How much to see it doesn't happen again?"

"Blackmail," Allisun whispered. "I knew he was up to—"

Hunter clapped a hand over her mouth. "Shh," he hissed in her ear. "If they find us here, we're dead." She grunted in assent, but he kept her mouth covered just in case.

"Twenty pounds," Derk Neville told Maxwell.

"On top of what I already pay to see my own lands are not raided?" Maxwell's eyes rounded then narrowed as Derk nodded. "That's robbery. Might as well take our chances fighting off the Bells as beggar ourselves paying the black rent."

Mutters of agreement came from the Humes, Nixons and other Borderers who stood behind him. Studying their faces, and the sacks they carried over their shoulders, Hunter reasoned that they were also here to pay the blackmail.

Derk rose and braced his hands on the table. "Is this the thanks we get for protecting you from your enemies?"

"Damn, ye're as bad as Ill Will."

"I've never done you any harm," Derk exclaimed. "Granted paying the rent costs you dear, but better to part with a few coins and spare your property, your lives and your loved ones."

"English bastard," someone shouted. The words ruffled through the crowd. Men shifted forward, hands falling to the weapons at their sides, only to be stopped by a wall of Nevilles brandishing bare swords.

"Easy, lads. Ian...Tommy, keep your men in check," Derk called out, halting them all. "If you kill me, Will Bell'll only find another to take my place. One who may not be as accommodating when it comes to taking goods in place of silver." He gestured toward the casks, chests and bags stacked along the walls. Above them were shelves crammed with blankets and clothing. Plunder, aye, and black rent payments.

Hunter's skin shrank away from his own borrowed tunic. Had the former owner parted with it willingly or been killed?

Allisun shivered and swiveled her head to look up at him. Moving his hand from her mouth, she murmured, "I told you."

"Aye, you did," Hunter whispered.

"What are we going to do?"

"Get back to our room."

"But..."

"We can do nothing to stop this," he said softly, regretfully. Not at the moment, anyway. But once they were away from here, he intended to launch a full inquiry. "Come, we'd best leave before the guards return."

Chapter Twelve

"What are we going to do?" Allisun demanded the moment they were back in their bedchamber.

Hunter added a few chunks of peat to the coals in the hearth and hobbled over to the chair. "Help me get my boot off, will you?" He extended his left foot.

Allisun glared at him. "I'm not your lackey."

"Nay, you are my wife."

"I am n—"

"Gently, love." Hunter jerked his head toward the door. *Someone might be listening,* his eyes warned.

Drat, she'd not thought of that. "Oh, very well." Grudgingly she grabbed hold of his heel and tugged.

"Ouch! Easy, there, I think it's swollen again."

Instantly her pique vanished. He'd reinjured himself coming to her aid. "I'm sorry." She carefully worked the low leather boot off, then examined his foot. "It is a little swollen, but the bruising is better. I'll bandage it again." She fetched the small stool and basket of medicines. "Put your foot up here," she ordered, kneeling before him. The room filled with the scent of vinegar as she unstoppered the vial of pennyroyal concoction. Working quickly but gently, she applied the leaves to his ankle and bound it with a cloth. "There, that should—"

The chamber door suddenly opened. Lady Morna stood in the doorway, looking not at all the genial hostess. "My men said ye were wandering about behind the stables."

Before Hunter could reply, Allisun stood, anxious to avert the disaster she had brought upon them. Sighing dolefully, she quickly improvised. "Aye. We had a bit of a row earlier, and I ran out. This…this daft idiot came after me." The loving glance she graced him with was at odds with her censorious words. "I fear he's strained his ankle again."

Hunter smiled up at her. *Clever, clever lass,* his eyes said this time. "But we did mend the quarrel."

Allisun felt her cheeks heat as the memory of that kiss burned between them. Flustered, she ducked her head. "Aye, we did. Though Hunt picked the most inappropriate place to…to…"

"Hmm." Lady Morna's suspicious gaze bounced between the two of them. "'Twas most incautious of you, Sir Hunt," she grumbled.

"I do not think my ankle's taken any permanent hurt," he said. "'Twas kind of you to take time from your guests for me."

"Hmm," Morna said again. "They will be departing in an hour or so. Then we can all have a nice little chat about your future here at Hawkehill."

The implied threat filled Allisun with dread. She did not dare look at Hunter.

"We are at your service, my lady," Hunter said blandly.

"Aye, you are." Lady Morna smiled thinly, like a cat with a cornered mouse. "I worry that you have strained your ankle, Sir Hunt. John shall remain outside your chamber in case you need anything." Without waiting for their reply, she departed.

The moment the door clicked shut, Allisun rounded on him. "Hateful old witch. How dare she treat us like prisoners?"

"Keep your voice down," Hunter murmured.

"Well," she whispered. "We have to get away. Now."

"That is the worst thing we could do, for it would confirm their suspicions."

"We have to do something." Hands clenched at her sides, Allisun began to pace before the hearth.

Knowing she'd not listen to reason till her temper had cooled, Hunter sat and watched his irate love. Dieu, she was magnificent, he thought, captivated by the play of firelight over her delicate features and slender body. The thigh-length tunic concealed her torso, but the hose faithfully outlined the long legs that had tangled so sensuously with his. She looked much too fragile to bear the heavy burdens life had heaped upon her. She should be safe at home, tending her keep and her babes.

His keep. His babes.

Hunter's gaze moved to her belly, hidden by the loose tunic. He knew it was flat and velvety soft. Imagining it swollen with his child made his heart do a slow roll in his chest. He wanted that more than he'd ever thought possible. How his friends and family would laugh, for he had always claimed that marriage was not for him. He could not be a good husband and father if he was away for long stretches at a time hunting down criminals. And he'd thought that any other life would bore him inside a fortnight. But that was before he'd met Allie. Life with her would never bore.

"I have got to get that ledger," Allisun whispered. She stood at his elbow, one eye on the door. "That's the key."

Hunter started, his pleasant image of wedded bliss shattered by grim reality. "Do not even think of trying to get it." He seized her wrist to keep her from rushing off and doing something foolish. "We are two against a hundred, and, thanks to your snooping, the Nevilles are even more suspicious of us.''

''If I had not gone looking, we'd not know what evil people they are,'' she muttered.

''Ill Will and his band are the evil ones. Oh, I grant that Neville and his men are accomplices.'' And his Uncle Jock was somehow involved, too, judging by Ian's comment. Pray God Jock was only a collector of the Bells' black rents, but whatever his connection, Hunter would see Jock was also punished. It occurred to him that if Jock were arrested for dealing in blackmail, he'd be unable to pursue his vendetta against the Murrays. That might be the only good thing to come out of all this.

''I am going to stop them.''

''Shh.'' Hunter tugged her down into his lap. ''Be still, dammit,'' he hissed in her ear. ''God alone knows if John is listening at the keyhole. If we sit like this and keep our voices low, he cannot hear what we are saying.''

''I am going to stop them,'' she whispered.

''You are going to do nothing,'' Hunter replied in a low, firm voice. ''We will stay right here till summoned to dinner, thence we will cheerfully go down to the hall and eat.''

''How could you break bread with such—?''

Hunter cut off her words with a quick, hard kiss. ''Do you think this is what I want, love?'' he said harshly. ''I'd like to see them all in hell for what they've done to these innocent men, women and bairns. But,'' he added in a softer voice, ''how would it aid them if we were caught and killed ourselves?''

Allisun's fury lessened. What he said was true. More than that, knowing he shared her hatred of this whole business somehow eased the gnawing frustration. ''What can we do?''

''Get safely away from here. While we are inside Hawkehill—''

"Keastwicke."

"Whatever. As long as we are here, the truth is a prisoner with us. 'Tis our duty to get free and take the truth with us."

Allisun nodded grudging acceptance. "But we stand a better chance of convincing the warden, or whoever, to issue a warrant against Neville if we have the ledger."

"I can get a warrant for his arrest without it."

"How?"

Hunter hesitated, wanting to tell her who and what he was, but conscious that he dared not while they were in Neville's hands. Think of the power Ill Will could wield if he had the king's chief justice in his dungeon. "I can do it."

"Hmm." Hope and skepticism warred inside Allisun. She wanted to believe him, to believe in him.

Hunter took both of her icy hands in his warm ones. "Trust me, I will not let you down this time. You were right to be suspicious of the Nevilles, and I was wrong to come here."

"We had no choice when Derk offered us transport."

"So it seemed to me at the time, but being desperate for a horse and in pain is no excuse. I pride myself on being a good judge of people's character, but Derk fooled me completely."

She squeezed his hand. "You are not used to Border ways. Papa used to say that along the Tweed there was no man who did not dabble in thievery from time to time. Whether it was taking a bit more than your due when you went to reclaim a stolen herd or attacking a convoy of merchants."

"Or kidnapping another man's wife." Hunter touched her cheek. "Forgive me. I do not know why I said that."

"Because it is true, in a way."

"You have said Aunt Brenna went willingly, and I believe you. But why did she not tell me she planned to leave? We were close,'' he added, voice harsh.

''Mayhap she feared she'd endanger you, too.''

''Too? What was she involved in?''

Allisun went cold inside. How could she have slipped? She had not thought about those tally sticks in years. She was not even sure where they were. It was because what was happening now so closely mirrored the past. Jock McKie and blackmail, hand in hand again. Only this time, Allisun would get irrefutable proof of Jock's guilt. She would not fail as Brenna had.

''She was not involved in anything that I know of,'' Allisun said slowly. ''I but speculated that she might have worried you'd try to follow her when she left and be hurt. Which you were.''

''Which I was.'' His eyes were glazed, obviously focused on that fateful day and the pain it still caused all of them.

''I am sorry,'' Allisun said gently.

He sighed, the shadows lifting from his eyes as he looked at her. ''I, too. But one good thing has come of this, and that is meeting you. Together we can put an end to this.''

''There can be no end till Jock is dead,'' Allisun hissed, wrenching free of his grasp and lurching to her feet.

''I think I can force him to give up his obsession with eliminating your family.''

''How?'' she demanded.

''I have not yet worked out all the details.''

''But…''

He shook his head and looked toward the door.

Frustrated, sick of being hemmed in, Allisun whirled and walked to the window. The sky had darkened, though it was only midafternoon, and the fog had not lessened one wit. Undaunted by the damp, a family of pigs rooted in the garbage heap. A few servants moved about in the courtyard, taking down the trestle tables and carrying away the remnants of the refreshments.

"Are the guests still here?" he asked.

Her gaze strayed to the storage building where two Nevilles stood by the half-open door. "Aye."

"Let me know when they leave." He bent to pluck writing materials from his saddle pouch. The scratching of quill on paper grated on her already frayed nerves.

Tension and lack of sleep, she thought. But she knew it was more than that. It was Hunter's presence that made her edgy.

He sat with his foot propped on the stool, the wash of candlelight making his hair gleam like newly minted coins. His ruggedly handsome face was somber as he bent over his work, the scholarly occupation at odds with the warrior's physique her men would have envied. Encased in close-fitting hose, his long, muscular legs bespoke an active life. His broad shoulders strained at the seams of his borrowed tunic, evidencing his ability to wield the claymore that rested against the side of his chair. Close at hand, in case he needed it.

Hunter Carmichael was a man who left little to chance, a trait her father would have much admired.

But when she looked at Hunter, she did not think of strength or of intelligence. She remembered the passion that had flared between them, hot, unexpected, overwhelming. He had not tried to touch her since they'd returned to the room, nor had he spoken of what they'd shared last night. But she'd seen the memories heating his gaze when he looked at her.

Shivering, Allisun wrapped her arms around her waist and tried desperately to control her wayward thoughts. But the subtle ache in heretofore unused muscles was a constant reminder of their loving. It was impossible to forget what it had felt like to be held fast in those strong arms, to be kissed and caressed as though she were the most beautiful, most desirable woman in the world. Impossible not to remember what it felt like to be well and truly loved. Yet somehow she must.

"There, that is done."

Allisun flinched. "What?"

"Come here, and I'll show you."

Against her better judgment, Allisun went to him.

He took his foot from the stool, drew it up beside the chair and motioned for her to sit. "I've found it helps to record the facts in a case when they are fresh," he said, tone low, conspiratorial. "So that I do not forget anything. This is a list of who was here, what we saw and heard."

Allisun was taken aback by this official-sounding talk of facts and cases. "Is that not dangerous? What if this list should fall into the Nevilles' hands?"

"I am hoping it will not matter. Do you read?"

"Mama taught me to. She and Papa put store in learning, though I've had little chance to practice the skill." She took the sheets and scanned. The words were an unintelligible jumble. "What is this?"

"French." He smiled. "I'm hoping few hereabouts know it."

"Not many read English or Scots, much less this." She handed the sheets back to him. "A clever trick."

He grinned. "I pray so." He rolled the parchment tightly, then wedged it inside a flap concealed on the backside of his wide leather belt.

Curious. All the more so when she considered some of the other things he'd said. Like being able to get a warrant without the ledger. And his talk of cases and evidence. "Tell me again what it is that you do?"

"I raise horses."

"And?"

The sounds of activity from outside had her turning back

to the window. The courtyard was filled with milling men, pawing horses. "The guests are leaving."

Hunter got up and joined her, his steps slow and careful. "Look at Derk, smiling and chatting like an Edinburgh courtier trying to curry favor," he grumbled.

"He is not making a dent in his *guests'* resentment. They look wane as men after a bloodletting."

"'Tis no fit way to live. Giving most of what you make in a year just to keep the cutthroats and reivers at bay." Hunter's hand tightened on the sill. "I will find a way to help them."

Allisun glanced up at Hunter's rugged profile, his squared jaw and blazing eyes, and knew he would do just that. For the first time in a long time, she felt the stirrings of hope.

"Someone is arriving," Hunter said suddenly.

Allisun swung her head toward the gate just as a band of hard-faced men cantered in. At their head rode a red-haired devil she knew only too well. "'Tis Red Rowy," she gasped.

"Bloody hell. Get back." Hunter grabbed hold of her and whirled her away from the window.

"What are the McKies doing here?" Allisun whispered.

"Likely they are searching for me."

"I've got to get away." She spun toward the trunk, wrenched the lid up and rooted around till she found her knife. Straightening, she thrust the weapon into her belt.

"You cannot run. They would catch you before—"

"I can reach the stables without anyone seeing me." She fought to keep her voice low, her nerves steady. "The Maxwells and the others have left their horses there, saddled and ready to depart. I will blend in with them when they go, no one—"

"Too dangerous." He looked deep into her eyes. "Lady

Morna is already wary of us. If the Nevilles catch you, there is no telling what they might do.''

''Well, I know what Red Rowy would do if he caught me.''

Hunter's face went gray, and he caught hold of her shoulders. ''He will do nothing. I am Jock's nephew. Rowy will have to obey me when I tell him to leave you alone. I will go down now, make my presence known to Rowy, and—''

''What will Derk say when it comes out you are Hunter Carmichael, not Hunt Sutherland?''

''I will tell him I hid my identity out of fear we'd be held for ransom.''

Allisun studied his face closely. ''You are not surprised to see Rowy here.''

''Well.'' He shrugged. '''Twas to be expected Jock would have men out looking for me. My own men may be with them, though I did not see them ride in.'' His eyes held hers, but there was something in them, some shadows that shouldn't be.

''Jock is part of this,'' she hissed.

''I do not know that.''

''But you suspect it.'' She had an ally. Her heart tripped a little faster. ''If we can prove the McKies are partners with Ill Will and an English blackmailer…'' The possibility dazzled.

''Allie. We must move carefully here.''

Reality dashed her excitement. ''Of course you would say that. He is your kin.'' She tried to wrench free, but his grip was unbreakable. ''Let me go,'' she coldly demanded.

''I will not let any harm befall you.''

''You cannot control Red Rowy McKie.''

''Aye, I can,'' Hunter replied, born to power and position, used to wielding both to achieve his ends. ''He will not cross me in this. None of them will.'' Unable to bear the separation any longer, he dragged her up against his chest and held her there. "Trust me, Allie," he whispered into her hair, drinking in the unique scent of herbs and woman that was his lass.

"I want to, but…but how…"

"Leave that to me." Conscious each minute was valuable, he reluctantly eased his hold on her. Curling his fingers beneath her chin, he lifted it till their gazes met. Frightened yet determined blue clashed with equally stoic brown. "I want your promise you will remain here with the door barred while I go down and treat with Rowy."

Her eyes slipped away from his. "If you think that best."

"I do." Hunter brushed a quick kiss across her mouth, moved by the way her lips trembled. Picking up his cane, he crossed to the door. "Lock the door behind me."

She stood straight and tall, her red hair a burnished brand in the gloomy room. "I will," she replied.

Hunter nodded and went out to face the first of many trials. John refused to let him leave unescorted. "I'd rather you stayed to watch my lass," Hunter said.

John straightened his narrow shoulders. "I've my orders. Ye're not to walk about without a guard."

Hunter bowed to inevitable and made his way through the hall with John clumping along behind. At the top of the entryway, Hunter paused to assess the situation.

Ian Maxwell and the others were on the point of leaving, horses milling, men shouting orders. Across the way, in the shadow of the storage building, Red Rowy stood with Derk and Lady Morna. The sight of their three heads bent together fairly screamed conspiracy. Judging by the looks cast their way by the departing men, Rowy was part of this blackmail scheme. Which likely put Uncle Jock square in the center of things.

His mind racing over what he would say to extricate Allie and himself from this, Hunter carefully descended the steps. He reached the bottom without attracting Rowy's notice. Excellent, for it gave him the element of surprise.

"Rowy!" Hunter shouted, pitching his voice over the din.

The older man jumped and spun about. All other activity in the courtyard came to an abrupt halt.

"Hunter?" Rowy's shaggy brows rose.

"You know him?" Derk and Morna said in unison.

"Aye." Rowy frowned as he hurried across the fog-choked courtyard. "How the hell did ye end up here?"

Hunter pasted on a self-deprecating smile, conscious that Maxwell and the others had paused to watch the unfolding drama. "Well, 'tis a long story. I hurt my ankle." He lifted his bandaged foot out of the fog. "And lost my horse. The Nevilles were kind enough to take me in."

"Ye might have sent word, mon," Rowy exclaimed. "Old Jock's been tearing the countryside apart looking for ye."

"Jock...McKie?" Derk asked faintly.

"Aye. Hunter here is Jock's nephie."

The news whispered through the crowd. If looks could indeed kill, Hunter would have died a dozen times. Cursing and growling amongst themselves, the men began to mount their waiting horses.

"Why did you not say so?" Morna demanded of Hunter.

Hunter contrived to look even more sheepish. "Well, I was just a wee bit concerned you might try to ransom me."

"Ransom?" Derk hooted. "Why, I'd be about as likely to chop off my own foot as hold my dear friend's kin for profit."

Well, that answered that, Hunter thought with a sinking heart. "But I did not know of your association with Jock."

Derk chuckled. "To think, we offered you a post here."

Rowy paled. "Ye told him about our business?"

"What business?" Hunter asked with wide-eyed innocence while the Nevilles sputtered for an answer.

"Sheep. Derk is selling our sheep in Kelso," Rowy said, proving he was not as slow-witted as he looked.

"Ah." Hunter gazed about at the rapidly clearing courtyard as though dismissing the subject. "Your guests will find the ride hard in this fog," he remarked.

"What? Oh, aye." Derk glanced absently about, then his gaze sharpened. "Say, is that not your wife leaving with the Humes?"

"Wife?" Rowy asked sharply.

"Where?" Hunter swiveled his head and spied Allisun's white face as she sped by in the wake of a dozen leatherjacketed men.

Rowy spotted her at the same moment. "Dod! That's Allisun Murray." He sprang to snag the bridle of her stolen horse.

"Nay!" Allisun kicked out. Her toe caught Rowy in the chin and sent him sprawling.

"Allie! Wait!" Hunter stumbled after her, but she did not even pause in her headlong dash after the Humes. "Bloody hell." He spun on his heel, grabbed the reins of the nearest horse from an openmouthed McKie and swung into the saddle. Pain shot up his leg. He ignored it as he urged the horse out of the inner bailey in pursuit of his wife.

"Dinna just stand there!" Rowy roared. "To horse! Get her!"

Chapter Thirteen

Allisun had been afraid before…most of her life, it seemed. But she'd never been as terrified as she was now—wet, cold and hunted. The possibly hostile Borderers were somewhere up ahead in the fog, the hated McKies most certainly following behind.

The fog made everything worse. It cloaked whatever landmarks she might have recognized in a veil of gray. And yet, nature might become her ally if she could only find the entrance to the ravine and hide among the rocks.

There to the left she suddenly spied a mass of black stone jutting out of the fog. She urged her horse toward it, praying her memory was not faulty. As she drew closer, the boulders grew larger, looming over her in a seemingly impenetrable wall, but she knew there was a narrow opening. Her brothers had found it long ago, and together the three of them had explored this ancient cut in the land. Oh, the booty they'd dragged home of a summer—birds' eggs, colored stones, wildflowers for her mother and a few dried bones, which she had made them throw away.

Desperately aware of the fleeting time, Allisun gave the horse its head, trusting more to its instincts than her own eyes. He proved her right, heading deftly between the boulders and into the ravine. Here the fog had barely invaded, held back by the rocky walls. All was silent. Peaceful. Safe. Yet she knew it was an illusion. She dared not linger.

Allisun sent the hobbler down the belly of the ravine. The trail twisted through a maze of dark boulders, each one tall enough to hide her from view. Behind her, she heard a sound that made her quicken the pace: the ominous rattle of hooves on rock.

Hunter? Or Rowy McKie?

Either man was a danger to her.

She had to return to Tadlow and her family. Hunter would try to prevent that. Rowy would kill her.

Panicky now, she headed the horse into what seemed a dead end, but Danny and Sandie had poked about in the labyrinth till they'd discovered the way out. The horse balked at entering the narrow cleft, but Allisun urged him on with gentle words and a firm hand. Moments later, they emerged into a fog-choked meadow. Farther up the hill, the mist thinned to reveal a line of trees set out black against the darkening sky.

Cocking her head back the way she'd come, she listened intently. All she heard was the thudding of her heart and the raspy breathing of her mount. Whoever was after her had not found the way out of the maze. Yet.

"Good lad." Allisun patted his sweaty neck and swung his head toward home. As she approached the trees, a shape detached itself from the shadows. She skidded to a halt, then relaxed when she recognized Black Gil's scowling face. Hysterical laughter bubbled inside her. Who would think she'd be rescued by her most severe critic? "Gil, you're a welcome sight."

"Am I?" He drew rein beside her. His lip curled back over yellowed teeth. "Damn, but ye are a hardy thing. Here I had ye dead, and don't ye turn up looking fit as ever."

Apprehension iced her spine. Shivering, Allisun backed her horse up a step. "Where are the others?"

"About." He fingered the scar on his cheek. "'Tis not that I wished ye ill, ye ken, but I've gotten used to how things could be with ye gone and me in charge."

He was going to kill her. Allisun read the murderous intent in his narrowed eyes. On instinct, she jerked her mount's head about and set her heels into its ribs in a desperate ploy to escape. But she'd left it too late. Black Gil made a grab for her horse's bridle. A scream ripping from her throat, Allisun dragged back on the reins. The horse reared.

Allisun slid off and hit her head. The world went black.

A woman's scream shattered the stillness.

Allie!

Hunter swung his head around, scanning the fog-clogged landscape for some sign of where she'd gone.

The scream came again, higher, more panicked.

He turned toward it, urging his stolen mount up a steep slope and onto a high meadow. The fog was naught but a thin mist here, still he could not see her. Which way? Which way? Frantic, he stood in his stirrups, ignoring the flash of pain up his left leg. Where? Dear God, where was she?

A flicker of movement near the trees caught his attention. Two riderless horses silhouetted against the woods. One must be Allisun's. And the other...friend or foe?

Hunter drew his sword and nudged his horse into a gallop. As they closed the distance, he saw a man kneeling over something in the grass and caught the glint of upraised steel.

"Nay! Hold, hold I say!" Hunter screamed.

The assailant leaped up and turned toward him, the

weapon still gleaming in his hand. A hoarse curse rang out over the land. He crouched, clearly intending to fight.

"'A Carmichael!" Hunter roared. "To me, lads!" Let the bastard think he had a horde to contend with.

The ruse worked. Her assailant turned, mounted and disappeared into the trees long minutes before Hunter reached the other horse and the figure lying prone on the ground.

"Allie?" Hunter vaulted from the saddle, cursed as his ankle threatened to buckle, and hobbled to the form lying still in the grass. So still. So small.

Dear God, it was her.

Hunter prayed as he knelt beside her. His hand trembled as he touched her shoulder. "'Tis all right, Allie. I'm here." Gently he rolled her over. His heart sank when he saw the ominous trickle of blood running across her forehead.

"Nay, dear God, she cannot be dead." He felt for her pulse, found it thin and thready. Bandages. He had to stop the blood, then get her someplace safe and warm where he could—

"Hunter? Hunter?" shouted a frantic voice.

Stumbling to his feet, Hunter beheld the most welcome of sights. A score of mounted men thundered up the hill through the fog, their armor shimmering in the gloom. His men.

"Gavin! Gavin," he cried, picking out his cousin in the lead. "By all that's holy, I am glad to see you."

"And I you." Gavin reined in, slid from his mount and enveloped Hunter in a bone-crushing hug. "Dieu, when we heard your battle cry, we came as quickly as we could. Where the hell have you been? We've searched these hills till our arses are—"

"Never mind that now." Hunter extricated himself from his cousin's grasp and went back to Allisun. "I've a woman hurt, here.'' Gently he felt along her slender limbs, grateful to find no sign anything was broken.

"Who is it?" Gavin hunkered down on her other side.

"'Tis a long story, and we've not much time." He had left the tower a short distance in front of the McKies and Nevilles, certain that they'd overtake him. Then he'd heard Rowy order the men to fan out and search the rocky ravine just off the road. They could finish there and come this way at any time. "We've got to get Allie to a physician or a skilled herb woman."

"There's naught hereabout but poor crofts," said Gavin. "Kelso is the nearest town, a few hours' ride to the northeast."

Ah, there they'd find an inn with a bed, medical care and food. Best of all, it was far from Jock McKie's home turf. "We'll make for Kelso, then," Hunter said. "I'll bind her head before we do. While I tend to her, have the men hide themselves and the horses in yon trees."

"Have you hit *your* head?" Gavin asked.

"Nay, but we are in serious trouble. There are men after us—my uncle's and another man's. We cannot afford to be caught or seen. All else, I'll explain when we have Allie safely away from here. Have you something I can use to clean her head? And a spare blanket to wrap her in?"

"We came fully supplied with bandages, food and water, not knowing in what sort of condition we'd find you." He turned away long enough to secure the supplies and send the men into hiding. "I've posted one guard."

Hunter nodded, grateful for his cousin's foresightedness and forbearance. He washed the blood from Allie's head as best he could and wrapped it in clean linen.

"Riders moving along the main road," the guard said softly.

"Into the woods." Hunter swung Allie into his arms and hobbled into hiding. Behind him, a trooper efficiently whisked a pine branch over the ground, plumping up the grass they'd trampled. Not that there was much chance of anyone noticing, for night was fast falling. But Hunter left little to chance.

Deep in the concealing shadows, Hunter sat on a large boulder, Allie cradled in his lap. His men stood round about, hands on their sword hilts. The tension in the air was thick as the fog in the valley below. At the first sign their presence had been noted, they'd be on the attack. In absolute silence, he listened as a trio of scouts crested the hill.

They scanned the area, found nothing to rouse their suspicions and left, grousing about the damp weather and their empty bellies.

A few minutes later, Hunter gave the order to mount up. Allie did not stir when Gavin handed her up to Hunter, but as the horses began to move along the woodland trail, she whimpered and burrowed into his embrace.

"'Tis all right, sweetheart," he murmured, stroking her back. "I've got you, and I'll keep you safe." He whispered the words, but when he looked up, he saw that Gavin, who rode beside them, stared at them intently.

"What is she to you?" Gavin muttered.

"The lass who saved my life." And changed it, in ways he did not yet fully understand.

Gavin grunted, his eyes brimming with questions he was too good a friend to voice.

They rode in silence for several miles. The wind had freshened, blowing the clouds away from the moon. As the cavalcade made its way down a gentle slope and out onto what appeared to be a main road, Hunter recognized several landmarks and realized they were only a few miles from Kelso."

In his arms, Allie started and opened her eyes.

"Shh. 'Tis all right," he whispered, fearing she'd take fright and scream.

She moaned and raised a shaky hand to the bandage. "Not all right. I hurt."

"You fell from your horse and hit your head."

"Where…where am I?"

"Lie still. I'm taking you to a place where you can rest."

Her eyes were huge, dark pools in a face bleached white by the moonlight. "Wh-who are you?"

"Hunter."

"Oh." No recognition flickered in her eyes.

Dieu, had the fall addled her wits?

"Good, she is awake," Gavin said. "How do you feel, lass?"

"Hurt…confused."

"Understandable," Gavin said gently. "You must have taken quite a crack. You've been unconscious for a long while, but do not worry, we'll see you get well." He flashed another smile, then urged his horse toward the front of the band.

"Who is he?" Allie whispered.

"My cousin, Gavin."

"I do not know him."

"Nay, you do not. He only just—"

She sobbed, her eyes filling with tears. "I do not know anything or anyone. Not even me."

Hunter stared at her, aghast. His first instinct was to offer sympathy and hope. "'Tis this blow you took." He knew men who'd been knocked unconscious in battle. They'd awakened later with no memory at all of the fight just waged. "With time and rest, it will come back." But even as he soothed her, urged her to lie still in his arms while they rode to Kelso, another possibility hovered in the back of his mind.

What if she did not regain her memory?

Owen barely missed being captured by Rowy McKie. He was just passing the mouth of the ravine a mile from

Keastwicke when he heard hoofbeats thundering down the narrow cleft. Owen dismounted, tugged his mount behind a huge boulder and prayed the fog would hide him. From his vantage point, he watched men trot into the open, led by his longtime enemy.

"Idiot." Red Rowy scowled at the pudgy man beside him. "What possessed ye to send us into that blind canyon?"

"I thought I saw her go that way."

"Well, if she did, Allisun Murray's a witch who can change herself into a bird and fly up yon walls."

Owen came to full attention, straining to hear more.

"What do we do now?" asked Rowy's companion.

"We send men up the road for a look-see. Much good it'll do," Rowy grumbled. "She's likely long gone."

"And Jock's nephew?"

Rowy grunted and scrubbed a filthy hand over his droopy red beard. "He's out there somewhere, too. Damn fool. Who'd have thought that while we was combing the hills for him, he was holed up at Hawkehill swiving Alex Murray's daughter."

Owen's hand curled into a tight fist. Rowy was wrong. Allisun would not have let a McKie kin touch her. Willingly. The idea that she'd been raped made him sick.

"Well, best be at it. If we dinna find Hunter and Allisun here, I'm pressing on for Luncarty," Rowy said. "Jock'll be wanting to know what's happened."

Owen stayed where he was, shaking with fury, until they had ridden off. Then he stepped from hiding, crept around the rock and watched as the main body of the party headed down the road. Three men galloped up the hill to the high meadow. He waited till they came back down, empty-handed, and followed the others before he moved from the shadow of the rocks.

The scream he had heard, the one that had drawn him from his surveillance of the tower, had come from this direction. He'd had a feeling it was Allisun. And Red Rowy's comments seemed to confirm that. Allisun was out here, somewhere, at the mercy of a McKie. He had to find her.

Owen set off up the slope. Once he had known these hills well, but in the past five years, the brush had grown thicker, and new trees had sprung up. And the fog made everything worse. As he approached the crest, a thrush called out.

Owen halted and replied in kind. To his left, a pair of figures moved out of the shadows.

"Owen?" one whispered.

"Aye."

Black Gil and Dale moved closer. "We heard a woman scream."

"As did I. Did you see anyone?"

"Nay," replied Black Gil. "I got here just ahead of Dale. If there had been anyone about, they were gone by then."

"I came in from the west. Thought I heard men riding down the hill," said Dale. "But with the fog and the trees, I could see naught."

Owen nodded grimly and told the men what he'd overheard. "Allisun is out here somewhere, and we are going to find her."

Dale Murray was a rare tracker. It was he who found the faint signs of a scuffle near the woods. "Someone tried to wipe out the marks, but they are there." Kneeling, he poked through the long grass. "Blood...here...on this rock."

Owen leaped down. "There's only a bit."

"Aye. From the signs, I'd wager a horse reared, the rider fell back and hit his head."

"Or her head," murmured Owen.

Dale's frown deepened. "You think it was our Allisun?"

"Could be." Owen stared down the hill toward the road. "Curse this fog. It will make finding their trail impossible."

"The McKies took the road, that's sure," Dale said. "But the men who wiped out these tracks went north, over the ridge."

"How can ye know that?" Black Gil snapped.

"I know," Dale said. "I know. There was a score of them, two bearing heavy burdens."

"Or riding double?" asked Owen. At Dale's nod, Owen gave the order to mount and follow. Black Gil did not like it much, but Owen was so heartily sick of the man's complaints he scarcely heard them. "We are not giving up till we find her."

The physician, a gaunt man who smelled of onions and sour ale, tapped on her head with his knuckles. "Does this hurt?"

"Of course it does." She slapped his hand away.

"The humors are out of balance," Master Esley announced, straightening to address the man who stood at the end of her bed, arms folded over his wide chest, hooded gaze watching the physician as he examined her.

Hunter Carmichael...her husband.

How could she know what that meant yet not remember him? Not even remember her own name. Annie, he'd said it was, but the name was as unfamiliar to her as everything else. It was as though she had gone to sleep and awakened in another world.

Husband. The word conjured up a host of others in Annie's poor, aching head. Lord. Master. Mate. In her mind's eye, she saw a couple embracing, kissing. A blond-haired woman and a man with red hair like hers. Her parents? Hunter had told her they were dead. She was an orphan, alone except for him.

A man she did not remember. He was very handsome, in a cool, reserved way, tall and broad shouldered, with thick, sun-streaked brown hair and ruggedly chiseled features. Everything about him bespoke a man of action, from the way he ordered folk about to the aura of suppressed vitality he exuded.

Her husband?

Annie looked at his full, unsmiling lips and tried to imagine what it felt like to kiss him.

The only thing that stirred inside her was fear. Fear of him? Or fear she'd never regain her memory?

Annie looked at his dark, piercing eyes and tried to recall if she'd seen them shining with love.

Did he love her? Or had they wed for some other reason? It amazed her that she knew there were other reasons. In an effort to block out the physician's probing fingers, she tried to list the reasons. Land. Money. Was she wealthy? The worn tunic and filthy hose she'd been wearing when they arrived at this inn did not seem to her the clothes of a wealthy woman.

"Nay!" bellowed the object of her thoughts. Eyes ablaze with fury, her husband rounded the bed, seized the physician by the shoulder and pushed him away.

"But she must be bled, my lord," Master Esley whined, clasping a metal cup to his sunken chest.

"The hell she will! Get out."

The physician swept his instruments into a small wooden trunk and fled without a backward glance.

Hunter Carmichael shoved a hand through his hair, then turned toward her. "Bloody bastard."

For some reason, the sight of the man rushing off, cloak flapping, made her giggle. "He looks like a scraggly old crow."

"Aye. He does." One corner of his mouth hiked up, setting an intriguing dimple in his cheek. The smile made him appear younger, more approachable. "But I shouldn't have chased him off before I found out how best to treat you."

"Not bleeding me sounds like a good start."

"I suppose." He sat down on the side of the bed, his eyes gentle yet concerned. "Does your head still pain you?"

"A bit. More so when I try to remember."

"Do not, then." He took her hands, their warmth enveloping her. "Your memory will return when it is meant to."

Annie clung to his hands. "What if that is never?"

"Then we will live in the present, and live for the future. Would that be so bad?"

"I do not know. I know almost as little about the present as I do the past. Do we live at this inn?"

"Nay. We were on our way to my home. Renfrew, it is called."

"Renfrew. I do not remember it."

"You've never been there. In fact, I have not visited the place for some time, but my castellan is a capable fellow, who sends me regular reports. We will find things in good order."

"What will we do there?"

He shrugged. "You will manage the keep."

"That sounds intimidating. Do I know how?" she asked.

"Sadye, the housekeeper, will show you how things are done. There are servants aplenty to carry out your commands."

"Now it sounds dull. What will you be doing while I am ordering these servants about?"

"Raising horses."

"Really? That sounds far more appealing." She levered herself up against the pillows. "Can it be I like horses?"

"Indeed. You are a fine rider."

For some reason, the tears that never seemed far from the surface, welled in her eyes. "I am glad I am good for something besides lying here."

"Shh, none of that." He cradled her face in his palms, flicking away her tears with his thumbs. "Things will be better once we are at Renfrew."

"Can I help with the horses?"

He hesitated. "It is hard work, men's work."

"But if I am a fine rider, there might be something…"

"Shameless," he said softly. "Using those beautiful eyes of yours to bend me to your will."

"Can I really?" She was amazed that anyone could make this big, compelling man do anything he did not want to.

"Oh, aye." He grinned ruefully, his mouth only a scant inch from hers, his breath warm and scented with wine. "'Tis been this way between us from the first."

"It has?" She saw her dazed expression reflected in his dark, smoky eyes.

"Aye." One of his hands slid down her neck, leaving tingling flesh in its wake.

Her mouth tingled, too.

"Just like this." He lowered his head, brushing her lips with his, gently, so gently it made her ache for more.

"Again," she whispered.

"With pleasure." His mouth settled over hers, warm, firm and so achingly familiar.

Sighing, she put her arms around his neck. As natural as breathing, her lips parted, her tongue sought his. The groan that rumbled through his chest as he deepened the kiss made her shiver. Oh, it was too wonderful, this spreading heat, the delicious mating of their mouths. Even more wonderful was the overwhelming sense of rightness, of belonging.

When he raised his head, she whimpered and tried to draw him back again. "Nay, 'tis enough for now."

She opened her eyes. "All you've said must be true, for I remember doing this. I remember your kiss."

"I am glad." Yet his gaze was somber. "You must rest." Gently he disengaged her arms from his neck and settled her on the pillows. "Sleep is the best healer." He dropped a swift kiss on her forehead. "I will be in the next room if you need me."

Hunter shut the door to the adjoining room and leaned against it, his mind at war with his conscience.

"What did the physician say?" Gavin asked, rising from a stool before the small peat fire.

"I sent him away. Bastard wanted to bleed her." Hunter forced himself to move

"How is she, then?"

"Better. Much better." He clung to that.

"Her memory?"

Hunter shook his head and turned to pour a cup of ale. The cool liquid didn't ease the tightness in his throat and chest. Guilt. He did not like lying to Allie, but on the long ride to the inn he had decided that telling her who she was would not only sadden her, it might endanger her, as well. So he had buried Allisun Murray's tortured past and woven for her a new one as his orphaned bride. She even had a new name—Annie—for Hunter feared that hearing her own name might jar her mind.

"It would be a blessing if she never remembered the terrible losses she has suffered," Gavin said.

"So I keep telling myself." Walking to the tiny window, he stared down at the muddy street on which the inn fronted. The rain that had begun just after they'd arrived at dawn had let up, and the sun was trying to poke through

the clouds. His mood had not made such an improvement.
"But do I have the right to withhold the truth from her?"

Gavin joined him. "What good would it do for her to
learn most of her family died in a long, bloody feud with
yours?"

"None, I suppose." In the dark hour while they waited
for the innkeeper to locate the physician, he had told his
cousin everything that had happened from the aborted cattle
raid till he'd saved Allisun from the would-be assassin.

"She needs help and a quiet place in which to heal, not
more turmoil. If her memory did return, she might try to
rejoin her kin and place herself in danger."

"I would not let her go back," Hunter growled.

"You are in love with her."

"Aye, I am." Hunter raked an unsteady hand through
his hair. "For all the good it will do me. She is a stubborn
little thing, who wants nothing to do with me."

"That was before she lost her memory."

"Aye." Hunter sighed. "But have I the right to let her
think all is sunshine and roses between us just because I
wish it were so?"

Gavin smiled sympathetically. "'Tis not an easy choice
for a man who values the truth as you do. But my point is,
Cousin, that because you love her, you will not only give
her the protection she needs, but you will do your utmost
to make her happy. She deserves some happiness," he
added softly.

"That, I cannot deny." Hunter sighed. "And I do not
see any other way to keep her safe."

"Agreed. Now what will you do about Derk Neville's
little blackmail scheme?"

"It is neither little nor solely Derk's." Grateful to have
something else to occupy his mind besides his conflicting
emotions over Allie, nay, Annie, Hunter pulled from his
belt the list he'd compiled. He took it to the table, motion-

ing for Gavin to join him. "I want to put a stop to this. We need the names of victims, the dates of attacks and witnesses willing to testify. These men—" he tapped the list "—may provide all that and more."

Gavin took the list and studied it. "What of the ledger?"

"Getting it would be too risky. Derk Neville is soft and slow, but his wife is a distant cousin of Uncle Jock's. She'd order a man killed on the slightest suspicion."

"Lovely family."

"Hmm. I am just beginning to find that out." Hunter exhaled sharply. "I wish I knew why my aunt left Jock. Could the blackmailing have been going on way back then and she have found out about it? If so, why go to Alex Murray and not my father?"

"Lack of time. Or mayhap she thought Murray had more influence there in the Borders." Gavin stood and reached for his cloak. "I'll send word to Carmichael that we need more men."

"I'd like some who are Border bred."

"Leith of the Tweed. Robbie McNar. And Dugald Carmichael, if they are available."

"Have them meet us at Renfrew. We'll send out two groups. One to look into the blackmail, the other to find the Murrays' hideaway."

"Jock has been looking for it for years."

"Aye, but he has used the wrong tactics. These people have perfected the art of concealment. Like ferrets they are, quick, clever and skilled at going to ground at the first sign of trouble. The only way to catch one is to bait your trap with something irresistible. The Murrays are short of supplies, desperate enough for food that they attempted a raid on Jock's herd. When you go looking for them, take a small force and enough supplies to feed an army. Let them find you."

"Me?" Gavin grumbled. "I thought I'd go after the big game—Neville and your uncle."

"They may be bigger, but the Murrays are more important to me. Let Robbie see what he can learn from watching Hawkehill. Send Dugald to question Maxwell and the others who have been blackmailed. They will be skeptical, but if we can get even one to testify, we may yet put a stop to this."

Chapter Fourteen

*T*he fog was thick and stifling, cutting her off from the rest of the world. Leafless trees stood out black against it, some straight and tall as sentinels, others twisted monsters poised to spring.

She turned in a slow circle, trying to pierce the gloom, trying to find some way out, some safe haven.

"Help me," she whispered. "I am lost."

The silence pressed in around her, but she knew that something waited in that gray mist. Something dangerous.

Flee, urged her common sense. *Get away before it comes.*

Mouth dry, her breath trapped in her throat, she began to back away. She kept her gaze pinned to the grotesque trees, feeling they posed the greatest threat. Out of the corner of her eye, she saw that a tall shape moved from behind one of the sentinels and began to stalk toward her.

"You cannot escape me," whispered a deep voice.

"I must." Hiking up her skirts, she darted away, stumbling over roots and rocks concealed in the blanket of fog. Behind her, she heard heavy footfalls. "Nay! Nay!"

"Aye."

Hard hands grabbed her from behind and wrenched her around, pinning her to the ground.

"Nay!" She fought with every fiber of her being.

"Annie! Annie, wake up!"

She opened her eyes and stared up into the face that had been her anchor in a world gone mad. "H-Hunter?"

"Aye." Light from the bedside candle flickered over his rugged features, drawn with worry. "Bad dream?"

"The same one." Her heart still racing, she wrapped her arms around his neck and clung. "Hold me."

He obliged by hugging her so tightly her bones creaked. "Better?" he asked after a few moments.

"Aye." She tipped her head back and managed a faint smile. "I am sorry to be such a bother."

"You are not." His large hands caressed her back through the fine night shift she wore. The gesture, undoubtedly intended to soothe, made her feel restless and wriggly inside. "I only wish there was more I could do to help."

"This is enough," she murmured, suddenly aware that his chest was bare, separated from hers only by a layer of linen. He seemed to radiate heat, the warmth soaking in to melt away her fears. How different his body was from hers, his skin tanned a golden bronze and covered with whorls of brown hair, while hers was pale and smooth. Most of all, she was fascinated by his size and strength. She slid her hand over his shoulder, delighted by the sleekly corded muscles flexing beneath her palm.

He trembled. "What are you doing?"

"I've been lonely for you. This is the first time you've held me in days." Ten, to be precise, for it had been that long since they had arrived at Renfrew. He'd carried her up to this bed in the master chamber. Since then, she'd been fussed over by Sadye, the housekeeper, and a gaggle of maids.

"I held you all the way here."

"My point exactly. I miss that. I miss you. You are up and gone about your business before I awake each day and come to bed after I'm asleep.'' She glared at the pallet before the hearth. ''Sadye says that wedded couples do share a bed.''

''You have been injured.''

''The cut has healed.'' She tipped her head toward the light. ''Sadye says I'll have a wee scar, but my hair will hide it.''

''That is good. But what of your memory? Have you remembered anything?'' His voice was tight, angry almost.

''Do you not think I have tried?'' she snapped, exasperated. ''There is this great void inside me where my past...my life...should be. I want to fill it, dammit. I think and think till my head aches, but nothing comes.''

''Stop, then.''

''You do not want me to remember?''

''Of course I do.'' His expression was still guarded. ''But I cannot stand having you in pain.''

''Oh.'' That rang true, for his every word and gesture was aimed toward helping her. ''I am sorry I shouted at you.''

He stroked her hair, his hand resting gently on her cheek. ''No offense taken. This is very hard for you.''

''I am fortunate to have you to protect me and teach me what I must know.'' She turned her face and kissed his palm. When she looked up at him, his face had gone red. ''But grateful as I am, if you do not let me get up tomorrow, I'll strangle you.''

He choked on a spurt of laughter. ''We shall see.''

''Please.'' She stroked his chest, delighting in the ripples that spread beneath her fingers.

''Annie.'' He sucked in a harsh breath and grabbed her hands. The teasing light in his eyes had changed to fire. The blaze seemed to kindle something deep inside her.

''What is it?'' she whispered. ''What is this overwhelming need I have to be close to you? Why do I only feel alive when I'm with you like this?''

"Passion…desire. 'Tis the same for me."

Annie smiled. "One of the maids—Janet, her name is—sang yesterday of love and passion. Is that why we wed so quickly? Because our desire for each other burned as hotly as it did for the knight and lady in the song?''

"Burned hotly?'' His face went a charming shade of red. He turned their hands, linking them, his large, blunt fingers engulfing her slender ones. "Aye, there was fire between us. Still I do not want you to feel constrained by that.''

"What are you saying?''

"You do not remember me or the feelings we had for each other. I would not hold you to this marriage if—''

"You do not want me?'' The words came out a horrified whisper, for it seemed she'd been shoved from the one secure perch in her precarious world.

"Of course I do,'' he said harshly. "I am just trying to do the honorable thing and not force you—''

"Oh, Hunter.'' She squeezed his hands, eyes brimming with tears. "You are the most wonderful of men. The only thing you've forced me to do is remain in bed when I'd be up and about.''

He nodded, but his mouth still looked pinched and grim. "Go to sleep, then, and tomorrow you may go down to the hall. For a short time, only, lest you tire,'' he added.

"Will you show me around Renfrew? I had only a quick glimpse when we arrived.''

"Aye.'' He released her hands and gently set her back against the pillows.

She bounced up. "I want to see everything. Every chamber and storeroom, the gardens and the orchards. Sadye says they are under my direction now, and promised to show me how things are done at Renfrew.'' A polite way of covering the fact that Annie had no idea how to do anything. But she would learn. She had no past, but she would have a future here with Hunter and his people. Their people. "I especially want to see the stables and these horses you spend so much time caring for."

"I am sorry you've felt neglected, but I've not been here in some years, and there is much I must see to."

"I do not mind at all, only let me be part of it."

His warm, dazzling smile made her heart lurch. "You are. A most important part. It pleases me that you feel comfortable here. You will see everything, I promise, but only a little each day. I do not want you to make yourself sick by overdoing." He laid her down again, brushed her forehead with a kiss, then stood and walked back to his pallet.

"Hunter?"

"Aye." He turned toward her, his strong body, clad only in close-fitting hose, silhouetted against the glowing embers. He seemed like some pagan god, broad shouldered, long limbed, exuding grace and power.

Well she remembered what it felt like to be held by him, kissed by him. An odd shiver slithered down her spine, followed by a familiar warmth. "Will you not share the bed?"

Shadows hid his expression, but his fists clenched at his sides. "Not tonight."

"Did we sleep together before?"

"Aye, we did." The memory of that moment must have pleased him, for he smiled. "Though we got little enough sleep."

The notion dazzled. "Then why? Do you not desire me?"

"Of course I do. I am trying to be noble, dammit," he snarled. The first time he'd raised his voice to her. "I'm trying to give you time to get to know me again."

Annie smiled. Truly he was even more noble and honorable than the knight in Janet's song. "I know all I need to.'' Her gaze locked on his, she raised her arms, welcoming, beseeching.

"Lass." He was beside her in an instant, crushing her to him with such satisfying fierceness it drove out the last of her doubts. "Are you certain?" he asked.

"I am." Blindly she sought his mouth, sighing when it slanted over hers. This kiss was as different from the few they'd shared as day from night. She relished the hunger with which he devoured her, the possessiveness with which his hands splayed across her back and hips, molding them together. The feel of his warm, hard body pressed against hers washed through her like a healing balm, so right. So familiar. "I remember. I remember," she murmured when he let her up for air.

Hunter stiffened. "What?"

"This. I remember this." She ran her hands over his lightly furred chest, marveling at the corded muscles beneath his sleek skin. "'Tis not so much a memory as a feeling. A feeling that I've been with you like this before."

"Oh? And did you like it?"

Annie looked up at him through her lashes. "Very much, I think, judging by the way my heart is racing." She took one of his hands and placed it over her heart. "See?"

"Aye." He spread his fingers so they brushed the swells of her breasts. The heat and the weight were tantalizing.

"Hunter, I…I want."

"Anything," he whispered. "Tell me what you want, and I will do it."

"You. I want you."

"Lass." He kissed her again, light brushes on her eyes, cheeks, lips. "I want you, too. So very, very much." His fingers shook as he traced the arch of her brow, the curve of her cheek. "You are so precious." He ran the backs of his fingers down her neck and over her collarbone to the swell of her breast.

If her heart had raced before, it thundered now in anticipation of the moment she instinctively knew was coming. "Aye," she whispered, moaning softly as his hand closed over her breast. Her pulse quickened as he caught hold of the tip and stroked it. As though connected by some invisible chord, the sensual rhythm echoed down through her body to the cleft at the top of her thighs.

Hunter drank the little cries that fell from her lips as he teased her nipples into hard nubs. She had lost her memory, but not the passionate side of her nature. If anything, she was more relaxed, more uninhibited, her tongue dueling so erotically with his that his control slipped further and further till all he could think of was burying himself in her.

Nay. He forced himself back from the brink of madness, fought to remember how close he'd come to losing her. How innocent she was in mind, if not in body.

She whimpered in protest when he broke the kiss.

"Easy, easy, love. We have all night."

She gazed up at him, cheeks flushed, eyes dark with passion, yet in the depths was a vulnerability that cried out for care and soothing. "I cannot wait that long," said his imperious darling.

"Nor will you have to." Smothering a smile, Hunter unlaced the neck of her night shift. "But there is more...so much more I'd show you." He planted a kiss in the valley between her breasts, inhaling the tangy scent of herbs and woman.

Annie shivered, feeling the impact of that kiss clear to her toes. "Hurry, please hurry."

"Nay, it will be sweeter this way. Trust me."

It was, Annie discovered a moment later when his mouth closed over her nipple. Her gasp of surprise became a moan as he suckled with exquisite thoroughness, gentle, yet with a greediness that fueled her desire. She had not known such sweet torture existed, had not known she could want anything as badly as she did Hunter's touch. His hands and mouth were everywhere, stroking, tasting, driving her to the brink of madness.

"Please." She clutched at his shoulders, begging for some surcease from this storm of emotions.

"Aye, love." He parted her thighs and shifted. "'Tis time and past we were one again. Open your eyes. Look at me."

Annie forced her lashes up. The sight of him, poised above her in the candlelight, his features taut, his eyes blazing with what must be love jarred her. She had been here before. With him. Just like this. "I love you," she whispered.

"And I you, with all my heart." He came to her then, filling her so slowly, driving out the aching emptiness.

Hunter wanted to pause, to savor the moment, to tutor her in the ways of love with all the tenderness and care she deserved. But her hands turned greedy as she reached for him, her hips hungry as they began to move. She stole his will and his reason, showing him that an untried lass could teach a worldly man much.

Passion raced and climbed, shooting through her like little licks of fire. She strained toward the pleasure he promised her without words, finding it as his last subtle caress drew her over the edge. She cried out, fearing the unknown, but he was there, wrapping his arms around her, murmuring words of praise and love as she cleared the final crest.

With her cry of astonishment ringing in his ears, Hunter followed her into a triumph of rapture.

Moments later, hours later, his mind rejoined his sated body. They were still tangled together, her legs around him, their bodies joined. "Sweetheart?" he whispered. "Are you all right?" When she didn't answer, he moved so he could see her.

She slept, a half smile curving her lips.

This was as it should be. Hunter knew in his heart that it was the same for her, that she was at peace for the first time in years. Her happiness justified what he had done, he told himself. If his conscience pricked him, if he worried about what would happen should her memory return, he had only to remember this moment, and know he had done the right thing.

For both their sakes.

The bubble of pride in Hunter's chest expanded as he watched Annie with his people the next morning.

Dressed in a simple gown of light blue wool, her hair a shiny red coronet atop her head, she moved with him about the great hall as he introduced her to his retainers. She had a smile and a kind word for each person.

"The stewed chicken you prepared for my dinner last night was delicious," Annie told the cook. "Sadye tells me you ran a prosperous tavern in Edinburgh before coming here. The city folk must greatly miss your fine food."

George, a grizzled man of some fifty years, puffed out his chest. "Aye, well, 'tis true I never had food left over at the end of the night, but the city's a rough place." He scowled. "Did she tell ye a pack of Campbells burned down my inn and would have killed me if not for young Hunter?"

"Aye, she did. I am sorry for that, but glad you came here to cook for us." Annie smiled at Hunter as they left the cook. "You have a talent for rescuing people, my lord. Sadye tells me you tracked down the Campbells and had them punished."

"I was just doing my duty." Embarrassed, Hunter hurried Annie toward a pair of young maids, twins, they must be, with long brown braids and identical round faces. "Here are—" He searched in vain for their names. It had been so long since he'd been to Renfrew that Hamish had had to reintroduce him to his own people that first night.

"I know Janet and Jean," Annie said. "They have the sweetest voices. 'Tis thanks to them I did not expire of boredom these past few days."

"I am grateful to you both," Hunter said with a smile.

"We would do anything to repay you, my lord," the girl on the left said in a soft, urgent rush.

"Repay?" Hunter stared at them blankly.

"You sent us here from Stirling," added the girl to the right. "Th-that is where you found us after..."

Stirling. Twin girls. The ugly details poured into his mind. Two girls abducted, abused by a wealthy lord with twisted tastes. It had taken Hunter four months to find them. He'd killed their captor in self-defense, sparing the crown the cost of a trial. That victory had seemed hollow when the victims' parents had refused to take back their soiled girls.

"Aye, well." Hunter cleared his throat. "Seeing you both so hale and hearty is all the thanks I need." He reached out to pat the nearest one on the head.

Both girls gasped and ran off like timid mice.

"Damn, I did not mean to startle them."

"It is not you," Annie said. "Sadye told me that they were frightened by a man some years ago and are skittish now."

Hunter's jaw tightened, thinking of what they'd suffered, but they were safe now. He put it from his mind and went on to complete the introductions. He listened as Annie praised Callum the gardener for the tidiness of the herb patch and the orchards she could see from her chamber window. To Alyce and Isla, she remarked on the cleanliness of the linens on her bed.

"'Tis wonderful to sleep with the scent of lavender on my pillow."

"Aye, 'tis," Hunter winked suggestively at Annie.

Her cheeks turned a becoming pink. "Do not look at me like that, my lord," she whispered. "Else I may take you up on that invitation you are flashing me, and spirit you off to bed and keep you prisoner."

"I would die a happy man."

She giggled and cuffed him on the arm, much to the delight of the servants. In fact, Hunter had not seen the people of Renfrew so full of smiles ever. It must be Allie…damn, Annie's infectious charm.

Finally he and Annie came to the end of the line and took their places at a table set perpendicular to the others. At Carmichael, his parents' high table was set upon a dais, but Hunter did not like lording it over these folk, most of whom came of simple stock.

Annie sighed as she settled herself on the bench he'd pulled out for them.

"Are you tired?"

"Nay. Just a little dazed." She laughed ruefully. "Ah, you are thinking I've been more than a little dazed for days, but this is different. Happier."

"You are happy here, then?"

She glanced around the hall then up at him. "Aye. Much happier than I ever expected to be. When I woke up two weeks ago and realized I had no memory, I was devastated. I had no idea who I was or what was going to happen to me. But that was before I knew that I could trust you to help me."

A shaft of remorse pricked Hunter. He wanted her trust, but he felt he'd gained it under false pretenses. Even if he had lied out of concern for her safety and happiness. "I—"

"I have no past, but you are my future."

Hunter stared down into her bright, expectant face and knew he must hold fast to the lies he'd spun. It had not been easy to build for her a past that left her alone in the world except for himself. But, clever dog that he was, he had told her she was an orphan, raised in a Border convent. The convent had, conveniently, burned down, killing all except for Annie. They had met when he rescued her from the fire and fallen instantly in love. Wed within a fortnight, they had been on their way to Renfrew when a rabbit frightened her horse.

Not terribly imaginative, that, but it accounted for her head injury and memory loss. She had believed him. Trusted him. It was what he had wanted, but the victory seemed tainted. Or maybe it was fear, fear that she'd one day remember...

"Hunter? Did you hear me?"

"I am sorry, love, my mind wandered. I want you to be happy and comfortable here."

"How could I not be?" Her smile was dazzling. "You are the kindest of men, one who has saved all these people." Her gesture encompassed the hall, where fifty souls bent over their porridge bowls. "You snatched some of these folk from the very jaws of death," she whispered dramatically, no doubt more of what Sadye had told her. "I am proud to be your wife."

"I hope you always feel that way," Hunter said.

"What do ye mean, he's with Allisun Murray?" Jock shouted, levering himself up in bed to glower at Red Rowy.

"Well..." Rowy gulped down the cup of ale someone handed him and wiped his mouth on a grimy sleeve. "I'd no more than arrived at Derk Neville's tower—"

"'Tis my tower, ye idiot. He's but got the use of it."

"Aye, well. I was standing in the courtyard, listening to Derk tell what went on at the Lammas rite. Ian Maxwell's going to be trouble, mark my—"

"Devil take Maxwell. What of my nephie?"

Rowy grunted. "Down the steps Hunter came, limping

like, cause he wrenched his ankle. Well, ye could have knocked me over with a strong breath. He said as how he'd been hurt in that bloody cattle raid, and Derk had brought him to Hawkehill.''

"Why did Neville not send word to me?"

"Hunter didn't tell him who he was. Says he feared Derk'd hold him to ransom or some such."

"And the lass...Murray's get?" Jock asked darkly.

"She was with Hunter." Red Rowy shifted uncomfortably. "He...Hunter, that is...claimed they was wed."

"Wed! Wed!" Jock's roar shook the rafters overhead.

Red Rowy backed out of reach. Jock had been known to strike more than one messenger bearing ill tidings. "It could be a lie. Or maybe he doesn't know who she is."

"Hmm." Some of the unreasoning fury left Jock's eyes. "She's enslaved him, the way her da did my Brenna. But I'll put a stop to that. Where are they now?"

"Dunno. Allisun Murray stole a horse and escaped while I was talking with Hunter. He took out after her, and the rest of us hard after both of them, but with the fog and the dark..."

"Ye lost them's what ye're saying."

Rowy nodded glumly.

"Damn yer incompetent—"

"If I was ye," Rowy snapped, "I'd be more worried about what Hunter saw and heard at Hawkehill. Yer precious nephew was there whilst Derk was brokering our rent money."

Jock's mouth fell open. "He heard and saw everything?"

"Derk don't know that for sure. The Englishman's too wily to do his business in the open, but..."

"Dod." Jock's head fell back against the pillow. When he lifted it a moment later, his eyes were hard and flat. "It's happening again. Another Murray mucking up my business. The last time cost me dear. Five years it took me to recover.''

''Aye, men are not obligated to pay if ye've no tally.''

''I want ye to find Hunter. Overturn every rock till ye find him and find out what he knows.''

''And?''

''If ye think he's a danger to us, make sure he can't tell anyone what he saw and heard.''

Chapter Fifteen

"Well, here we are," Hunter said, pausing outside a large barn set in its own walled barmkin to deter thieves. "But just a short visit, mind. Can't have you tiring yourself."

Annie nodded and tried not to be annoyed by his lack of enthusiasm for the excursion. He'd put her off yesterday, insisting she rest. And would have today, too, if she hadn't donned her cloak after breakfast and walked out of the hall at his side, saying, "If you will not take me to see the horses, I'll be forced to find the stables by myself."

Annie stepped into the barn and stopped, eyes closing as the warm air, heavy with the scent of straw and horses, washed over her. "Oh, this is so familiar," she whispered.

An image flickered in her mind: a tall, redheaded man carried her on his shoulders through a place that smelled like this. She could feel his muscles bunch as he bent to show her something. A newborn horse. *"Look here, Allisun, when this lass is old enough you'll be just the right size to ride her."*

"Annie?"

She jerked, and the image shattered. Sighing, she opened her eyes. "I remembered something." She looked up at

Hunter. His features had tightened with…fear? Nay, it was likely concern.

"What? What did you remember?"

"A man." She told him what she'd seen and felt. "I think he was my father, but he called me Allisun."

"Your name is Annie," he said firmly.

"But I thought the man said—"

"You are doubtless tired and confused." He swept her into his arms. "I'll take you ba—"

This time, Annie objected. "Hunter, you must stop hoisting me about. I've lost my memory, not the use of my legs. Please." She laid her hand on his chest. "I want to be here. This is the first thing, other than you, that has seemed familiar. Maybe I will recall something else."

He frowned and clasped her a little closer. "I do not like it. Trying to remember makes your head ache."

"Sadye says pain is often a necessary part of life."

"Not for you."

"Hunter." She smiled into his scowling face. He could be annoyingly fierce when it came to her safety. "You cannot keep me from every little hurt."

"Aye, I can."

Annie sighed. The knights in Janet's songs were not half as chivalrous as her Hunter. "I need to remember."

"Why? What is there in your past except more pain?" he growled. "The pain and loneliness of losing your family."

"And the fear I must have felt when fire destroyed the convent," Annie added before he could. "Sadye would agree with you. She says I should leave well enough alone."

"For once I agree with that busybody."

"I cannot. I think there is danger in my past."

"Danger?" His eyes widened. "What sort of danger?"

"I do not know, but it is somehow wrapped up in that

cursed nightmare. If only I could see the face of the man who is chasing me.'' She closed her eyes, trying to capture the moment when she turned and looked back. All that came was searing pain, lancing across her temples, making her gasp.

"Stop!" Hunter pressed her face into his shoulder.

Annie clung to him till the agonizing wave had passed, then she raised her head. "I am sorry, I—"

"*You* are sorry?" He still sounded angry or frightened.

"Aye, for causing you to worry."

"Then promise me you will stop trying to remember."

"I will." But how could she stop the nightmares from coming? "I love you," she whispered to counter her fears.

His frown vanished. "And I you. Shall I take you back to our chamber and show you how much?"

"'Tis daylight."

"So it is." Sensual promise shimmered in his eyes.

Annie felt the familiar syrupy heat spiral through her. It was tempting, but thus far bed was their only common ground. She wanted more. If she could not know her past, she would know the man who was her present and future. "What of the horses?"

"We would have trouble getting them up the stairs and through our chamber door. But if that is your wish…"

Annie laughed and swatted his chest. "Idiot."

"That may be, but I am your idiot." Still grinning, he kissed her quick and set her feet on the ground. "Come, my lady, your subjects await."

Annie took his arm, her spirits lighter than they had been in days. The silly exchange had taught her something valuable. "We both enjoy a jest, it would seem."

"Aye. You've a dry wit and a clever mind to match my own."

"Hopefully I am less boastful."

"'Tis truth, not vanity I speak.'' He chuckled. ''Neither of us is lacking in pride.''

Sadye had told her as much. Valuable as the housekeeper's help had been these past few days, Annie wished she had someone else to speak with. Someone who knew more of Hunter's world.

''He spends most of his time in Edinburgh.'' Sadye had explained that was a huge city, with thousands and thousands of people living in it. ''His family has a home there and a castle about two days' ride from here.''

Carmichael Castle, Annie had learned, was vastly larger than Renfrew. Though Sadye had never been there, she had met Hunter's sire, Lord Ross. From her description, Annie envisioned a black-haired god who wore clothes encrusted with gems.

Would they go to Carmichael and visit his parents? Annie looked down at the blue wool gown the maids had sewn from the cloth Hunter sent twice yearly for his retainers' garments. It fit well, but even to her untutored eye, it looked very plain. She would hate to disgrace or shame him with her dowdiness.

''Here, this is Dancer's Pride.''

Annie looked up just as an immense black head appeared over the stall's half door. Instinctively she reached out to stroke the satiny muzzle. ''Oh, he's beau—''

''Nay.'' Hunter snatched her hand back inches shy of snapping white teeth. ''Easy, easy, lad.'' He caught the strap across Dancer's nose and held fast.

The horse snorted and shivered, eyes rolling white in their sockets as he glared at Annie.

''I am sorry,'' she murmured. ''I thought he was trained.''

''He is. Trained to attack anything that is not his master.''

''Oh.''

"They were first brought to England by my cousins, the Sommervilles. My father brought some to Carmichael and began raising them there. They are bred for size and stamina, and can carry a man in full armor all day without tiring. In battle, they help their master by striking out with teeth and hooves at anything that comes near. If the rider should fall from the saddle, a warhorse will stand over him and defend him."

"They are truly wonderful animals."

Hunter's smile set the tone for the rest of the visit. She was careful to admire his horses from a safe distance, until they reached the last stall, that is. There they were greeted by a colt with wobbly knees and velvety eyes.

"Oh, 'tis a wee babe," Annie exclaimed.

"Not so wee. The colt weighs as much as you do."

"Can I go in?" At his nod, Annie opened the stall and entered. The colt tottered over and butted her in the stomach. She nearly went down, but Hunter steadied her from behind.

"He's looking for a meal. His mama died birthing him, so we've been raising him by hand."

"Could I feed him?"

"Are you sure you want to? He's a messy eater."

Annie took one look into those pleading eyes and nodded.

Hunter fetched a leather pouch and bucket of milk. "Pinch off that hole in the end of the pouch and hold the top open. I'll put in a bit of milk, and we'll see how it goes."

Annie did as instructed, then turned. The colt latched onto the makeshift nipple so eagerly he dragged her forward. "Wait!"

Laughing, Hunter snagged her around the waist and countered the pull of the colt. "He's a strong one."

"How old is he?" she asked, only too happy to lean against Hunter, for the moment, at least.

"Born the day after we arrived."

"So this is what has kept you so busy."

"That and reacquainting myself with Renfrew."

"Why do you not spend more time here?"

She felt him shrug, felt, too, the way he seemed to tense. "My duties take me elsewhere."

He could have come here between time. Sadye had said so, bemoaning the burden his absence had placed on her Hamish. "We're right glad his lordship has settled down."

Annie was glad, too. Snuggling a little deeper into Hunter's embrace, she watched the colt feed, enjoying his rhythmic tugs. A sense of contentment crept in to fill her empty heart. Caring for the colt gave her a sense of purpose that had been lacking here at Renfrew. The feel of Hunter's arms around her created a cocoon of contentment. The quiet moment formed a bond between them.

With a great sucking noise, the colt drained the last of the milk and spat out the nipple.

Annie suppressed a sigh of disappointment as Hunter released her and took the pouch. "When is his next feeding?"

"He eats every two hours or so."

"Excellent." Annie brushed the milk from her skirts and followed Hunter from the stall. "I'll have to see if Sadye has some old clothing I can borrow."

Hunter frowned. "You are coming back?"

"Certainly. I would like to take over his feeding."

"You cannot traipse out here in the middle of the night."

"Very well, then, just the day feedings." She swept past him before he could voice the protest she knew was coming.

He caught her at the door. "'Tis not fit work for a lady."

She tilted her chin up to meet the challenge glittering in

his eyes. Obviously Hunter was used to getting his own way. Everyone here certainly deferred to him. If she did not take a stand now, she'd find herself under his thumb, too. Something inside her rebelled at that notion. "I do not see why not," she said tartly. "I have no other duties to occupy my time."

He blinked in surprise. "What of running the keep?"

"I cannot take over Sadye's job."

"Needlework?"

"I tried. Alas, I stuck the needle in my own fingers more often than the cloth." She shook her head in mock sadness.

"Cooking?" he asked desperately.

"George puffed up like a wet hen when I suggested his meat pies might use more salt. I've been banned from the kitchens."

"He cannot do that. You are the lady here."

"Well, 'twas either that or find another cook. Come, now," she said, smiling at him through her lashes. "All I want to do is help, and I do so enjoy it."

Hunter groaned, knowing he was doomed to failure. She might have lost her memory, but not her stubbornness. "All right, but at the first sign that you are tiring…"

"I won't." She danced away from him. "I am going up to the keep to see about some old clothes. But I'll be back." She dashed away with the carefree abandon of a young lass.

Something tightened in Hunter's chest as he watched her go. Pride, he decided. Pride in Allisun Murray. He'd been right to think she was special.

Beaming, Hunter followed her progress across the grassy outer ward to the keep, a gray stone sentinel against the cloudy sky. When she passed through the back gate and disappeared from sight, a pang of fear clutched at his belly.

What if she left him for good?

Dieu, he could not think of that or he would go mad. He could not, would not lose her. He, who had never thought to settle down, wanted to stay at Renfrew with her. He wanted to be here each morn when she awakened. He wanted to share in her joyful discoveries. He wanted to hold her each night while she slept. He wanted to watch her swell with their child and guide its first steps. He wanted a lifetime with her.

But he was sore afraid he'd not get it.

Hunter closed his eyes, reliving that awful moment when they'd stepped inside the stables and she'd remembered...

I think he was my papa. He called me Allisun.

How could he keep her from remembering when the littlest things seemed to jar her memory? One day something would happen and the whole thing would come back to her. Could he bear having her turn and look at him with hatred instead of love?

Nay. Hunter bowed his head against the weight of the pain that clawed inside him.

"Is aught wrong?" called a gravelly voice.

Hunter turned to find Hamish at his elbow. Shaken, he scrubbed a hand over his face and shoved these troubling thoughts into the back of his mind. "Nay, I was but watching to make certain Annie returned safely to the keep."

"What did the lady think of the horses?"

"She has taken over the colt."

"Has she, now?" His castellan grinned. "Sadye says your lady is a rare one."

"She is that." Rare and precious. Hunter smiled faintly, thinking of the way she'd faced him down. "Stubborn, though."

"Hmm. Sadye says 'twill take a strong-willed lass to stand up to you, my lord."

"Is that her way of saying I am a tyrant?"

"She would never say anything against ye, my lord."

"I was jesting, Hamish."

"Oh?" Hamish eyed him edgily.

It occurred to Hunter that he'd never seen Hamish laugh. Or Sadye, either, for that matter. "Did you want something of me?"

"Aye." Hamish pulled on his beard, which was now more gray than brown. "If ye've a moment, I wanted to show ye the plans for strengthening the west wall."

"Of course." The project was one his father had recommended after an English raiding party had burned down their neighbor's tower. "Did my father draw up the plans?"

"Aye, came himself in the summer and looked everything over. 'Twas good having him here, for I've no head for that sort of thing." As the castellan led the way to the keep, his steps seemed slower than usual.

"Have you hurt your leg?"

"Now the weather's turning cooler and wetter, that old wound pains me. You'll remember the one..."

Hunter did, indeed. He'd first met Sadye and Hamish when he went to relieve the siege on a tower belonging to a cousin. The cousin had been killed by a greedy enemy and his tower nearly destroyed by the time Hunter arrived. Hamish the steward, his leg smashed in two places, had been directing the defense from the walls. Hunter had made short work of the attackers, deemed the tower a total loss and taken the survivors home to Renfrew with him. The first of what his parents called his waifs.

"I'm glad ye've decided to settle," Hamish said. "We've need of ye here."

And he wanted to be here. But if Allie remembered... "Is there trouble brewing you've not told me about?"

"Nothing specific. But I'm no warrior. If there is trouble, the men will need a leader such as yerself," Hamish said as he labored up the wooden stairs and into the keep.

Hunter was shocked to see how old and stiff Hamish had become in the past few years. "I could get someone else to—"

Hamish gasped and stopped in the narrow entryway, the dimness accentuating the lines in his face. "M-my lord!"

"I did not mean I'd turn you out," Hunter said quickly. "Just find a man to assist you."

Hamish straightened. "I'll not be taking charity. If I cannot do my duty, I'll leave."

Where would he go? Hunter thought. Who would take in a crippled steward? "What difference would it make if I hire someone to advise you or do it myself?"

"Ye're the lord. 'Tis yer place to give the orders. Another man would be...another man." That was pride talking.

Hunter understood that. Respected it. But he suddenly realized that he'd been remiss in not attending more closely to things at Renfrew. He was not certain why, exactly, but for some reason he'd never felt comfortable here. Till now, till Allie. *Annie. Annie,* he reminded himself. Dieu, what if he slipped and ruined everything? "Well, let us take one step at a time. Show me the plans my father drew up, and we'll see what needs doing." That way, if he did leave, things would be in good order.

"'Tis not seemly for the lady of the keep to run about in such mean rags," Sadye grumbled, a stout woman with steel gray braids to match her iron will.

"But I've already soiled my only good gown." Annie shook the wrinkles from the skirt of the brown gown unearthed from the storeroom. It was a castoff of Janet's, but fit her right well. The coarse wool prickled yet felt oddly right. "I was raised in a convent, and so am doubtless used to such garments."

"Hunter's spent time at the king's court. *He's* doubtless used to ladies dressed in fine silks and velvets." Sadye's sharp brown eyes narrowed assessingly.

That gave Annie pause. "I do want to please him."

"Aye, we all do." Sadye's expression turned wistful. "Has he said anything about when he'll leave?"

"Leave Renfrew? Nay, do you think he will?"

"He always does. His work, ye know."

Nay, she did not. "I thought he raised horses."

"Hamish and the lads do that, with occasional visits from Lord Ross, Hunter's da. Hunter's a justice. A thief catcher."

"How long is he usually away?"

"Well, it has been two years since we've seen him."

Two years! Annie's knees went weak, and she sank onto the bed. "I would wither and die if he were gone that long. I wonder if he will take me with him?" she whispered.

"That would be no life for a lass."

"Staying here alone would be far worse."

"Ye'd have us," Sadye said. "We'll look out for ye, same as we do each other. Hunter may abandon us, but we stick together."

Abandoned. The word cut Annie to the quick. So cold. So bleak. Yet who could blame them for feeling that way? Each person here had survived some sort of tragedy. Each had lost a home, a family, a whole way of life. Hunter had rescued them and given them sanctuary, but he had not given them the one thing they needed most.

A sense of belonging. A feeling of being loved.

Annie cast her mind back over these past few days. "Hunter means well by you," she murmured. "He has seen to it you have food to eat, a sound roof and stout walls to protect you."

"He's a good lord," Sadye said defensively. "He never shouts if a thing's not done right. His orders are never unreasonable, and he's never had a one of us beaten."

These folk held him in as much awe as if he had, jumping to do his bidding almost before the words left his mouth. Yet for some reason Hunter distanced himself from them. "He does not even remember some of their names."

"Oh, he's got more important matters on his mind than the name of a stray maid or two." But Sadye looked a trifle pained. "Besides, he's hardly ever here."

"Why? Why would he stay away from his own home?"

"He can find no peace," Sadye said softly. "'Tis because of the woman."

"Woman?" Annie clutched her heart to keep it from leaping out of her chest. "Sweet Mary, what woman?"

"Oh, I did not mean he had a mistress." Sadye grabbed hold of Annie's icy hands and chafed them. "She was family."

"A sister?"

"Aunt, I think. Ralf, the old man who was castellan here when we came, mentioned Hunter had an aunt who died a violent death. 'Twas years ago, when Hunter was only a lad."

"He must have loved her greatly if it affects him still."

Sadye nodded slowly. "He was with her when it happened."

"How awful for him."

"He tried to save her, but could not."

"Oh, my poor Hunter."

"Aye, the guilt's a terrible thing," Sadye said. "It eats at ye, the wondering why ye were spared while others died. The fearing ye could have done more and didn't." Her eyes were glazed with pain, focused on some distant hurt.

Annie guessed it was not only Hunter's tragic loss Sadye spoke of but her own, as well. The urge to heal rose in Annie, as natural as breathing, as strong as the beat of her heart. "I must go to Hunter and see if I can ease his suffering."

"Nay." Sadye sprang up. "He never speaks of it."

"Mayhap that is part of the problem," Annie said. "'Tis like a festering wound that will not heal till it's lanced."

Sadye shook her head. "Wounds like this are best left alone. I know, believe me, I know."

"But," Annie began, then she realized it was her own past Sadye spoke of, and felt even sadder. "I would see him happy."

"He is. Hamish remarked only this morn that he's never seen the lord smile as much as he has since bringing you here."

Annie smiled herself, recalling the jest they'd shared at the stables. "Laughter is a balm for the soul," she murmured.

"Why, that's very profound, my lady."

"Aye, it is. I can almost hear someone saying it to me." She frowned, concentrating. "A woman, I think."

"Well, whoever it was had the right of it."

"Then we must find something that will make everyone laugh. What could it be, do you suppose?"

"A jest?"

"Too small. We need something bigger, grander."

"Hunter's cousin, the one we served before coming here, used to have entertainments after the feasting."

"Explain," Annie demanded. "Explain what these words mean, for I do not remember." As she listened to Sadye talk about fine food, music and dancing, a plan took shape in her mind.

Chapter Sixteen

Hunter knew something was amiss the moment he stepped into the hall. Though it was not nearly time for supper, the torches in the rings along the walls had been lit, casting a blaze of light over an unprecedented swirl of activity.

The menservants who should have been mucking out the stables or toting water for the horses were wrestling the trestle tables into straight lines that ran perpendicular to a lone table. The maids darted to and fro like minnows in a barrel, some spreading sheets atop the tables, others laying out spoons and raggedy hunks of bread.

The long room rang with the sounds of orders and counterorders, of lads arguing over where the benches should go and lasses bemoaning the lack of fine cups.

"Whatever is going on?" Hunter asked of the nearest maid.

She whirled, paled and cried, "'Tis Lord Hunter!"

The others froze, eyes wide as deer facing down a wolf.

Alarmed now, Hunter repeated his question.

Sadye worked her way through the crowd. "Ye're early."

He did not like the sound of that. "Where is my wife?"

If possible, Sadye went whiter. "Well…"

"Where?" Hunter roared.

"Up-upstairs, but ye canna go—"

Hunter did not wait to hear more. If Annie had regained her memory, at least she had not yet left him. He raced to the stairwell and took the narrow curving steps at a reckless pace. Outside his chamber door he hesitated, gathered his courage and entered. The sight that greeted him stopped him in his tracks.

Annie, clad only in her shift, was bent over at the waist rummaging through the trunk at the end of the bed.

Fear left him in a rush, replaced by a fierce surge of desire. Crossing the room on silent feet, he wrapped both arms around her waist.

"Oh!" She straightened with a little shriek and tried to wriggle free.

"Easy, lass."

"Hunter! 'Tis you."

"Aye." He nuzzled her neck. "Have I told you what a tempting backside you have?"

"Nay, I..." She shivered. "You are early."

"So everyone keeps telling me. But it seems to me I've arrived at just the right time." He pulled her back against the hard length of his body, so she'd have no doubt what he meant.

Despite the familiar melting heat spilling through her veins, Annie tried to maintain her perspective. There was still much to do before dinner. Chiefly, she had to unearth a garment suitable for the occasion. "I have no time for this."

"Surely there is always time for this."

Annie moaned softly as his hand closed over her breast. "I must find something to wear," she murmured, her argument ruined by the speed with which her nipple swelled into his palm.

"A wasted effort, for I'd only have to take it off. I want you, Annie. Now," he whispered into her hair.

"I want you, too," she replied, her pulse soaring as he picked her up and carried her the few steps to the bed. He laid her down with infinite care. Eyes locked on hers, he straightened and pulled off his own clothes with a haste that bordered on frantic. His hunger fueled her own. Senses humming, she lifted her arms to welcome him.

Desperation seemed to edge Hunter's lovemaking. Oh, he was no less gentle with her, but his kisses were fierce, his touch fire, as though he sought to bind her to him with the force of his passion. She greedily took what he offered, her cries both surrender and triumph as he guided her over that first crest.

Giddy with happiness, she rose above him, wanting to share her joy. "Let me love you," she whispered.

He groaned as she hesitantly touched him, taking the lead in their loving for the first time. "Annie...oh!"

Laughing softly, she turned the tender skills he had taught her into the seeds of his own conquest. But before she could see the game through, he rolled her onto her back, pinning her beneath him, filling her so slowly they both groaned aloud.

"Now!" she commanded, arching into each stroke.

"Now!" he echoed, and they clung together as ecstasy claimed them.

In the sweet aftermath, Hunter tugged the coverlet over their cooling bodies and held her close.

"We cannot fall asleep," she warned.

"Why?"

"Dinner. They expect us down for dinner."

Hunter frowned, recalling the turmoil in the hall. "Has some guest come, and I was not told?"

"Nay, only we are having a feast."

"In honor of what?"

Uncertain now, Annie toyed with the hair on his chest. "For us. All of us. To make us feel better."

He held her a little away, eyes probing hers in the rapidly darkening chamber. "You are ill?"

"Nay. Well, except for the fact that I have no memory. But," she added, seeing an opening. "In that, mayhap, I am the luckiest person at Renfrew, for I am not haunted by my past."

"And others are?"

"Everyone here is. Even you."

"Me?" The shutters dropped down over his eyes, rendering them blank and cool. "What about me?"

"Sadye told me of your aunt who died."

"She what?" Hunter leaped out of bed. The body that had so recently loved hers radiated pain and tension.

Alarmed, Annie sat up and clutched the blanket to her chest. She longed to reach for him, to offer comfort, but feared he'd reject her help. "Why is it wrong for me to know you had an aunt who died?"

"Did Sadye say how she died?"

Annie shook her head, praying for the right words. "She said that you were there. She said..." Annie choked on a sob. "She said you tried to save your aunt and could not."

Without uttering a word, he turned away from her and walked to the window. Bracing his hands on either side of the narrow opening, he stood there. The pale scars on his broad, suntanned back were mute testimony to the battles he'd fought. But that one important fight he had not won.

Drawn by his silent suffering, Annie climbed out of bed, and went to him, wrapping both arms around his waist, as he had done to her earlier. "I only want to comfort you, as you have comforted me countless times these past weeks."

"You are a comfort, but..."

"Nothing can take the pain away. I understand that. And

I know you must feel you failed your aunt, but look at all
the others you have saved. Surely they count for something.''

"Aye,'' he replied, voice low and harsh.

"And me. You saved me from the fire. It cannot mean
as much to you as saving your aunt would have, but God
works in myster—''

"You mean everything to me.'' He turned then, and
slipped his arms around her. "Never doubt that.''

"I do not.'' They clung together, closer in some ways,
Annie thought, than they had been while they loved. "I
wish I could ease all of the suffering.''

He looked down at her, eyes soft again. "In the world?''

"Here at Renfrew. As you are troubled by what happened to your aunt, so these folk are haunted by their
pasts.''

"What have they to feel guilty about?'' he asked gruffly.
"They were victims, one and all.''

"I do not know,'' Annie began, then something Sadye
had said nudged her brain. "Mayhap they feel guilty for
surviving.''

"That makes no sense.''

"I know.'' Feelings were not always logical. If they
were, she'd not be so obsessed with remembering her past
when her present and future were so rosy. Or were they?
Suddenly Annie felt cold inside. "Sadye says you will be
leaving.''

"Where the hell did she get that notion?''

A shudder racked her. "You always do.''

"Ah, well that was because I was searching for something.'' His hands soothed the gooseflesh from her back.
"You. Now that I have found you, I am never leaving.''

"Truly?'' Annie asked, tears welling again. Joyful tears.

"Truly.''

"Oh, I am so happy.'' She hugged him tight. "Everyone

will be happy. Now we really have something to celebrate. Sweet Mary, I nearly forgot." She pushed free of his embrace, raced to the trunk and picked up the blue gown draped over it. "Jean did a fine job getting out the milk stains, but I wish I had something finer than this to wear."

"I like you in what you have on." He strolled over and reached for her again.

Annie swatted his hand from her hip. "Now we really do not have time." Her words were punctuated by the sound of the horn summoning them to dinner. "Oh dear." She looked at the gown again. "I guess it will have to do."

"First thing tomorrow, I'll send a message to Mama and ask if she has any bolts of cloth suitable for the lady of Renfrew."

"I would not want to deprive her of—"

"There are always supplies aplenty at home." He cocked his head. "Perhaps we should invite them to visit."

Annie gasped. "Oh, nay."

"Do not look so frightened. You will like them right well."

But what would they think of the convent-raised orphan their son had so hastily wed? A woman who could not even organize a fete because she had no memories to guide her, no skills. "I think we should wait till we are more settled."

"Coward," Hunter chided.

"Aye, I am afraid they will not think me good enough."

"Nonsense. They will love you as I do."

Annie was worried, but the visit of Hunter's parents was tomorrow's worry. Tonight they had to get through the banquet.

Hunter paused in the doorway to the great hall, his eyes round with wonder as he surveyed the assembled retainers, each decked out in his or her best garments. "My God, what is this?"

Hamish stepped out of the crowd and bowed low. "Welcome, my lord and lady, to the dinner in honor of your recent marriage."

"Thank you," Hunter replied just as gravely. He extended his arm to Annie, then led her inside.

"Say something about the hall," Annie softly prompted. "They have worked hard to make it beautiful for you."

"Dieu," Hunter exclaimed. "Cloths and candles on the tables, fresh rushes on the floor. Why even my old war banners look to have been cleaned," he added, gazing at the scraps of silk hanging from the ceiling.

"Laying it on a bit thick, aren't you?" Annie mumbled.

"I doubt that is possible." Indeed, the sight of so many anxious faces was a bit daunting. And touching. Deeply moved, Hunter settled Annie on the bench at the head table and sat beside her. "Whatever gave them the idea to hold a celebration in our honor?"

"They wanted to do something for you. In payment for all you have done for them."

"I was only doing my duty."

Annie shook her head, her gaze full of admiration. "Saving their lives was your duty. Giving them a home was a kindness."

"Food and shelter were all I provided," Hunter said. "Renfrew did not become a home till I brought you here."

"I have not done anything," she protested.

"You have changed my life completely," Hunter said. "And theirs, too."

A flourish of trumpets blasted through the hall. George himself preceded two menservants bearing a haunch of venison on a large metal tray. They paraded around the hall, then stopped in front of Hunter. Whereupon George produced a huge carving knife. "If you will permit me to serve you."

Hunter nodded, waited gravely while the cook took off

two generous slices and deposited them on the brown bread trencher the lord and lady would share. The servants moved on to offer the meat to the other diners, but George stayed to supervise the presentation of the other dishes. Boiled kale, herring fried in oatmeal, and hotchpotch, a flavorful vegetable stew.

Hunter took some of everything, even the despised kale, conscious that not only was George watching him, but so was everyone else in the hall. No one ate or drank or laughed or talked. "What are they waiting for?" he whispered to Annie when George had at last gone to his own place at a nearby table.

"To see if you approve of the meal."

Hunter stood and raised his ale cup. "My thanks for this wonderful feast. I would propose a toast—to Annie, the love of my life and the lady of Renfrew."

"To Lady Annie!" they cried in unison.

"To Lord Hunter!" Hamish roared. "Long may he rule us."

Smiling, Hunter inclined his head in acknowledgment. "I am glad to see you have not found me an onerous lord."

Their shouts to the contrary were deafening. And touching.

"I did not realize they cared that much," he murmured.

"They love you dearly," Annie said softly. "Because you saved them and showed them kindness. Tell them you will stay. It would mean so much to know they'll not be abandoned again."

"Abandoned? Is that how they have felt?"

"Aye. I think it is."

Hunter shuddered, reliving the moment when he'd awakened and realized his aunt was gone. It was a terrible thing to care about someone and have them leave you. "I did not know."

"There is time to make amends."

"Aye." He banged his cup on the table. When all fell silent he said, "As you know, my duties have often taken me away from Renfrew, but from now on I will be staying to raise horses and—"

A whoop of joy sang through the hall. It was followed by another and another till the rafters shook. Men hooted and stomped their feet. Women fell on their knees and prayed. There was not a dry eye in the house. Hunter's included. Overwhelmed, he sank onto the bench, wrapped an arm around Annie and held her close while chaos reigned in his hall.

Long minutes later, Hamish finally called for order and was heard above the merrymaking. "This is indeed a night to remember," the steward said when the noise subsided. "Let us eat, drink and rejoice."

"Amen," said Sadye.

"Always does have to have the last word," Hamish grumbled.

Hunter chuckled. Annie giggled. A round of laughter ruffled through the room before they all set to eating.

Healing laughter, Hunter thought, sealing wounds he had not even been aware existed. But Annie had known.

"Thank you for what you've done for our people," he said.

"Our people. I like the sound of that." She accepted the hunk of venison he held out on the tip of his eating knife and pronounced the meat delicious.

Hunter ate and drank absently, captivated by Annie's laughter, her obvious joy. As the servants came forward to clear away the gravy-soaked trenchers, he took Annie's hand. "Come, let us retire," he whispered in her ear.

"Nay." She looked stricken. "The entertainment…"

"Oh, I will keep you entertained." He wiggled his eyebrows.

Her cheeks turned a charming shade of red. "I fear it must be later, for the juggler and the singers and—"

As if on cue, a tall man in shocking red hose and tunic bounded into the hall, executed a series of somersaults and wound up on his feet before the head table. "Good eve to ye, my lord, my lady," he intoned, bowing low.

"Good eve to you..." Hunter fumbled for a name.

"Malcolm, you look very fine in your minstrel's garb," Annie said smoothly.

Hunter gave her hand a grateful squeeze. "Aye, he does."

In truth, Malcolm was skinny, gaunt and pale, a shadow of the virile man Hunter had saved from bandits two, or was it three, years ago. Recalling that Malcolm's wife had died at the hands of those thugs brought a spurt of sympathy.

"Are you in charge of this evening's revels?" asked Hunter.

"Aye, if it please ye, my lord."

What pleased Hunter was the spark of life he saw in Malcolm's eyes. "It does, indeed."

What followed was not a professional performance by any means, but what they lacked in polish the entertainers more than made up for in enthusiasm. Malcolm told a ribald series of stories that had men and women rolling on the floor, laughing so hard tears coursed down their cheeks.

Janet sang of love while Jean accompanied her on the harp. Then they both told a tale of valor and knightly daring. At its conclusion, cheers filled the old hall.

When the evening came to an end, Hunter thanked his people—their people—took Annie's hand and together they climbed the stairs to their chamber. There he undressed her, laid her gently on the bed and made love to her with all the skill at his command. As they drifted off to sleep in each other's arms, he thanked God for having brought them together.

That she was safe and happy eased a measure of the guilt that had plagued him since he'd embarked upon this course.

The tiny village of Renfrew slept under a slender moon, its neat wattle-and-daub huts surrounded by a sturdy stone wall. The hamlet boasted no inn, but the tavern keeper had gladly rented a corner of his stable loft to the weary traveler.

And weary he was, Owen thought as he stared out at the silent community. Four days it had taken them to track down the Kelso physician who had treated a lass of Allisun's description. What a relief it had been to learn she was not badly hurt. From Master Esley, Owen had gotten Hunter Carmichael's name. The innkeeper had supplied the less welcome news that Carmichael lived many days to the north.

Gil had been for going home then, certain Allisun was lost to them. Owen had agreed, to a point. Afraid to leave the clan vulnerable with winter coming and old Jock sniffing about, Owen had sent the men back to Tadlow. He had continued on to Renfrew alone, determined to rescue Allisun from Hunter Carmichael.

A shiver went down Owen's spine. Odd how things had come full circle. Alexander Murray had taken Brenna Carmichael, now her nephew held Allisun prisoner in his great walled tower.

The cold settled in the pit of Owen's stomach as he tried to imagine what Allisun was going through. This Hunter had every reason to exact vengeance on Alexander's daughter, yet the villagers claimed he was a compassionate overlord.

Looking out over this peaceful land, Owen almost believed that. The hills beyond the village walls were lush, the trees laden with fruit waiting to be harvested. It was a stark contrast to the burned fields of the wasted Border country. The villagers were well dressed, well fed and went about their tasks with good cheer, not the fear Owen was used to seeing.

These signs of a caring lord eased a wee bit of Owen's concern for Allisun, but did not lessen his determination to free her. With his dying breath, Alex Murray had begged Owen to guard his clan and his children. That Owen would do—to his dying breath.

Sighing wearily, Owen turned away from the haymow door and sought the pallet he'd laid in the straw. The innkeeper had told him Lord Hunter was in need of men to help with the horses. At first light tomorrow, Owen would apply for the post.

Chapter Seventeen

Hunter stopped outside the stable door, his hand resting on the small of Annie's back. "Are you sure you are not too tired to feed the colt?"

"I am not tired at all," she assured him, though they had kept each other awake half the night. "Who could think of sleeping on such a beautiful morn?" She lifted her face to the clear blue sky and turned to examine the yellow sun just poking its head up over the distant hills. "'Tis perfect."

"Aye, you are." He brushed her lips with his, lingering in the corners, making her blood hum.

"Hmm." She went on tiptoe, looping her arms around his neck as she arched into his embrace. "This is perfect."

Hunter grinned, his hands sliding warmly along her spine. "Any more perfect and we will be back in bed."

"Tempting." She fluttered her lashes at him, sure of herself, secure in his love. The sense of rightness, of belonging was nearly as heady as the pleasure she found in their lovemaking. "But the colt is doubtless starving."

"And Hamish is waiting up at the tower with those drawings of Papa's." He kissed her quick, spun her about and gave her rump a playful swat. "Get along, temptress."

Giggling, Annie dashed into the stables. It was dark after the sun's glare, and she gasped as a figure moved in the gloom.

"'Tis just me, my lady." Clem stepped forward, the milk pouch dangling from one hand. A lanky lad of some fifteen years, with dark hair and a perpetual frown, he had been assigned to help her feed the colt.

"I did not see you at supper last night," she remarked as they started toward the back of the building.

"Nay, I didn't belong there."

"The feast was for everyone."

Clem grunted, handed her the milk pouch and opened the door to the colt's stall. "If ye'll brace yer back against the wall, I'll just steady Blackie."

Blackie. A shiver raced down her spine. She recognized the jolt as a forerunner of an image from her past. Clutching the milk pouch to her chest, she grappled with the elusive memory.

A man. She could see him, standing among the trees. Big. Burly. The man from her nightmare. If only she could see—

The colt butted her in the stomach.

Annie jumped as the vision shattered. "Hungry, are we?" She held out the makeshift nipple and laughed as the colt latched on. This time she was ready for the hard, twisting pull as he fed. "There is something so satisfying about feeding him."

"Aye. Puts me in mind of me own mam nursing my sisters."

"There are babes here?" She had not seen or heard any.

"Nay. We've had no weddings, and nor bairns birthed here."

"That is odd." Sadye was too old for childbearing, but there were other, younger men and women whom Sadye said had come to Renfrew with them from Hunter's cousin's estate. Why…?

"I was thinking of before." A shadow crossed his angular face. "Of my family. They were killed four years ago when reivers overran our village. Lord Hunter found me in the woods."

"Oh, I am so sorry," Annie said, saddened by the all too familiar tale of violence. "You were fortunate to survive."

"I must have run away." Clem lowered his head, his voice falling to a mumble. "I do not remember, but I must have."

"You must not blame yourself. You were only a lad."

"Lord Hunter would not have run."

Annie felt the lad's guilt. "He is a man, and you—"

"Blackie's finished eating." Clem took the empty pouch from her and fled without a backward glance.

"The poor thing." Annie absently stroked the colt's head.

"Who? The colt?" Hunter peered at her over the top of the door.

"Nay. Clem."

Hunter frowned. "Who? Oh, the lad I sent to help you."

"The lad you saved from reivers four years ago."

"Ah, I remember. The village had been burned out. He was the only survivor, and he nearly died of starvation."

"He blames himself for not saving them."

"That is ridiculous. He was only ten or so."

"Nonetheless, he feels he should have done something."

"Guilt is a terrible, clawing monster."

Annie knew he was thinking of the aunt he had failed to save. "You understand. Mayhap if you spoke to him?"

"I cannot absolve him of his guilt. That is between a man and his conscience."

"Or his God." Annie was not certain where the notion

came from, but a host of images flooded her mind: the sweet smell of incense, a gentle voice murmuring words in some foreign tongue and a gold cross before which she had knelt on a cold stone floor. But more than that, there had been joy and peace. She wanted that for these people.

There was a chapel at Renfrew. Sadye had showed it to her. A small, musty chamber through whose high windows light slanted in on an empty stone altar and dusty benches.

"There is no priest here," Annie suddenly blurted out.

"Father Gregory died shortly after I inherited this estate from my grandsire. I told Hamish he could find a new one." Hunter took her hand and led her from the stall. "Come, I've finished with the drawings and thought we might take a ride."

"Hmm," she said absently. "You should have seen to it."

"The priest? You are right. That I was not here to see the lack of one is no excuse."

"Why did you never stay here?" Annie asked as he shut the door to the colt's stall.

"I was too restless, I guess." He looped an arm over her shoulders and guided her through the stables. "Always there was another challenge beckoning. A battle to fight..."

"A wrong to right?" she quipped.

Hunter's steps slowed. "Aye, damn my arrogance. I thought if I saved enough people, I could forgive myself for failing."

"Your aunt?" she asked gingerly.

He nodded. "But I failed to give these people what they needed most. Heart. Hope. A sense of belonging." He shrugged. "I am not certain what to call it, but there was something vital missing till you came here. You are the heart and soul of Renfrew."

Annie felt tears well but smiled in spite of them. "What a lovely thing to say."

"My lord? A moment." Malcolm stood in the stable doorway, a tall stranger at his side. "This is Ned of Abington, come looking for work."

"Have you worked around horses?" Hunter asked pleasantly.

"Aye." Ned's voice was sharp and curt.

"We've been down to the paddock," Malcolm added. "He has a good hand, and he's not intimidated by the great beasties."

Hunter chuckled. "There's much to be said for that. We'll give it a try then, Ned, see if you are suited to the work. Malcolm can explain your duties, show you where to sleep."

"Thank ye, my lord," said Malcolm. "If ye'll come with me, Ned." He led the way into the stables.

Ned said not a word as he passed by them. Annie could not see his face clearly in the gloom, but something about his size, the shape of his head seemed familiar. As he walked by, he turned his head. His pale eyes seemed to leap out at her.

Annie shivered and stepped closer to Hunter.

"What is it?" Hunter asked.

"Nothing, I...that man is...odd."

"If he frightens you, we can let him go."

"Nay." She could not deprive a man of work on a whim.

"Well, what say we take that ride?" Hunter asked heartily.

Annie shook off her mood and readily agreed.

"Do you have something else to wear?"

She looked down at her rumpled, milk-stained gown and sighed. "Not unless I steal one from the maids."

"'Tis all right." Hunter kissed her nose. "But when we get back, I'm writing to ask Mama if she has any cloth I may buy."

Annie frowned. "I suppose we should ask them to visit."

"Truth to tell, I'm surprised they've not already come. When we arrived, I sent word we'd wed, and—"

"Wretch." Annie punched him in the arm. "Why did you not tell me so?"

Hunter rubbed his arm. "What difference does it—"

"I know nothing of entertaining such grand people."

"They are not royalty, they are just my—"

"Hunter!" A tall, dark-haired man hurried into the stables.

"Papa! We were just speaking of you." Hunter embraced his sire heartily.

"It has been too long." His father thumped him on the back.

Touching as the reunion was, Annie wanted nothing more than to flee the scene and repair her appearance. She tried to edge past them, but before she'd gotten more than a couple of steps, Lord Ross whirled away from his son and seized her shoulders.

"You must be Hunter's Annie." Tears glistening in bright blue eyes, he kissed her on both cheeks. "My dear, you are mose welcome to the family."

"Milk stains and all?" she asked faintly.

"Eh?" Lord Ross, clad in fine crimson wool, looked down at her filthy, sodden skirts and frowned.

"We were feeding Dancer's colt," Hunter began.

"Really?" His father fairly rubbed his hands together. "When was he born?" Some of his glee dissipated when he heard they had lost the mother.

"Annie has been helping to raise the colt."

"Ach, what a bonny lass. Hunter, did you know that your mother once helped me save a foal that was caught crosswise in its mother's belly?"

"I have heard the story. A thousand times," Hunter added, winking at Annie. "According to Papa, he fell in love with Mama at that very moment."

"And I've not stopped to this day," Ross admitted. "I'd see the little lad before we join your mother."

"L-Lady Megan is with you?" Annie asked faintly.

"She would not miss meeting you for anything. Come along, which stall is the colt in?"

"Last on the left." Hunter hung back with Annie as his father strode on ahead. "I am sorry, love."

"Me, too. I so wanted to make a good impression on them."

"My parents are not so shallow as to be swayed by what you are wearing."

"I just do not want to embarrass you."

"You will not," he assured her quietly. "What you wear on your back is less important than what is in your heart."

Annie sighed and nodded. "I hope you are right." She reluctantly took Hunter's arm and returned to the stall. But a few moments in Lord Ross's company and she forgot about her dirty gown, for he was clearly more interested in the colt than in her clothes. He seemed to like her, smiling at her often, including her in the conversation about horse rearing and training.

By the time they were walking up the steps to the keep, she had actually relaxed and was looking forward to meeting Lady Megan, whom Lord Ross obviously adored. But the moment she walked into the great hall, her contentment vanished.

The trestle tables had not been set up for the noon meal. The servants, who should have been seeing to that and many other tasks, stood in a knot outside the door leading to the pantry and thence the kitchens.

"Ah, there is Mama." Hunter, obviously unaware something was wrong, dragged her toward the hearth, where a lone woman sat, still clad in her dusty travel cloak.

Lady Megan rose as they approached, a small, delicate figure in green wool with the smooth cheeks of a lass. The few strands of gray in her tawny hair were the only clue she was old enough to be Hunter's mother. But the resemblance was striking. Though he had his father's size and powerful build, he'd inherited his mother's hair and sultry brown eyes. She, however, had not a bit of reserve.

"Hunter!" Lady Megan threw her arms around him. "Oh, it is so good to see you, my love. I feared—"

"Shh." Hunter let go of Annie and hugged his mother. "I am fine, as you can see."

The sight of them locked in each other's arms affected Annie deeply. Had her parents loved her this much? Had she grieved when they died? For once, she was glad she could not remember the pain of losing them.

Hunter let go of his mother and stepped back, his eyes suspiciously moist. "Mama, this is my Annie."

"My lady." Annie started to curtsy, but the lady seized her hands and drew her up.

"None of that. Oh, you are so lovely."

"I fear I'm a bit dirty at the moment, my lady."

"Megan." Her eyes twinkled. "If I know my son, he's got you slaving away with those horses of his."

"Oh, but I want to help," Annie exclaimed.

"That is as it should be." Megan's smile widened as her husband came and put his arm around her. "I am sorry that we did not send word of our arrival," she added. "We seem to have thrown your household into a bit of turmoil."

"Aye." Belatedly remembering the tables, Annie turned and nearly tripped over Janet.

"Annie," the maid whispered. "We need yer help."

"Of course." Annie smiled at her new relatives. "If you will excuse me, I'll see to dinner." Taking Janet's arm, she steered the maid toward the pantry door. "Why are the tables not set up?"

"Because Sadye said we had to have a dais on which to set Lord Ross's table."

"What in the world is that?"

"Sadye said 'twas a big step. She's gone out to show Hob the carpenter what to build."

"Hmm. That sounds like a lengthy project. I will ask Hunter if we can do without for this one meal." She made to turn away, but Janet grabbed her arm.

"We've worse trouble than that. There's no supper."

"No supper?" Annie sniffed the air. "I smell something."

"Venison pie."

"Excellent."

"Not according to George. He says 'tis not a fit dish to set before the likes of Lord Ross and Lady Megan."

"That is ridiculous. They will understand. Begin setting up the tables in the usual manner, only see if there are any more sheets to cover them."

"The way we did last night." Janet nodded.

To Annie's surprise, the other servants seemed to calm, hurrying away without a moment's hesitation. She kept Jean back. "Will you go and take Lady Megan's cloak?"

"Me?" Jean squeaked. "I'm not fit to wait on her."

"Of course you are. Whatever gave you that idea?"

"She'll know," Jean whispered, tears in her eyes. "She'll look at me and know I am…soiled."

Annie nearly pointed to her own stained gown, then she realized of what Jean spoke. The abuses she and Janet had suffered at the hands of that perverted nobleman. Her heart cracked. Salvaging dinner no longer seemed important. But what could she say to ease Jean's suffering? Her first instinct was to call Hunter over. He was good with words. He had saved Janet and Jean. But she could see him laughing with his parents. Later, mayhap, he would speak with the twins and ease their lingering pain. For now, it was up to her.

Annie cleared her throat. "Jean," she began gently.

"You look no different from any other lass here. I did not know you had been...hurt...and neither will Hunter's parents. They are kindly people, who did not turn up their noses at my stained gown."

"Well." Jean glanced toward the hearth.

"We must put aside our own feelings. Hunter is counting on us to make his family welcome."

"I owe him so much." Jean squared her shoulders and marched toward the trio.

Bolstered by that small success, Annie hurried through the pantry where the dishes were readied for the table and out the back door to the kitchen. The door to the low building was open. The two potboys and three serving maids, all of whom had once worked in George's tavern, were huddled just inside. Beyond them, George sat at the worktable, face buried in his hands.

"What is going on?" Annie demanded.

Everyone but George jumped and turned to her. The maids had been weeping; the lads were grim faced.

"George says we'll be turned out," one boy murmured. "'Cause we've nothing fit to serve."

"That's ridiculous. The venison pie—"

"Happened before," the lad grumbled. "That fire, the one that destroyed the tavern. Them that set it were angry because they wanted a grand feast. All we had was mutton stew."

Oh. "Well, that is not going to happen here. Lord Ross particularly asked if there'd be meat pie for supper."

George raised his head, his eyes red rimmed. "He did?"

Annie nodded, hoping God would forgive the lies she was about to tell. "He remembered your pies fondly from his last visit. Now," she added before they lost their nerve again, "here is what we are going to do. We will turn this simple but delicious meal into another celebration."

"We used all the fine food last night," George grumbled.

"We will contrive. What else have you got to serve?"

"I've an apple pudding." George stood. "There's smoked salmon left from yesterday. And cheese aplenty."

"What of the walnuts we gathered last week?" a lad asked.

"That would be lovely," Annie said. "I'll leave it to you, then." She turned and found Sadye standing behind her. "Oh, there you are. I was just coming to look for you."

"Ye're doing right well without me," the older woman said. "Ye've remembered how it's done from before."

"I guess I have." Annie smiled. "Thanks to all of you for helping make this dinner special for Hunter's parents." Well pleased with what she'd accomplished, Annie hurried back to the hall. Jean had not only taken their guests' cloaks, she'd added wood to the fire and provided them with cups of ale.

Hunter stood as Annie approached. "Is everything all right? I was about to come looking for you."

"There was some confusion in the kitchen." Annie sat on the bench he'd drawn up opposite his parents, who occupied the only two chairs. "We will eat shortly. I apologize for not changing my clothes, but my other gown is also soiled."

"Do not fret about it, my dear." Megan's smile was tender and compassionate. "Hunter told us you'd been set upon by thieves and lost…everything."

Annie realized he'd told them about her loss of memory and felt vulnerable, flawed. She wanted to run. Coward. She'd just finished coercing his people into overcoming their demons. She could not do less. "I count myself fortunate to have had Hunter's support. Without it, I fear I'd have been truly lost."

His father smiled. "And we are glad he has you."

"Aye. Very glad." Lady Megan fairly beamed.

Annie relaxed. It was going to be all right. She did not

even mind when Lord Ross said he had papers for Hunter and the two men went off, leaving her with her new mother.

"Annie is absolutely lovely," his father said the moment they were private in Hunter's counting chamber.

"Aye, she is."

"You have only to see her with the colt to know she is kind and generous. Animals are better judges of people than we are."

"So you've often said." What would his father say if he knew she was Alex Murray's daughter? Dieu, he had chided Annie for being nervous about this visit, yet here he was with sweaty palms. There was nothing to fear. His father had never met the Murray and could not note any resemblance.

"Do you plan to stay at Renfrew?"

"Aye."

"I am glad." Ross clasped his shoulder and squeezed, his relief evident. "Your mother worried about you."

"And you did not?"

"Logically, I know you can take care of yourself, but…" He shrugged. "Bad things do happen to good people. If they did not, there'd be no need of a king's justicular. What of your post?"

"The king will find another as zealous as I was."

"But not as canny or as compassionate."

"I disagree. I plan to propose Gavin for the task."

"Ah, he would make a good choice." Ross slid the saddle pouch from his shoulder to the desk and freed the laces. "Speaking of justice, I have brought the warrants you wanted."

Hunter unrolled the parchments and scanned them eagerly. Three precious pieces of paper, one for each miscreant. "My thanks. You had no trouble getting them?"

"Your notes and the strength of your reputation were

enough. Though I never liked him, it was a surprise seeing Jock's name on the request.''

"So far, the evidence against him is weak. God knows I do not want to think he is part of this blackmail scheme. I always liked the old reprobate, rough though he is.''

"I suppose he is no worse than any Borderer. I did believe him an honest man. Otherwise I'd not have agreed when he asked for Brenna's hand. Losing her drove him a bit mad, I think. Right along with the rest of us.''

Hunter nodded. Much as he longed to tell his father Brenna had not been kidnapped, he feared talk of it might spill over into dinner and jar Annie's memory. If he was wrong about Jock, he'd burn the warrant without using it, and no one need be the wiser.

"Well, since all is settled, let us rejoin the ladies.'' Hunter clapped his father on the back as they walked to the door. "Again, my thanks for securing the warrants.''

"You've amply repaid me by taking a bride.'' Winking, his father opened the door. "Your mother was beginning to worry.''

"And you were not?''

"Not a bit. I'm just glad you did not wed one of those shallow, flirtatious wenches who hung on you at court.'' As they walked down the short corridor, Ross's expression turned serious again. "Will you go to Luncarty yourself?''

"I will have to. I've got two parties of men gathering evidence.'' And Gavin looking for the Murrays. "When we are ready to move, I will have to be there.''

"Mayhap Annie would like to visit us while you're gone.''

"I am certain she would. Now that she has seen for herself that you and Mama accept her.''

"Why would we not?''

If you only knew. Hunter cleared his throat. "Partly it is her loss of memory. There are many things she does not remember how to do. She feels inadequate, fears shaming me.''

''And herself. I would guess she is a proud lass.''

''Aye, she is. If Mama would be willing to teach her the things a lady should know to run a household…''

''I'd say they have already made a start.''

The sight of Annie and his mother sitting together, heads bent close as they chatted, made Hunter smile. His steps lighter than they'd been in months…years…he wove his way through the trestle tables and dropped a kiss on his wife's head.

''Oh, Hunter.'' Annie's smile dazzled. ''It is the most amazing thing. I can read and write.''

''Indeed.'' Hunter glanced at the parchment on her lap. It was covered with haphazard practice letters and words.

Annie fairly bounced in her chair. ''Aye, Megan was showing me this book of ancient legends she has been compiling.''

''Mama!'' Hunter gave an exaggerated groan and rolled his eyes. ''Trying to recruit slave labor to copy your manuscripts?''

''She volunteered,'' his mama replied, looking affronted.

''I did.'' Annie was so excited she jumped up. ''The stories are even more thrilling and touching than Janet's ballads. It would be a crime if they were lost,'' she added, echoing her new mother's earlier words. Megan's acceptance of her meant even more than Lord Ross's. The dear woman had promised to teach her everything she needed to know to be a fitting wife for Hunter. ''Megan wants one set for each member of the clan, so we need not rely solely on memory. I am going to help.''

''I will send to Edinburgh for the finest parchment and inks,'' Hunter said.

...Annie's glad cry of glee was drowned out by a horn

blast. Turning, she spotted Hamish hovering outside the pantry door. "I think dinner is served."

As they moved toward the table, Annie noticed that Megan limped slightly. Too much time in the saddle, no doubt. "After supper, would you like a hot bath to ease your aches?"

"Aches? Oh, 'tis a kind offer, but I am lame from a fall, not sore from riding."

"Oh, my lady. I am sorry. Would you rather have a tray in your room? Should you lie down?"

"Nay." Megan smiled wryly. "The accident happened long ago. The leg does not pain me, but 'tis often stiff. For a time, they did not think I would walk again. And some said I'd bear no babes. I worked very hard to learn to walk, and I prayed for a child. The good Lord saw fit to grant both my wishes. So all and all, I've come out better than I might have."

"What a good way of looking at things." Annie vowed she would enjoy the present and stop feeling sorry she could not remember her past.

"Oh, this is lovely." Megan slid onto one of the chairs the servants had moved to the table for the honored guests.

Indeed, it did. Annie, seated on a bench with Hunter, beamed with pride as the servants entered the hall.

The meal passed pleasantly. George was just serving the apple tart when Hamish approached the table.

"I am sorry to disturb ye, my lord, but there's a churlish fellow at the gate demanding admittance."

"Did he give a name?" Hunter asked warily.

"Rowy Mc—"

"Damn." Hunter leaped up, nearly toppling the bench he and Annie shared. Steadying her with one hand, he growled, "There's something I must see to. Go on with the meal. I will be back."

His father rose, also. "I will come along."

"Nay! That is, stay and finish your tart."

Ross Carmichael was no fool. He knew something was up and gave Hunter a look that said so, a look that made Hunter feel like a lad being put in his place. "I will come."

And that, of course, was that. Short of tying his father to the chair, there was no going alone.

"What is wrong?" Annie murmured. "Who is this—"

"No one you know." Hunter pasted on a smile for Annie's benefit and gave her a quick kiss. "Save some of the tart for us," he teased, and stalked from the room with his father sticking to his side like a clump of thistle.

Bloody hell. What could have brought Red Rowy here? Nothing good, that was sure.

Chapter Eighteen

Every minute that Hunter was gone seemed like an hour. The slight queasiness that had plagued her this morn returned. Annie tried to eat George's apple tart, but her stomach threatened to rebel. Finally she gave up and set her spoon aside.

"Do not fret," Megan said, patting Annie's hand. "Hunter and Ross will return shortly. I am certain it is nothing."

"I'm not worried, but the man's name is familiar."

"Red Rowy is related to Hunter's uncle. Jock McKie."

McKie. Jock McKie. Annie flinched as a wave of cold shot through her. Fear, stark and terrible.

"It is possible you met him," Megan added. "Did Hunter take you to Luncarty after the fire at the convent?"

"Not…not that I recall," Annie managed to say. *Jock McKie.* Was he the man in her nightmare? Was that why his name terrified her? Her head began to ache as she pushed for answers.

"Likely Hunter will bring Rowy in to sup when they have finished their business. Seeing him may jar your memory."

For days that had been her fondest wish. Now, with fear

grinding in her belly, she was not sure she wanted to remember.

"Oh, look. Here is Ross now," Megan exclaimed.

Annie's gaze snapped to the doorway.

The man striding into the hall bore no resemblance to the smiling lord who had left. His lips were set in a grim line. His once gentle blue eyes narrow and hard, he advanced to their table. "Come, Meggie, we are leaving."

"Leaving? But...but..."

"I will not stay under the same roof with Alexander Murray's daughter."

Annie gasped, struck by his vehemence and by the images that swept through her.

A tall, redheaded man with laughing eyes. She could see him carrying her into the stables, teaching her to ride. Her father? If so, why did Ross hate him?

"Papa." Hunter came up beside his father, his face pale and haggard. "Papa, if you would only listen."

"Listen?" Ross snarled. "What excuse could you possibly give for wedding *her?*"

"I love her." Hunter spared Annie a glance, his eyes dark pools of misery. "And she is innocent, Papa. An innocent victim who does not deserve your hatred."

"Aye. That may be true." Some of the fury left Ross's face, yet the pain lingered. "But I cannot forget who she is." He held out his hand to Megan. "Come, we are leaving."

Instead of obeying, Megan reached for Annie's hand. "I am not going till I have heard what Hunter has to say." Softly spoken, the words were edged with steel.

Air hissed out between Ross's clenched teeth. "Very well. Meggie, Hunter, we will talk in your counting room."

Hunter sighed and nodded. "All right. Annie—"

"She stays here." Ross spun about and left.

Hunter came around the table and took Annie's other

hand. "I am sorry, sweetheart. Mama, will you stay with Annie?"

"If she wishes."

"Nay," Annie said quickly. "It will only anger Lord Ross. And you will wish to hear..." This horrible thing that had made Lord Ross despise her. Moreover, she craved solitude to sort out the memories assailing her. "I will take a nap."

"Annie." Hunter knelt beside her, his hand on her back, warm and reassuring as always. "Try not to worry."

"I will be fine," she lied, hanging on to her composure by a slim thread.

"I will be back quick as I can." He took his mother's arm and escorted her from the hall. No sooner had they gone than Sadye rushed up to Annie.

"Oh, my lady! Whatever is going on?"

"I am not certain. Just some misunderstanding," Annie mumbled. "Hunter will straighten it out." The knot in her stomach rose into her throat, and she knew she was shortly going to lose George's venison pie. "I am going down to the stables to feed Blackie." And lick my wounds in private.

Hunter waited till his mother was settled in the chair beside the empty hearth before he spoke. "Her name is Allisun Murray, and none of this is her fault."

"I know." Ross walked slowly to the window and looked out. "It is myself I blame. Poor Brenna. She had ill luck with men. Thrice a widow before she wed Jock, and look where that landed her. I never should have let her go. I knew the Border was wild and untamed. It haunts me still, thinking she ended her days in fear and misery." He lowered his head, as though the weight of his pain was too great to bear.

"Papa." Unable to stand his father's grief, Hunter went

to stand beside him. "I have spoken with some people, and I now believe it possible that Aunt Brenna was not kidnapped."

His father turned, eyes wide with disbelief. "What?"

"'Tis said she knew Alex Murray, that she loved him."

"I thought she was happy with Jock."

"She wed him willingly," his mother added.

"Aye, she did. But was she happy with him?" Hunter sighed. Casting back, he told them what he remembered of that summer he'd spent at Luncarty. "He did not abuse her, that I knew of, but when they argued, he shouted and made her cry."

Ross scowled. "I am sorry for that, but a few angry words are not unusual. Still, if she was miserable, why did she not complain to me? I would have found a way to bring her home."

"Pride," his mother said. "She chose Jock, and likely felt she must make the best of things."

"If only I had not been such a green youth, she might have confided in me," Hunter said. "Instead, she turned to Murray."

"But you were there when Brenna was taken," Ross said, clearly not convinced. "You said she had been kidnapped."

"When I came upon them Murray was holding her. I heard her say she could not go with him. He insisted, she resisted." Hunter shook his head. "And I, God help me, assumed the worst."

"But his men attacked and beat you."

Hunter raked a hand through his hair. "I was struck and knocked unconscious, but only after I pulled my sword and challenged Alex Murray. The cuts and bruises came later. I fell trying to get back to Luncarty."

"But Jock said—"

"He either leaped to that conclusion or lied to strengthen his case against the Murrays."

His father snorted. "It did not need strengthening."

"Aye, if my suspicions about Jock are correct, it did. You yourself thought it excessive to pursue a kidnapping so long and so ruthlessly. I think it was more than that. I think Aunt Brenna left Jock for Alex Murray, and I think that when she went, she took with her Jock's ledger and tally sticks."

"You never mentioned this before."

"I did not remember it. I've seen the like often enough in my work. Victims of a crime sometimes do not recall details till months or years later. I was young, frightened and in pain when Jock found me. I told him two men had taken Aunt Brenna. Until recently, I did not recall his first question to me. He did not ask after her. He wanted to know if she had had with her a ledger and tally sticks. I had seen neither, but that morn she had spent time in his counting room. She emerged with a covered basket, which she carried away from the tower."

"She put these thoughts into your mind," his father snarled. "That red-haired wench you have wed."

"Easy, Papa, Allie is the woman I love. But aye, she did make me think about things I had forgotten. And she made me believe her father was no kidnapper. Not by singing Alex's praises, but by telling me she hated Aunt Brenna for stealing her father's love and bringing so much trouble upon her people."

"Humph. It is not easy to think of Brenna as an adulteress. What of these tally sticks? I know it is inconvenient if your records go missing, for you do not know who owes you what, but why would Jock be so obsessed about getting them back?"

"Because they detailed his illegal activities." Briefly Hunter told his parents about the blackmail scheme. "I think that Jock has been at this for a long time. Aunt Brenna found out. They may have been arguing about it that last night. She may even have feared he'd harm her.''

"Why go to Murray instead of her family?" Ross growled.

"There may not have been time. And too, if she was in love with Alex, it would be natural to turn to him."

"If she had proof Jock was involved in something, why has it not come to light?" Ross demanded.

"Maybe she lost them," Megan said.

Hunter swung toward her, encouraged by her sympathetic support. "When Gavin finds the Murrays' hiding place, I think I will have the answers to all our questions."

"'Twould be good to know what really happened." Ross sighed. "I apologize for my outburst in the hall."

"Hunter is not the one who needs to hear that." Megan walked over to her husband. "You have always been a fair man, love. Do you not agree that Annie is innocent of any crime?"

"Aye. I cannot feel as warmly toward her as I did before I knew who her father was, but I'd make amends for hurting her."

Annie stepped from sunlight into the darkened stables and waited a moment for her eyes to adjust. She had lost the battle with her stomach on the way down from the tower, and her insides felt even more hollow and achy.

"Allisun?" a man whispered from the gloom.

Allisun. Allisun. The name rang over and over in her head, pounding against the barrier that kept her from remembering.

"Allisun." Warm hands gripped her shoulders. "By all that's holy, what has he done to ye?"

"Done?" Dizzy, she stared at the square, weathered face

hovering above hers. "Do I know you?" She should. The memory was there, just out of reach.

"Bloody hell! 'Tis Owen."

"Owen." The thunder in her temples was unbearable. Moaning, she put her hands up to keep her head from shattering.

"Oh, lass." He picked her up and cradled her in his arms. "Ach, my poor wee Allie. What has he done to ye?"

"I hit my head." She looked up at him and was suddenly swept by a sense of déjà vu. "You picked me up like this before, when I fell from the apple tree."

"Aye." A tear ran down his furrowed face.

"Owen." She lifted her hand to his cheek. "I remember. I remember." She was Allisun...Allisun Murray.

The memories flooded back in a pain-filled rush. The feud. Her parents' and brothers' deaths. The raid. The time at Keastwicke. "I fled the tower," she mumbled. "And... and something happened. Everything went black. Hunter...Hunter found me. He..." She drew in a quick breath, stabbed anew by his betrayal. "Oh, Owen. He lied to me," she cried bitterly. "He...he..."

"Do not fret about that, lass. I'm taking ye home."

"I'm not going till I confront him," Allisun said, fury crowding out her confusion. Hunter had kept the truth from her so he might have a convenient bedmate. The fiend.

"We cannot stay." Owen guided her deeper into the stables where two saddled horses waited. "A guard just rode in with news that Red Rowy is at the gates, and I was set to come find ye."

"Rowy, here?" Allisun swayed. Did Hunter plan to turn her over to Jock?

"Easy, lass, we'll be out of here in a moment." He jammed her braid into a wool hat and pulled it down low over her forehead. An old ratty cloak went around her next, stinking of mildew but covering most of her gown. "That'll have to do.'' He lifted her onto the saddle and swung up behind.

"We will need two horses."

"Aye. I'll lead the other one till ye're stronger." Owen urged their mount out of the stables and into the light.

"How will we get past the gate?" she murmured.

"I'm supposed to take this beast to the blacksmith in Renfrew to have a shoe repaired. I'll say ye're my helper."

The ruse got them through the gates and a quarter mile down the road before a shout from behind warned of pursuit.

Owen looked back. "Damn, 'tis Hunter." He sent the hobbler into a gallop, but the warhorse soon raced up beside them.

"Annie!" Hunter cried.

The name cut her to the quick, a symbol of all the lies he'd told. "Stop," she said to Owen. "He will not leave us alone till we've thrashed this out."

Dancer lived up to his name, prancing in a wide circle as Hunter reined in beside them. "Who is this man?" he demanded of her. "Where are you going with him?"

It was tempting to let Hunter think that she was running off with Owen, as his aunt had with her father. But weak fool that she was, some part of her still cared for him, despite what he had done. "This is Owen Murray, my captain."

"I'm taking her home," Owen growled.

Hunter ignored him, his intense gaze focused on her face. "Annie, what does this mean?" He looked as confused as she had felt these past few weeks. The knowledge that he could have spared her that, could have told her the truth yet withheld it, roused her temper even further.

"The name, as you well know, is Allisun," she said crisply. "Allisun Murray, and I am going home."

"You remembered." Pain darkened his eyes.

"I remembered," she echoed, shivering. Cold. She was so cold and empty inside. She fought to stay strong by remembering what he'd done. "You lied to me."

"I lied to protect you."

"You lied to further your desires." She knew by the way he flinched that her barb had wounded.

"I love you," he said in an agonized whisper. "I did not tell you who you were—"

"To protect your uncle and his cohorts."

Grief ravaged his features. "Jesu, you cannot think that."

"That and worse. You used me to end the feud."

"This cannot be happening," he cried, raking back his hair. "Come back to Renfrew with me, and we will talk."

"I am going back to my people, to continue the fight against your uncle." Lest he forget what stood between them.

Hunter shuddered. They had come full circle, from hate to love to hate again. Never had he felt more helpless than he did now, staring into her implacable gaze and fearing nothing he said would make a difference. "It does not have to be this way," he said in an agonized whisper. "I love you. Together we—"

"Get them! Get the Murrays!" screamed a rough voice.

Hunter whirled just as Red Rowy and his band of six came charging down the road. "Owen, get her back to the keep," Hunter cried, drawing his sword. Without waiting to see if Murray had followed orders, Hunter went on the attack.

He sent Dancer straight at the McKies. The warhorse bit the first man who came near him and kicked the mount out from under the next, clearing a path to the center of the band.

"Damn yer eyes," Rowy shouted as he brought his blade up to counter Hunter's. "I knew the Murrays was in there."

Shock reverberated up Hunter's arm, nearly numbing it. "You'll not be getting your hands on them." He thrust and parried with all his might, conscious that he was badly outnumbered. His only hope lay in capturing Rowy quickly and forcing the others to surrender.

But what Rowy lacked in skill, he made up for in brute strength, dragging out the battle till another McKie joined him on the left. Together they pressed Hunter, forcing him to divide his strokes. He eliminated one man, only to have another take his place. He sank his blade into Rowy's arm, drawing blood.

Roaring a curse, Rowy struck back. Fire sizzled in Hunter's left shoulder. He felt men jostle behind him, kept back only by Dancer's flailing legs and sharp iron shoes, and knew that they would not last long.

Then Hunter heard the most welcome of all sounds.

"'A Carmichael! To Hunter! To Hunter!"

A quick glance showed his father and a dozen knights racing to the rescue. It was too much for the McKies. They disengaged and fled with the Carmichaels hot after them.

Ross sheathed his sword as he rode up to Hunter. "Dieu, that was close. Are you all right, son?"

"Allie?" Hunter demanded, gasping for breath.

"Gone. She and the man rode into the hills after bringing us word you were in trouble."

"You did not try and stop her?" Hunter cried.

"My first priority was getting to you."

Hunter cursed and turned Dancer toward the hills.

"Where the hell do you think you are going?" his father demanded, grabbing hold of the stallion's bridle.

"After Allie." Hunter tried to wrench free.

Ross held tight. "Idiot! You are in no shape to ride."

"You are glad she is gone!" Hunter shouted.

"I am not," Ross roared. "Calm down and listen to me.

I know you are frantic to get her back, but you are like to bleed to death if you charge off like this.''

Hunter glanced at the blood dripping from his fingers. He scarcely felt the pain for the ache in his heart.

'''Tis up to the keep with you to have that arm bandaged.''

''All right, but then I am going to find Allie.''

''Stubborn fool,'' Ross grumbled, but there was a wealth of love in the words and gentleness in his touch as he tore his own tunic to bind up the bloody wound. ''There, that'll do till your mama can look at it.'' He herded Hunter toward the gatehouse.

Wes Carmichael, Ross's captain, awaited them there. ''Where shall we put him?'' He jerked his chin in the direction of the loudly protesting Rowy McKie.

''I need to question him,'' Hunter mumbled. The numbness had worn off. White-hot pain sizzled in his shoulder.

''We will see to it.'' Ross motioned one of his men forward. ''Get my son into Lady Megan's care. That wound looks deep.''

Not deep, thank God, but long. His mother had set twelve neat stitches in his shoulder and was just covering them with clean linen when his father joined them.

''What did you find out?'' Hunter asked, attempting to sit.

''Lie still.'' Megan pushed him back onto the bed.

''Tyrant,'' Ross said fondly. Leaning against the bedpost, he peered at the proceedings. ''How is his arm?''

''A clean cut. Little muscle damage.'' Her face was as pale as the bandages. ''With rest and care, he'll be up in a week.''

''He has ears and a tongue,'' Hunter snapped. ''And he will be in the saddle before dark.''

''You will not!'' his mother cried.

''Easy, love.'' Ross put a supportive hand on her shoulder and scowled at Hunter. "You told me Gavin was down there looking for the Murrays. Why not send word to him?"

"Nay. Gavin reports that there are increased McKie patrols in the area of Tadlow Mountain, near where he believes the Murrays are hiding. I have got to get there before the McKies find Allisun." He levered himself up on the pillow, teeth clenched against the burning in his arm. "Jock is obsessed with wiping out the Murrays, and she is the last of Alex's line."

Ross nodded. "He'll want the ledger and tally sticks, too. Even after all this time, such evidence could cost him dearly."

"Ross, you are not condoning his going!" Megan cried.

"Mama." Hunter took her hand. "I must. This is Allie's life we are talking about, and you said the wound was not deep."

She frowned. "The dressings will need changing."

"I will go with him to make certain he is cared for."

"Oh, you men. Always anxious to rush off and put yourselves in danger." Megan threw up her hands and left them.

"Thank you, Papa. I appreciate the support. What did you learn from Red Rowy?"

"He is a closemouthed man, but his eyes fair popped from their sockets when I said we had proof of the blackmailing. He went gray when I named names and dates. But he swore the McKies had never lifted a head of cattle nor raided a single croft."

"Likely it's the truth. They have Ill Will and the bloody Bells for that. And Derk Neville to collect the rent."

"Without Will Bell, there would be no black rent. Maybe we should go after him directly."

"I would love to find a way. But he is a force to be reckoned with, shrewd, fearless and ruthless. His men are cutthroats, his home an impregnable fortress. And he has proved too wily to be lured into a trap.''

"Could the warden rouse the Border against him?''

"The warden's daughter is Will's prisoner.''

"Hmm.''

"And it'll only get worse as Ill Will grows stronger and more daring. Dugald is down talking with Ian Maxwell and the other Border lords to see if any will testify against these bastards.''

"Well, we will take this a step at a time.'' Ross straightened away from the bedpost. "I will bid the men prepare to travel at first light tomorrow. Tomorrow,'' he said again before Hunter could protest.

Chapter Nineteen

Three days of hard riding it took for Allisun and Owen to reach the hills. Some of that time they had spent doubling back and laying false trails in case they were followed. The closer they got to Tadlow, the more circumspect their route.

"I am sorry for this, lass," Owen said when he called a halt in the woods a mile distant from their goal. "I know ye're tired, but we'd best wait till full dark before we ride in."

Allisun nodded and slid off her mount. Her legs were so weak she had to cling to the stirrup for support.

"Ach, lass." Owen was there, as he had been the whole journey, his hand under her arm to help her to a rock.

Allisun sank onto the cold stone with a sigh. "I am sorry to be such a bother, but I have not ridden in ages."

"Ye're no bother." He crouched beside her. "Ye need to eat." He rummaged in his sack and took out some dried meat.

One sniff and Allisun's belly rumbled. "Thank you, but I am not hungry just now."

"That's what ye said this morn."

"I am just tired." And miserable. How could she think of food when her heart was in turmoil? She feared that fatigue was not the only reason she could keep nothing down, especially in the morn. Morning sickness, Morna had called it when she'd brought Allisun custard and advice on childbearing. Then the pregnancy had been feigned. Now Allisun feared it was real.

It was early days, yet, little more than a month since that night at Keastwicke. But Morna had claimed she was sick the whole nine months with her first. Putting a hand to her flat stomach, Allisun tried to imagine it rounded and full of life.

Hunter's child. She had lost him, but she had his babe. The notion filled her with a bewildering jumble of emotions. The joy she should have felt was tainted by his lies. How could she carry it beneath her heart knowing the babe had been fathered by him? How could she raise it, love it, when every time she looked at the bairn she would remember Hunter's betrayal?

Allisun flinched. Listen to her. Sweet Mary, what sort of unnatural person was she to feel so about her own unborn child?

Not all women are destined to be good mothers.

Dimly Allisun recalled her father saying that of Brenna, for after Carina was born, Brenna had refused to nurse the babe. She had turned her face to the wall and slowly faded away. Childbed fever, the maids of Keastwicke had called it. But others whispered it was God's punishment for her adultery.

Clearer were Allisun's memories of poor Carina, growing up in the shadow of her mother's sins. Motherless, unloved, always the outsider. Allisun had done what she could to befriend her sister, but she had only been seven herself and beset by her own demons. *She should have done more, been a better person.*

Allisun closed her eyes on a wave of pain and regret. This babe, she would not fail. She splayed her fingers over her belly in silent pledge. This babe they had made together was innocent. It was hers. A fierce surge of possessiveness shook her. She would love this babe as she could not its sire.

"Are ye all right, lass?" Owen asked anxiously.

Allisun opened her eyes and turned her thoughts outward. "I am fine. Much better, actually." She had gone mad for a moment, but that was past. "I cannot wait to see everyone again."

At nightfall on the fourth day after Allie's escape, Hunter rode into his cousin's camp. He swept the neat encampment with a commander's eye. Guards had been posted, the horses and weapons secured nearby in case of surprise attack. Half the men were out, likely on patrol. The others were cooking the evening meal.

Gavin hurried to meet him. "You've been hurt," he said, no doubt spotting the huge bandage Megan had insisted on.

"A scratch." Hunter swung down, hiding a grimace as the healing stitches pulled. "What news?"

"We have not found their hideout." Gavin led the way to a tent erected in the center of the camp. "But we are expecting some interesting visitors." He ducked inside after Hunter.

Hunter tossed his gauntlets onto the cot. "McKies?"

"Nay." Gavin's eyes danced as he poured two cups of ale from the flagon on a low table. "Ian Maxwell and a few of his 'fellow victims' as he put it."

"Dugald has persuaded them to give testimony against Derk and the Bells?"

"Not yet. They are coming to talk."

"'Tis a start." Hunter downed the ale, then told Gavin about the warrants against his uncle, Will Bell and Derk. "Allisun has regained her memory." The words nearly choked him. "She fled Renfrew with her captain, and I fear for her safety. I've sent Papa to Luncarty to *visit* Uncle Jock.''

''Warrant in hand, in case the McKies do get your Allisun.'' Gavin cocked his head. ''I take it she was angry with you.''

''Furious. She hates me now for lying to her, but if I had it to do over again, I would do the same.''

''What other choice had you?''

''None, if I wanted to save her.'' He scrubbed a hand over his face. ''The hell of it is, she was happy. Likely for the first time in years, she was happy, carefree.'' *In love.* The little bit of heaven they had shared made losing her all the more painful. ''But I am not giving up. I am going to find her and take her back to Renfrew, will she, nill she.''

''Oh, that'll be bound to mend your quarrel, but I do agree she's not safe here. We've narrowed down the area where we think they are. I'll send Leith out to show you the way.''

As they left the tent, a group of men rode in. Hunter recognized Ian and several others from the Lammas swearing.

Ian recognized him, too. Pulling his mount to a halt, he glared down his nose at Hunter. ''I hear ye're the king's man.''

''I am. If you will testify against Derk Neville, Will Bell and Jock McKie, I can promise you they will be arrested.''

''Oh? And who'll see to it Nebless Dickie don't murder us so we cannot speak against his father?''

''I will,'' Hunter said. ''Give me the information I need, and I'll see them all brought in, tried and hanged.''

''It'll be no easy task,'' Ian grumbled. ''But I'd be willing to hear ye out. What say ye, lads?'' he called to the others.

''Jock McKie's your uncle. Do ye expect us to believe ye'll do for him, too?'' asked Sly Tom Nixon.

"I will if he's guilty," Hunter replied.

"What about the warden? Andy Kerr's in their pockets."

"The crown takes precedence over him," Hunter assured them. "And after the king reads my report, Andy will not be warden."

Ian Maxwell smiled faintly. "I like the sounds of that. We'll step down and listen to yer plan."

"Actually—" Hunter cast a desperate glance at Gavin "—you talk to them," he whispered. "I have to go after Allie."

"My words won't carry the weight yours do," Gavin murmured. "It should only take an hour or so."

Hunter bowed to the inevitable, but as he gathered the Borderers around the fire, he prayed Allie was somewhere safe.

As homecomings went, Allisun's was miserable.

It was dark by the time she and Owen finally crept into the secret caves beneath Tadlow Mountain. The musty caverns seemed even more dank and confining than she'd remembered. As she followed Owen through the maze of tunnels, she shivered and gathered her cloak close.

It was not much warmer in the low-ceilinged cave that served as their hall. The only heat came from a bit of peat glowing feebly in a single metal brazier. By its light, she made out the meager furnishings, crude tables, benches and storage chests. On the bare floor, the folk of Tadlow slept rolled in their blankets. The unadorned walls seemed especially stark when she remembered the bright tapestries hanging at Renfrew.

Renfrew. Hunter.

Sweet Mary, why could she not forget? A bubble of hysterical laughter swelled inside her. Once she had cried because she could not remember; now she was haunted by memories. Bitter memories of Hunter's betrayal. Poignant memories of what they had found together, the companionship, the laughter, the love that could never be.

"It's Allisun," someone cried.

One by one, the Murrays leaped up to welcome her back, looking every bit as gaunt and vulnerable as when she'd left.

They could have been at Renfrew, safe, warm and well fed, Allisun thought. If she had not been too proud, too steeped in hatred for Jock McKie, to accept Hunter's offer.

"I feared I'd never see ye again." Linnet, the housekeeper, dragged Allisun into her ample embrace and sobbed loudly.

"Here, here, ye're getting her all wet." Freda, Allisun's former nurse, gently pried her loose. "Let me look at ye." Her welcoming smile faded. "Ach, ye're fair done in. Come to bed."

"I am tired," Allisun admitted. But she could not sleep till she'd greeted each of her people.

Old Claire, who had been her mother's maid, tisked over Allisun's dirty clothes. Dora the cook said she was too thin. Myles, Linnet's husband and the steward here, launched into a list of supplies the men had *appropriated:* blankets, salt—

"You went raiding?" Allisun turned on Ralph, who was the senior guard on duty.

"Nay, Wee Harry wouldn't let us without Owen's sayso." He lowered his voice. "He and Black Gil argued about it, but in the end we didn't need to go raiding. The blankets, oats, salt and such were left in the woods by a party of armored knights."

Allisun gasped and looked at Owen, whose eyes were as wide as her own. "A trap," she whispered. "Jock set a damned trap."

"Or Hunter did," Owen said. "Jock has no knights."

Dale snorted. "They thought to trap us, but Gil was too

smart to get caught. We'd nip in, take the goods and run. If they followed, we'd drop the stuff and come back for it later.''

"Fools," Owen grumbled. "That the knights have stayed nearby means they won't give up till they find us."

His warning drew a chorus of protests and arguments. Under cover of the noise, Allisun turned to Owen. "Hunter offered to take all of us in at Renfrew. I think we should accept."

"Then why did ye leave with me?"

"Because I was furious with him." And she had not known about the babe. The child changed everything. It was one thing to live like a hunted animal, quite another to bring a bairn into this bleak world. Though she could never love or trust Hunter, she'd grudgingly accept his help, for the babe's sake.

"Here's Gil coming now," Dale shouted over the din.

As Allisun watched Gil step into the cavern she was swept back to the moment when he'd ridden out of the trees and attacked her. The missing memories fell into place. His was the face that had haunted her dreams.

"Gil," she whispered, unable to believe one of her men had tried to kill her.

His eyes rounded, mirroring her shock. "Ye're alive." He crossed to her in three strides and wrapped his arm around her.

To the rest, it might look like a hug, but Allisun felt his tension, smelled his fear and knew her life hung in the balance. "Aye, I'm alive. I suffered an accident that stole my memory."

His arm relaxed. "You remember nothing?"

"Nothing from the time of the stampede till Owen found me at Renfrew Castle." She stepped free of his embrace, conscious of his probing gaze, struggling to maintain her calm.

"That is...too bad."

"Aye, well." There was a scream lodged in her throat. She wanted to run, but dared not. Not yet.

"Gil!" Carina emerged from a side tunnel and rushed to Gil's side. She had her mother's waist-length black hair and expressive eyes a shade grayer than Brenna's. But her delicate features hinted she'd be as beautiful as her mother when she grew up. "Have you come to take me riding as you promised?"

"Hello, Carina," Allisun said softly.

Carina's head whipped around. Her eyes narrowed to sullen slits. "You are back."

"Aye." The sight of her sister clinging to that would-be murderer sickened Allisun. "It is too late for riding, Carina. Come here to me," she said.

"I will not." Carina pressed her slender, gawky body even closer to Gil's beefy one.

"Wanton," Linnet snapped. "She's always hanging on him."

"Aye, she's a harlot like her ma," said Freda.

"You'll not speak of my sister that way," Allisun cried.

"Why not? They say worse behind my back." Carina tossed her head, eyes flashing pain and defiance. "They all hate me. Even you, dear sister. You blame me, as you did her, for this..." Her gesture encompassed the cave in which they were forced to hide and the people who lived in constant fear. She licked her lips and looked adoringly up at Gil. "It doesn't matter. Gil is taking me away from here."

"Nay!" Allisun searched their faces, one young and rebellious, the other weathered and sly. What did Gil want with her sister? "I won't let you go with him." She reached for her sister. "You don't know what he—"

Gil snagged Allisun's arm and dragged her back against him. His dirk was out, cold and sharp against her throat.

"Don't!" he shouted as Owen and the others surged forward.

"G-Gil, what are you doing?" Carina whispered.

"Never you mind. Go down and get three horses ready."

"Three? But why do we have to bring her?"

"Because I said so. Now do it!"

Over the pounding of her heart, Allisun heard her sister scramble to obey. "Where are you going?"

"To join up with Will Bell, I'd guess," Owen snarled. "While we were away, he's been sneaking around, making deals."

Horrified gasps echoed through the cavern. Men who had once followed Black Gil slowly backed away.

Allisun kept her attention focused on the man who held her. "Will Bell is in league with Jock."

"Not anymore. Jock is old, crippled. Will is looking for new men. Strong, canny men."

Owen snorted. "Go then. Go make yer pact with the devil."

"But leave my sister here," Allisun demanded.

"Oh, I couldn't do that," Gil drawled. "Will's been looking forward to meeting her."

Allisun felt sick again. "Leave Carina here and take me," she pleaded. "Will Bell always fancied me."

"Oh, I'll be taking ye both. Double the reward, ye ken?"

Carina raced back, breathless and smiling. "Ready."

"The pack with yer mama's things?" Gil asked.

"In my saddle pouch, Gil."

The ledger and tally sticks, Allisun thought. Now she knew why Gil was interested in Carina. And she was even more afraid that Jock had a part in this.

"Go ahead to the horses, Carina." When she'd dashed off, Gil issued his warning. "If anyone follows us, Allisun dies."

* * *

The negotiations dragged on for hours. The moon rose, stars popped out of the sky and still the Border lords waffled, looking for assurances they would be protected.

"Bloody hell." Hunter surged up from the circle around the campfire. The woman he loved was out there somewhere in harm's way and these men haggled over what might be? "Sometimes you just have to take a chance in hopes of changing things."

Ian stood, too. "This is no horse race we're wagering on. This is our homes, our lives, our families we're risking."

"Aye, easy for ye to speak about taking chances when yer estates lie safely out of Ill Will's reach," Tom Nixon added.

"But if you all stick together, you outnumber the Bells."

"Ill Will's men fight like fiends," muttered Tom.

And that, Hunter supposed, was part of the problem. These were good, decent men, not thugs. "Dieu, I…" Hunter turned as a band of men rode in. Seeing his father in the lead, he smiled for the first time in hours and hurried to meet the one man who might sway these stubborn lords. "Papa, you are well come."

"My news will not be." Ross swung down from the saddle and tore off his helmet. "Jock is not at Luncarty."

"That's impossible," Hunter cried. "He was bedridden."

"Well, something forced him up and out."

"The Murrays," Hunter said in an agonized whisper. "His men must have found the Murrays."

"Jesu, I hope not." Ross frowned. "Who are these men?"

"The victims of the black rent." Hunter dragged a hand through his hair. "Word that Jock is riding will send them scurrying for their burrows like the rabbits they are."

"Easy." Ross laid a hand on his shoulder. "Not all men are cut out for fighting and killing. I will speak to—"

A Carmichael trooper galloped into the firelight, his face shiny with sweat. "Thought ye should know, Hunter, we spotted three people riding away from Tadlow Mountain. Two lasses and a man. Wee Artie's laying a trail we can follow if ye've a mind."

Allisun! Hunter wheeled away from the soldier, calling for his armor and horse.

"Where are ye going?" Ian Maxwell demanded.

"After my wife." Hunter turned, shouting for his horse and squire. "And pray God I am not too late."

"Wait," Johnny Carmichael shouted. "There's more. On my way here, I saw a band of men moving along the main road."

Hunter's pulse jumped. "McKies?"

"Too far off to tell, but they were riding slow-like."

"Go after Allisun," Ross urged. "My men and I will check this out." He looked over at Ian Maxwell. "It might help if you came along, for I'd not know if these men were friend or foe."

"I suppose we could, just for a look, mind," Ian allowed.

Her hands tied before her, Allisun clung to the pommel and the slim hope of rescue. It faded with each mile they traveled away from Tadlow. Gil's threat had served its purpose.

Four or five miles they'd come. Allisun had lost track, her slim store of energy focused on staying in the saddle as Gil pulled her horse along after his through the trees and up the side of a hillock. Along its narrow back they went, across a dry riverbed and into a steep-sided ravine.

The valley of death, Allisun thought and swayed momentarily in the saddle. Sweet Mary, she was afraid. For both of them, though Carina rode beside Gil with nary a backward glance to see how her sister fared. Strangely, Allisun blamed herself. She had failed Carina, failed to make her feel wanted. Black Gil had played on Carina's loneliness, used her, lied to her.

Ironic how Hunter's lies paled beside Black Gil's. Now, when it was nearly too late, Allisun realized that though Hunter had taken advantage of the situation, he had done so at least partly to protect her. If only she could tell him that she understood. That she still loved him.

"This is it." Black Gil drew rein in a small clearing bounded by huge black rocks and a fringe of low-growing pines.

Exhausted in spirit and body, Allisun drooped in the saddle. She had to make some attempt at escape. But how?

"Why are we stopping here?" Carina whined.

Gil dismounted. "I am meeting someone."

"Ill Will Bell," Allisun muttered.

Gil grabbed the front of her tunic and dragged her off the horse, laughing when she fell to her knees on the stony ground. "Ye'd best learn to mind yer tongue. Will does not like taking orders from a woman any more than I did."

The pain in her knees drove the cobwebs from her head. Will was coming; she had to have a plan. Surreptitiously she slid the wee dirk from her boot. As weapons go, it was not much, but she felt better holding it concealed in the folds of her cloak.

"Can't we leave her here and go?" Carina asked. "You promised to take me somewhere fine and warm. You said—"

"Shut up. Someone's coming." Gil drew his sword.

Allisun braced herself, but she was not prepared for the shock of seeing Jock McKie ride into the moonlit clearing.

Apparently, neither was Gil.

"What the hell are ye doing here?" Black Gil cried.

"Collecting a debt long due." Jock's broken leg stuck

straight out before him, tied to a plank. Silvery light limned his craggy features, emphasizing the dark sockets where his eyes blazed with malicious joy. "Will said ye'd have my ledger and tallies. Sly fox never let on ye'd have Allisun Murray, too."

Allisun's hand tightened on the haft of the dirk. If she could get close enough, she might plunge it into his black heart. Still on her knees, she watched Jock's men file in behind him, taking small consolation from the fact that Gil appeared nearly as afraid as she was.

"My deal is with Will." Gil sidled nearer to his mount.

Jock growled. "The ledgers are mine and so's the lass."

"Hold on, Jock." The speaker sat to Jock's right, a giant of a man and quite the ugliest Allisun had ever seen. His face had been mashed in so it seemed he had no nose at all. "The deal Da struck with ye was only for the ledgers and tallies."

"Allie?" Carina hunkered close beside her, shivering so her teeth chattered. "Wh-what is happening?"

"I'd say our betrayer has been betrayed."

"It is all my fault, if I hadn't wanted to leave—"

"The fault is mine. I knew what Gil was but spoke too late. Still all is not lost." She eyed the two men trading barbs and whispered, "Move a bit so you shield me from sight, then take my dirk and see if you can free my wrists."

"I'll try, but I'm so afraid." Carina swallowed hard and positioned herself so it looked as though she'd collapsed into Allisun's arms. It was tricky work, though, sawing through thick leather with a wee knife and unsteady hands.

"He agreed to sell me the tallies and ledgers," Jock said.

"For the next quarter's rents, aye, but Da wants the lass."

"Which lass? Not Allisun. She's mine," Jock snarled. "The last of Alex Murray's foul brood, and I mean to have her."

The bindings on Allisun's wrists gave.

Carina whimpered and burrowed her head into Allisun's shoulder. "He does not know about me," she whispered.

"Shh. Pray we can keep it that way," Allisun murmured. "My hands are still numb. Could you use the knife if you had to?"

Carina nodded. "Gil taught me."

"His one good deed." Though how much good one wee dirk would do, Allisun did not know. "Now, we are going to inch back toward the rocks. A bit at a time, and not a sound. Understand?"

Carina looked up, eyes wet and haunted. "I am sorry for—"

"You are not to blame for Gil's black heart." Allisun crawled steadily but slowly back, drawing Carina with her.

"But the feud...my mother..."

"All Jock McKie's fault." Allisun kept her eyes on the quarreling men. "If Jock was not so evil, your mother would not have fled him in fear of her life."

"If ye want Allisun, it'll cost ye extra," Gil shouted.

"Why should I pay for what's rightly mine?" Jock roared. Before Gil could react, Jock drew his sword and ran him through.

"Bastard," Black Gil wheezed. The curse ended on a gurgle as Jock pulled the blade free, and Gil slid to the ground.

Allisun gasped, felt Carina stiffen and quickly clamped a hand over her sister's mouth. "Shh, love, I know it is terrible, but you must not make a sound."

Silent tears streamed down Carina's cheeks. She shivered so violently it seemed she'd fly apart. Allisun prodded Carina into moving again, knowing they had little time, watching to see what these vile fiends would do next.

For a moment, none of them moved. Even these hardened reivers seemed stunned by the swiftness, the callousness with which Jock had dispatched his rival.

"Well, that's that." Jock smiled as he wiped the blade on his cloak and resheathed it. "We're agreed Allisun is mine."

Even by moonlight, Dickie's nebless face looked paler. "Da fancied her himself. There'll be no deal till he gets here."

Jock scowled. "When'll that be?"

"Soon. Real soon," Dickie growled. "He stopped by Hawkehill to teach the Nevilles a lesson. They was stealing from Da!"

Allisun glanced over her shoulder. The rocks were still twenty paces away. Too far.

Then came the moment she had dreaded. The moment when their captors stopped shouting and looked their way.

"Dod! They're getting away!" Jock kicked at his horse with his good leg.

Cursing, Dickie started for them, the McKies and Bells scrambling to follow.

Allisun stood and pushed Carina toward the rocks. "Run!"

Beneath her feet, the earth shook with the force of thirty mounted men. They'd never make it.

Suddenly a man popped out of the rocks.

Owen. Sword held aloft, he leaped from the boulders and raced toward them, screaming, "Hurry, Allie! Carina!"

Hope lent wings to Allisun's feet. Half dragging, half carrying Carina, she headed for Owen. But her soaring spirits dropped when she saw he was alone.

"Go back, Owen! Go back!"

He didn't. He kept coming.

A spear whizzed past Allisun, buried its tip in Owen's shoulder and carried him to the ground.

Everything seemed to stop...all sound...all movement...

all thought. Allisun stood transfixed, numbed by this latest loss. Her mentor. Her guardian. Her friend. She dropped down beside him, dimly aware of Carina screaming and clutching at her arm.

"Owen?" Allisun reached out to him, praying.

A callused hand grabbed her arm and yanked her to her feet.

"Well, well, if it ain't wee Allie Murray." Ill Will Bell leered down at her, lips curled into a feral smile, revealing sharp yellow teeth and breath worse than Rank Rolly's.

The scream went on and on, high, wild and bone chilling. Allie.

Hunter stood in the stirrups, head whipping about like a coursing hound's. "It came from up there." He pointed toward the narrow mouth of a rugged ravine.

"It leads up to the high meadow," Gavin said.

"Can you go around and come up behind the meadow?"

Gavin nodded. "Give me ten men and five minutes."

"Pray God we have that long." Hunter looked around at the ten men left behind with him and thought longingly of the thirty troopers with his father and the scores of Borderers. It would take too long to locate them. "Up we go, lads," he murmured. "Swords out, look sharp."

Every fiber of his being urged him to race up the slope and find out if Allie was in trouble. Inbred caution had him moving quickly but carefully. If they were outnumbered, surprise could be a valuable weapon. The wind had risen to whistle through the pines and, he hoped, cover the sound of their approach.

Hunter called a halt at the jumble of boulders rimming the lip of the meadow. Dismounting, he crept forward and peered around a massive rock.

Moonlight leached all color from the land, yet it was bright enough for him to make out thirty or more men ranged about the meadow. Of Allie, there was no sign, but Hunter recognized Jock at once, still on his horse, injured leg sticking out on a board. A bear of a man stood beside Jock's hobbler, arms waving as he argued. The streak of white in his black hair marked him as Ill Will Bell.

A gathering of thieves and villains, Hunter thought, but if they had Allie, where the hell was she?

Nerves taut, Hunter scanned the crowd again. Bells and McKies, shoulders hunched against the biting wind, taking no part in their chiefs' quarrel. Hunter supposed it was too much to hope the two old reprobates would do each other in.

"Bloody hell!" Will shouted. "Ye're that stubborn. Drag out the other lass, and I'll see if I want her instead of Allisun."

Hunter's heart jerked to a stop. Breath bated, he watched one man detach himself from a group near the rocks and cross the meadow with a small figure hanging limp in his arms. Her hair fluttered behind, long and black as the night.

Not Allie. Hunter looked back at the guards, trying to see if one of them held his Allie.

"Dod!" Jock cried. "It's…it's Brenna."

"Idiot. This lass is no more than ten," Will snapped.

"Alex got a bairn on my Brenna. Another blot to be wiped out." Jock's voice rose hysterically. "Give her to me! Give her—!"

"Nay!" Allie broke free and stumbled across the rough grass, her hands bound before her, her face wild with fear.

Hunter waited to see no more. "To me, lads!" Vaulting into Dancer's saddle, he drew his sword and roared his battle cry. It was taken up by Gavin on the other side of the field. As Hunter led the charge, he had the grim satisfaction of seeing both Jock and Ill Will freeze in place.

Their shock lasted only a moment, but it was enough time for Hunter's men to reach the first Bell troopers. Like a scythe mowing down ripe wheat, they cut a swath through the enemy.

"To arms! Get the bastards!" Will roared, swinging his sword free as he leaped into the saddle.

Hunter veered out of the pack, swept Allisun off her feet and carried her to the far side of the meadow. Holding her slight, trembling body reminded him of the night they had met. "You are all right, love," he crooned. "You are safe."

"Carina." Allie clutched at his arm. "My sister, Jock has her. You've got to get her."

Hunter looked back at the shapes parrying and thrusting at each other with deadly intent. "I'll find her. Get behind the rocks and out of sight, sweetheart." He set her on her feet and reluctantly left her. Even as he spurred toward the fight, he realized that the Bells did fight like fiends. Not only were his men outnumbered, they were in danger of being overrun by the hard-pressing Bells, urged on by Ill Will's hoarse shouts.

Roaring his battle cry, Hunter charged into the thick of things, counting on Dancer's help. Two men fell to them, but as Hunter turned to engage a third, he saw Jock heading toward the ravine with Carina in his arms.

Hunter instantly took up the chase, but just as Jock approached the trailhead, Ross and the Carmichaels swarmed out of the rocks.

Jock swore and dragged back on his horse's reins. The beast reared, but the old man kept his seat and his hold on Carina. "Stay back," he warned, holding the lass before him like a shield, his knife at her throat.

"Brenna," Ross whispered. "By all that's holy."

"Let go of me! Let go!" Carina screamed. Moonlight gleamed on shiny metal as she brought her hand up and struck at Jock's imprisoning arm.

Jock yelped. "Ye bitch, I—"

Hunter and Ross both started forward, but Carina did not wait for help. She kicked Jock's bad leg, tumbling onto the ground when he roared in pain and released her.

"Get him!" The voice was Ian Maxwell's. The spear that followed it out of the night caught Jock in the chest and carried him off the horse.

"Death to the reivers!" someone cried, and the Border lords swarmed out of the ravine to fall upon the Bells and McKies.

Seemingly oblivious to the battle, Ross dismounted and went to Carina. "Are you all right?"

She screamed and tried to scramble away.

"'Tis all right, lass." Ross extended a hand to her. "I am your uncle. Ross Carmichael. Your mother's brother."

"Her brother?" Carina's lower lip trembled. "Help me, please. Jock is..."

"'Tis all right, sweetheart." Ross picked her up and held her to his chest. "He cannot hurt you ever again."

Hunter relaxed when he saw Carina burrow into his father's embrace. He knew just how comforting those strong, steady arms of Ross's could be. With her in good hands, Hunter turned his attention back to the battle. He was not needed there, either, for the Borderers fought like men possessed.

Skirting the battlefield, Hunter went in search of Allie. He found her kneeling over a fallen man. Owen. Dismounting, Hunter hunkered down on Owen's other side. "How is he?"

"He had the spear out by the time I got here." Allie's hands fluttered over the makeshift bandage on his shoulder.

Owen's eyes opened. "Jock and Ill Will?" he rasped.

"Jock is dead, and Will maybe, too, by now."

"Good." Owen struggled to sit, brushing off Allie's hands when she tried to restrain him. "I need to see Jock's body."

Allisun scowled. "If Hunter says he's dead…"

"I understand." Hunter helped Owen up onto Dancer. The only men standing as they recrossed the trampled meadow were triumphant Maxwells, Humes and Nixons. Hunter supposed he should have tried to save a few reivers for the hangman's noose, but likely the outlaws had neither asked for nor expected quarter.

Ross was comforting Carina, and Allisun joined them.

Hunter helped Owen down and supported him over to the body sprawled in the waving grass.

Jock's eyes were closed, but even in death his features were stern and unrelenting.

"Ah, it does my heart good to see the old devil lying here," Owen said, one hand pressed to his shoulder.

Jock's eyes flew open, his blood-flecked lips curled when he looked up at them. "Gloat if ye will, Owen Murray. When I get to…to hell, it'll be filled with the Murrays I sent there."

Owen smiled bitterly. "That may be, but ye'll go to yer grave knowing this, Jock McKie. The lass—the one who's the image of Brenna—she's yer get, not Alex Murray's."

Hunter's cry of surprise was drowned by Jock's gasp.

"Lies." Jock's eyes were round with shock.

"'Tis God's truth," Owen hissed. "She did not know when she turned to us for help, but I swear Alex never touched her. The babe she bore is yers. Even has yer gray eyes, does Carina."

"Bring her…bring her here…got to see." The air rattled in Jock's chest as he struggled for breath.

"Nay," Hunter said, thinking of what this would do to Brenna's child, his cousin. But he need not have worried.

Owen shook his head. "I swore to Alex that I'd take the secret to my grave, so the lass would never know what evil seed she sprang from. And, by God, ye'll take it to yers." With that, Owen turned away.

Jock's roar of rage and pain filled the air. His hands clutched at the spear haft, but it was too late. His eyes rolled back, and his head lolled to the side. He was gone.

"It's done, then." Owen sagged into Hunter, but his eyes were clear and determined. "I'll want yer pledge that this goes no further."

Hunter looked over at Carina, sheltered on one side by the sister who was not of her blood and by his father, who was. "You've my word, Owen Murray, and my undying gratitude for keeping them both safe all these years."

Owen smiled through the pain. "Ach, well, 'tis pleased I am to be turning the duty over to a man such as yerself."

"And my father." Hunter smiled as he listened to his father cooing over Carina. "She'll not want for love again." His smile dimmed as he looked at Allie. What of her? Could she forgive the lies he'd told?

Epilogue

Hunter carried his three-month-old son to the window of the master chamber. Leaning one shoulder against the frame, he lifted Alex so he might see what would one day be his.

The mellowed gray stone of the old keep and its dependencies shimmered in the hot summer sun, neat and pristine. A far cry from the burned-out hulk they'd ridden into a year ago. Nearly all winter it had taken to undo the traces of Ill Will Bell's punishing raid against the Nevilles. But the Murrays and Hunter's folk from Renfrew had risen to the challenge. Working long hours, sometimes in the biting cold, they had resurrected Keastwicke. And found themselves.

Laughter bubbled up from the courtyard as Clem showed young John Murray the finer points of wrestling. A crowd encircled the sweaty, straining youths, Hunter's waifs and Allie's Murrays—their Murrays—all of them smiling and placing wagers on the outcome. George, still in his cook's apron, draped an arm about Dora Murray, his wife of two weeks. Malcolm stood behind Janet, one hand spread possessively over the mound that was their babe.

"Ah, 'tis a grand sight, is it not?"

Alexander Murray Carmichael waved a fat hand in the air and gurgled, as though in agreement.

"I wasn't just meaning the repair of Keastwicke, though that was important to your mama. Her way of safeguarding what little remains of her heritage so she could pass it on to you. It's the change in the people that matter." They were a family, now, his victims of violence and the persecuted Murrays, the common threads of their pasts woven together to make a future for all of them. "Your mama knew that, wise lass that she is." He ran a finger down Alex's forehead and tickled his nose.

Chortling, the babe grabbed the finger and stuck in into his mouth. He had a thatch of red-brown hair, his mother's blue eyes, and his father's kind nature. Or so Allisun claimed when the lad slept the night through at only one week.

"She's the one with the generous heart." Hunter brushed a kiss over his son's down head. How dear and precious they both were, his wife and his son. He'd have had neither if Allisun had not found it in her heart to forgive him for having lied to her.

"I can only hope she'll be as forbearing when she hears this news." He glanced over his shoulder at the parchment rolls he'd laid on the bed. The two messengers had arrived almost simultaneously, one from his father, the other from the king.

When he looked back, Hunter spotted Allie crossing the courtyard dressed for work in a plain brown gown, her thick red braid thumping against her back. Short and portly Father Matthew jogged along beside her, gesturing with his hands.

"Plans for expanding the chapel, no doubt," Hunter muttered. "God knows the poor man deserves it." Hearing the confessions of this motley crew had left the good father's florid face white for a week. But unburdening themselves had been good for all their souls. Another thing his perceptive Allie had been right about.

Grinning, he leaned out the window and called her name.

Allie stopped and looked up, shielding her eyes from the sun with one hand. "Hunter. Whatever are you doing up there?"

"Looking for you. Can you come up a moment?"

Instantly her smile vanished. "What is wrong?"

"Nothing." Or so he hoped. He was still gathering his thoughts when the door popped open and she dashed in.

"Is something wrong with Alex?" she asked anxiously, running over to touch their son's bare foot.

"Nay, he is fine."

"Then what?"

Hunter kissed the stiffness from her lips, then raised his head, letting his eyes wander over her. This past year of peace and plenty had changed her for the better, too. Her body was more curves than angles now, and her eyes had lost that haunted look. "Dieu, you are beautiful," he murmured, filled with wonder that this most special woman returned his love.

She giggled. Something she now did often. An even more telling mark of her inner peace. "You, sir, either have very low standards or very poor eyesight. I am filthy and rumpled."

"It matters not to me what you wear. In fact—" he waggled his eyebrows "—I prefer you with nothing at all."

"You are buttering me up for something." She cocked her head. "Let us see. You have decided that it's not enough your horses have taken over Derk's enormous storage building, now you want to house them in the great hall.''

He chuckled. ''Nay, and you'd not begrudge me if I did.''

''You've got me there, my lord.''

''I should hope so.'' He put his right arm around her and pulled her close, sighing as she curled into his embrace.

''You must be tired,'' she said softly. ''You've worked so hard putting Keastwicke to rights.''

''It was well worth the effort.'' Though at first, it had looked hopeless. Hunter had brought the Murrays home, intending to arrest Derk and reclaim the tower. He'd found the Neville troopers dead, and Derk, Morna and the maids trapped atop the burning tower. The Carmichaels had dragged the burning peat from the tower and rescued the Nevilles. The Nevilles' gratitude had turned to shock when Hunter ordered them out of Keastwicke with nothing save their clothes and horses. Some of the Murrays had been angered to see the Nevilles get off with their lives.

''I am glad now that you let Derk and Morna go,'' Allisun said, as though having guessed his thoughts, which seemed to happen often with them these days.

''They were not responsible for the Bells' raids nor for Jock's schemes. And from what Morna said, being sent back empty-handed to that wee sheep farm was severe punishment, indeed.''

''And you were wise enough to realize that.'' Going up on tiptoe, she laced her hands around his neck and tugged his mouth down to hers. What started out as a quick kiss soon flared out of control. They had resumed lovemaking a few weeks past, but still it seemed they could not get enough of each other.

Alex, scenting a snack nearby, set up a howl.

''Glutton.'' But already Allisun could feel her milk begin to flow. ''Give him here. It will be good to have him contentedly full when your parents arrive." She retreated to the bed, sat and reached for the laces up the front of her gown.

"Let me." Hunter slipped the ribbons free efficiently, yet his fingers lingered on the swell of her breast. "Beautiful."

He made her feel so. As wee Alex began to nurse, Allisun leaned against Hunter's chest. The thud of his heart against her back, the insistent tugging of the babe moved her.

"What is it?"

Too much to put into words. Allisun looked up into his calm brown eyes and knew, as always, that he understood. This winter, living in close quarters, working together on the repairs to the tower had taught them much about each other. Oh, he was still arrogant and she stubborn, but they had learned to compromise, to love, to trust. That was the most important thing he had done for her, with the exception of giving her wee Alex. "I was thinking how far we've come in a year."

Hunter grinned. "I wondered if you'd remember. 'Twas a year ago tonight that you came to me."

"And look where that led," she teased, glancing at Alex.

"Aye." Hunter touched his son's head. "Thank you."

"He is the most beautiful babe."

"I meant for giving me another chance." The eyes that glowed when he loved her and danced when he teased were solemn now. "I was afraid you would never give me a chance to explain."

"It is behind us, now. The feud, the hard times." Allie smiled up at him, basking in his love. "And we have so much." But there was something on his mind. Curious as she was, she waited till she'd finished feeding Alex. Laying her sleeping son in his cradle, she turned to his father. "Now, what is wrong?"

"I should have wed a less perceptive woman."

"You'd have been bored silly. Now tell me."

"We've had two messages."

She stiffened. "Bad news?"

"Nay. One was from Papa with word he and Mama will be here before dark."

"Everything is in readiness. I cannot wait for them to see how Alex has grown." Megan had come to Keastwicke in May for the babe's birth, and they had become very close.

"They are bringing Carina with them."

"Oh." Her smile dimmed. "That is...nice." And it was, in a way. Carina had bloomed under Ross and Megan's gentle nurturing.

"Tell me, love," Hunter whispered.

"You will think me a terrible person."

"I could never think that. I love you."

"And I you." Allisun took a breath to steady her nerves. "I want the best for Carina. I am so pleased she's found happiness with your parents. But when I look at her, I remember Papa lay with Brenna while my own mother...his wife...was dying."

Hunter nodded, his expression so grave she feared he did despise her. "I gave my word I would never speak of this, but I think silence is doing more damage." He took her hand and stroked it gently. "Carina is not your sister."

Allisun listened, stunned as Hunter told her what had really happened all those years ago. The truth eased old wounds and opened new ones. "She is Jock's daughter. Sired by the vicious old man who took so much from us," she cried.

"Brenna shared that sentiment. Apparently she went a little mad when she realized she was carrying the child of a man she despised, a man whose schemes she had planned to stop with the tallies, ledgers and her testimony."

"Why was the evidence never used against Jock?"

"Because Brenna was in no condition to testify against him. According to Owen, Brenna had confided her suspicions about Jock to your mother, who offered her sanctuary and support. But the child changed everything. Brenna tried to pretend it wasn't happening, then retreated from the world. She could not testify against Jock, and your father feared that if Jock learned she was expecting he'd try to take the babe."

"It explains so much." If she'd had momentary qualms about bearing Hunter's child, how must Brenna have felt? Allisun turned her hand and linked her slender fingers with Hunter's long, blunt ones. "Thank you for telling me. It does help."

"What will you do?"

She smiled faintly. "I will remember that Brenna's good Carmichael blood flows in her veins. I will remember Father Matthew saying that all bairns are born innocent of sin. And I will love her as I could not before."

"Then I did the right thing?"

"You usually do." She paused a moment, considering. "In a way, the warden is partly to blame. Had Andy Kerr not been taking Jock's bribes, my father could have laid the matter before him and been assured of justice." Andy had been hauled off to Edinburgh's dungeons for his part in all this. "I hope the next warden is more honest."

Hunter cleared his throat. "I like to think he is. The other message was from the king, naming the new warden."

"Oh. Who is it? Is it someone we know?"

"Aye." Hunter reached for the parchment scroll with its heavy wax seal and handed it to her.

The letters were thin and faint, the words long and pompous. Much like the king, so she'd been told. Squinting, she made her way to the bottom of the page and the name. *Hunter Carmichael.*

"Oh, Hunter." Allisun threw her arms around his neck, toppling him back onto the bed. "That is too wonderful."

He gazed up at her, grinning like a lad who'd stolen a prize. "Some days it may be. But it's sure to be hard, thankless work. With Ill Will dead and his band scattered, the Borders have been quiet this winter. But you can bet it won't last."

"Peace never does." Allisun shivered and hugged him tighter, thinking of the scars he already bore and those that might come. "But you can count on a lot of support."

"Aye. Ian Maxwell and his ilk will be glad of my appointment, I think." He stroked her back lazily, his mind whirling with plans. "I'm thinking nightly patrols would—"

Allisun cut off his words with a kiss that stole his breath and eventually his reason. "Later. Now I've a mind to see how the new Border Warden does make love."

"In broad daylight?" he teased, slanting her a slow, heated smile that made her bones melt.

"Aye. I'd like to see exactly what sort of man the king has foisted on us this time." In the long, lush moments that followed, she discovered that the king's new warden was thorough in everything he did, with quick, clever hands and an exquisitely knowing mouth. When the last pinnacle had been reached, she lay content in his arms, a syrupy sense of belonging curling through her limp body.

"Well?" he drawled when their hearts had slowed.

"Hmm." She summoned the strength to open one eye. "Oh, a vast improvement over the last warden."

"Cheeky wench."

Allisun giggled, then sobered. "If anyone can bring us a measure of peace, it is you, my love. For I do not know of a more honest, honorable man. I am proud to be your wife."

He cupped her cheek in his palm, deeply moved by her

faith in him. How like this land she was, bold and brash, yet surprisingly vulnerable. But for all their seeming fragility, she, and her Borders, would endure. "If so, then we are evenly matched, for you are my pride and joy."

* * * * *

Did Somebody Say Medievals?

This holiday season join Harlequin Historicals in celebrating the pageantry of the Middle Ages!

PRIDE OF LIONS
by Suzanne Barclay
January 1999

THE KNIGHT'S BRIDE
by Lyn Stone
January 1999

THE HIGHLANDER'S MAIDEN
by Elizabeth Mayne
February 1999

THE BRIDE OF WINDERMERE
by Margo Maguire
March 1999

Available at your favorite retail outlet.

HARLEQUIN®
Makes any time special ™

Look us up on-line at: http://www.romance.net

HHMED2

Take 2 bestselling love stories FREE
Plus get a FREE surprise gift!

Special Limited-Time Offer

Mail to Harlequin Reader Service®

P.O. Box 609
Fort Erie, Ontario
L2A 5X3

YES! Please send me 2 free Harlequin Historical™ novels and my free surprise gift. Then send me 4 brand-new novels every month, which I will receive before they appear in bookstores. Bill me at the low price of $4.19 each plus 25¢ delivery and GST*. That's the complete price, and a saving of over 10% off the cover prices—quite a bargain! I understand that accepting the books and gift places me under no obligation ever to buy any books. I can always return a shipment and cancel at any time. Even if I never buy another book from Harlequin, the 2 free books and the surprise gift are mine to keep forever.

347 HEN CH7M

Name	(PLEASE PRINT)	
Address	Apt. No.	
City	Province	Postal Code

This offer is limited to one order per household and not valid to present Harlequin Historical™ subscribers. *Terms and prices are subject to change without notice. Canadian residents will be charged applicable provincial taxes and GST.

CHIS-98   ©1990 Harlequin Enterprises Limited

Sexy, desirable and...a daddy?

THE AUSTRALIANS

Stories of romance Australian-style, guaranteed to fulfill that sense of adventure!

This February 1999 look for

Baby Down Under

by **Ann Charlton**

Riley Templeton was a hotshot Queensland lawyer with a reputation for ruthlessness and a weakness for curvaceous blondes. Alexandra Page was everything that Riley *wasn't* looking for in a woman, but when she finds a baby on her doorstep that leads her to the dashing lawyer, he begins to see the virtues of brunettes—and babies!

The Wonder from Down Under: where spirited women win the hearts of Australia's most independent men!

Available February 1999
at your favorite retail outlet.

HARLEQUIN®
Makes any time special ™

MEN *at* WORK

All work and no play?
Not these men!

January 1999
SOMETHING WORTH KEEPING by Kathleen Eagle
He worked with iron and steel, and was as wild as the mustangs that were his passion. She was a high-class horse trainer from the East. Was her gentle touch enough to tame his unruly heart?

MEN of STEEL

February 1999
HANDSOME DEVIL by Joan Hohl
His roguish good looks and intelligence drew women like magnets, but Luke Branson was having too much fun to marry again. Then Selena McInnes strolled before him and turned his life upside down!

TALL, DARK AND SMART
E=MC²

March 1999
STARK LIGHTNING by Elaine Barbieri
The boss's daughter was ornery, stubborn and off-limits for cowboy Branch Walker! But Valentine was also nearly impossible to resist. Could they negotiate a truce...or a surrender?

MEN OF THE WEST

Available at your favorite retail outlet!

MEN AT WORK™

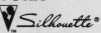

HARLEQUIN® ▼ *Silhouette*®

Look us up on-line at: http://www.romance.net   PMAW4

My Secret Admirer

**Savor the magic of love
with three new romances
from top-selling authors
Anne Stuart,
Vicki Lewis Thompson and
Marisa Carroll.**

My Secret Admirer is a unique collection
of three brand-new stories featuring passionate
secret admirers. Celebrate Valentine's Day with
these wonderfully romantic tales that are
ideally suited for this special time!

Available in February 1999 at your favorite retail outlet.

HARLEQUIN®
Makes any time special ™

COMING NEXT MONTH FROM

HARLEQUIN HISTORICALS

- **A ROSE AT MIDNIGHT**
by **Jacqueline Navin,** author of
THE FLOWER AND THE SWORD
A dashing earl and a beautiful gentlewoman find love
unexpectedly in a marriage of convenience.
> HH #447 ISBN# 29047-0 $4.99 U.S./$5.99 CAN.

- **FOR LOVE OF ANNA**
by **Sharon Harlow**
Ranch owner Anna Caldwell rescues handsome cowboy
Trent Malloy from a snowstorm, and through her love, rescues
him from a lifetime of loneliness.
> HH #448 ISBN# 29048-9 $4.99 U.S./$5.99 CAN.

- **THE HIGHLANDER'S MAIDEN**
by **Elizabeth Mayne,** author of LADY OF THE LAKE
When the king decrees that a female mountain guide must
protect a mapmaker from a warring clan, her loyalties are
divided, especially when they fall in love.
> HH #449 ISBN# 29049-7 $4.99 U.S./$5.99 CAN.

- **HAWKEN'S WIFE**
by **Rae Muir,** author of TWICE A BRIDE
In the third book of THE WEDDING TRAIL series, a tomboy
heroine changes her mind about marriage when an amnesiac
mountain man joins her wagon train.
> HH #450 ISBN# 29050-0 $4.99 U.S./$5.99 CAN.

DON'T MISS THESE FOUR GREAT TITLES AVAILABLE NOW:

HH #443 PRIDE OF LIONS
Suzanne Barclay

HH #444 THE HEART OF A HERO
Judith Stacy

HH #445 THE KNIGHT'S BRIDE
Lyn Stone

HH #446 BURKE'S RULES
Pat Tracy